Poacher's Moon

John D. Nesbitt

JOHN D. NESBITT

www.pronghornpress.org

for Bob McKee,
good friend and fellow writer

JOHN D. NESBITT

1

Wilf was riding the dark horse when he crested the hill and saw the serpent.

Off to the east, the grassland stretched away for a good ten miles, ending in a line of hills that squatted in the haze. Closer in, the county road ran parallel to the hills, north and south, across his field of vision. At the left edge, where a dirt road led from the main road into the ranch, movement caught his eye. It looked like a vehicle, the silvery color too light to be a game warden's pickup. He watched it for a moment. A giant worm of dust hung above the road as the thing made its way, glinting as if it were the head of a long, grey snake.

Downslope in front of him, nothing moved. The camp

trailers, the horse trailer, and the two pickups all sat in silence in the fragile warmth of an autumn afternoon. Wilf imagined the hunters were asleep. His nostrils still carried the smell of deer fat from the morning kill, and the two carcasses hanging in the shade between the horse trailer and the cedar trees should be firming up.

A tug on the lead rope reminded him of the sorrel. He glanced back, then put his heels to the dark horse and took them both down into camp at a walk, keeping his eye on the rangeland as he went. The shape had disappeared for a moment, but the dust told him it was still on the way.

Now he heard the sound of the engine as the vehicle came up out of a swale and leveled off. It was a late model sport utility vehicle, silvery bronze and clean-looking as the sunlight reflected off the hood, windshield, and roof. The machine veered left and then right, following the road. When it straightened out for the last two hundred yards, Wilf could see that it had Wyoming plates. It wasn't an out-of-stater, then, and it didn't look like a hunting outfit.

Wilf drew the horses to a stop next to the two camp trailers. He dismounted so he wouldn't be looking down at his visitor, and with a little handwork he ended up in front of the two horses with the reins in his left hand and the lead rope in his right. He glanced at the sorrel and saw that the packs were still riding even; then he turned back as the shiny Lincoln Navigator settled to a stop.

Unless there was someone out of view in the back of the vehicle, the driver was alone. He shut off the engine and got out of the car, a bright figure in clean town clothes. He was tall and well-built, somewhere in middle age, with a full head of light colored hair that at one time had probably been blonder. Wilf didn't recognize him, but he knew the type — well-off and self-assured, good looks and good hair and good country-club manners.

"Are you Wilf Kasmire?"

"I sure   nodded and passed the lead rope behind himself to his left hand, then stepped forward with his right hand free.

"I'm Scott Wentworth." The man walked forward, and with his light blue eyes steady, he reached out his hand and gave a firm shake.

Wilf glanced at the vehicle and back at the man. "Something I can do for you?"

"They tell me you're a hunting guide."

Wilf nodded. "I've done some of it."

"Well, I've got some hunters coming in, and I need someone to guide 'em."

"Is that right? Do you have your own place, then?"

Wentworth raised his head half a notch. "Yes, I do. I bought the Bonnell ranch a little while back, and I've invited some of my friends to come and hunt."

"I see. Are they from out of state?"

"Oh, yeah. They're all fellows I know from down in Colorado."

Wilf glanced at the Wyoming license plate and figured it must be pretty new. Then, meeting Wentworth's eyes again, he said, "They've got permits and all that, I suppose."

"Sure. I just thought it would be good to have someone to keep things organized."

"You mean take 'em out, get 'em lined up, and then take care of their animals as they get 'em?"

"Yeah. Whatever you do when you guide someone."

"Have they hunted before? How many are there?"

"I've got three of 'em coming. They've all hunted a little bit before, but I want someone to make things go smooth for 'em."

"Hmm." Wilf looked at the ground and back up at the newcomer. "The season's half over. When do they plan to get started?"

"The first one's already here. The other two are coming in tonight."

Wilf hesitated. "I don't know. I usually try to get things planned a little bit farther ahead than that."

"So do I. But I just found out they were coming, and I thought I'd better get someone." Wentworth tightened his brows and gave a short, confidential nod. "They tell me you're the best."

"Your hunters did?"

"No. I asked in a couple of places in town, including Norm Lang's office, and they recommended you. Said I could probably find you out here."

"Oh." Wilf felt like saying that if anyone had said anything, it was probably that he would take the work. "Well," he went on, "today's the seventh. The season lasts fourteen days. I've had six hunters here, and they all got their deer. All but these last two are gone, and I think they'll pull out this afternoon." He paused. "I don't know. It sounds tight. I've got to take all this stuff back to my place, and then I'll need the last two days to get ready for elk season and meet my hunters. That starts on the fifteenth."

"Oh, I bet you can get these guys taken care of in three days. A day each at the most. But I'd like to hire you for five days, just in case."

Wilf scraped his teeth against his upper lip. "I don't know. It just sounds tight. And I still need to hunt my own deer."

"Ah, hell," said Wentworth, with a jerk of the head, "c'mon and kill him at my ranch."

"Well, it's part of my lease here, and I'd rather get it while I'm entitled to it."

"Suit yourself. We can take care of that detail later if we need to. But I think we can make things work."

"Maybe." Wilf shrugged.

Wentworth paused for a second. "You tell me how much you need, and I'll see if I can do that." With a steady gaze he added, "I like to put a price on things."

Wilf cleared his throat. "It's usually two-fifty a day each, when I provide everything—the camp, the meals, and all the guiding. But even with something like you're talking about, I've got work on either end of it, so I couldn't do it for less than a hundred and fifty a day for each hunter. That's for the days I work, not the comin' and goin'."

"So that's four hundred and fifty a day."

"A hundred and fifty per gun. If someone fills, he doesn't have to keep paying while the others hunt."

"Sure. I see. So if they were paying individually, you might make anywhere from nine hundred to eighteen hundred, depending."

"Something like that. It could actually work out even less, but then I wouldn't have the time crunch, so it wouldn't be all bad."

Wentworth pulled a cigarette from his shirt pocket, rapped the filter against a chrome-plated lighter that appeared in his left hand, put the cigarette in his mouth, and lit it.

"How about this, to make it worth your while? I'll

give you a minimum of four hundred and fifty a day for every day you're there, up to four days."

Wilf gave it a thought. "Well, if I don't have to be there for more than four days, I might be able to fit it in."

Wentworth took a drag on his cigarette and nodded as he blew away the smoke. "So when do you think you can show up?"

"Well, I still need to take care of all this stuff, and like I said, I need to hunt for myself, so I'd say day after tomorrow, first thing in the morning."

"You know, you can always get your deer on my place. I already said that."

"I know, but I couldn't get there by tomorrow morning anyway. I can by the following morning, though, and if I don't get my deer in the meantime, I may have to take you up on your offer. I do appreciate it."

"Well, the sooner you can come, the better. The day after tomorrow is fine." Wentworth motioned with his head toward the sorrel. "Nice-looking horse."

"Thanks. He's been a good one for me." Then a thought flickered. "You didn't mention whether you wanted horses. I didn't have that figured in."

"Oh, no. We don't need any of that. I've got a ranch pickup that needs a little work, and a four-wheeler, and I assume you have a pickup, too."

"Yeah, that one over there. "Wilf pointed with his chin, and as he did so he squinted at the glare of the sun coming off the camp trailers. "I take it you've got room for your hunters. Or should I bring along one or two of these trailers to sleep in? That gooseneck sleeps up to six, but three or four is better. At the very least I could bring along the smaller one and sleep in it myself."

Wentworth lifted the cigarette to his lips. He frowned and then said, "Well, bring something for yourself."

"Sure. I'll just pull that one along. It won't be any bother, especially if I'm not hauling a horse trailer."

"That sounds good enough. "Wentworth moved his head again in the direction of the sorrel. "What do you have in the packs?"

"Oh, I've got a fifty-pound bag of grain in each side for right now—just some dead weight for practice. As it turned out, I fetched all the deer with my pickup and didn't use the horses, so I thought I'd get in a little practice before I broke camp."

"I see. But you do use the packs for hunting?"

"Oh, yeah. That's why they're orange. They call 'em panniers. You drape 'em right over the saddle and tie 'em down, then load 'em and snug 'em up."

"I can see that." Wentworth smiled. "I can tell you do everything first rate."

So that's what it was. Just buttering him up. The guy didn't really care about the horses. Wilf gave a half-smile. "Well," he said, "I guess we've got it all square. I'll be out at your place early in the morning on the ninth."

"You know where it is, then?"

"Sure. I've even hunted on it before, as far as that goes. Been a few years, maybe three or four."

The easy smile came back. "Then you probably know the place better than I do."

"I doubt that, but I always remember where I see deer and where we kill 'em."

"Good. I'm glad you're able make it work, then."

"It's a little bit of a squeeze, but it's what I want to be doing, so it's worth it."

"I'll make sure it is. It sounds like we're goin' to do fine."

"I'm sure we will, Mr. Wentworth."

"Call me Scott." He dropped what was left of his cigarette, stepped on it, and held out his hand to seal the deal.

The engine of the Navigator hummed as Wentworth turned the vehicle around and drove out the way he'd come in. Wilf stood and watched until the bright object dropped out of sight in the first low spot. Then he led the horses to the rear end of the horse trailer and tied one animal to each side. He went to the packhorse to unload it first, and as he picked at the ropes that ran up and across the saddle and lashed the two packs, he sifted his prospects.

He had done all right with his antelope hunters, and he had gotten this set of deer hunters taken care of, but he hadn't made all that much. It cost money to set up and run a camp, and he always had to think about investing in more equipment. The horses and the trailer and all the tack — none of that was cheap. His tents and such were paid off, and so was the smaller of the two camp trailers. With a little new money, he might be able to buy something.

As the ropes came loose and the pack sagged, he pushed against the dead weight and lifted the bag of grain up and out of the pannier. He flipped the bag onto his shoulder and carried it over to the tailgate of his pickup. As he turned back around, he glanced at the larger of the two campers, the gooseneck. He hated to pay rent on something like that because he barely broke even, but if he went in the hole to buy it, it would take a long time to pay itself off. He shook his head and went back to the packhorse. Well, that was business.

Everything cost something. This extra work he was picking up would help, and it was another connection. This fellow Wentworth seemed like something of a wheeler-dealer type, and maybe more pushy than he needed to be, but it was good to get lined up on a private ranch. A guy didn't want to turn that down unless he had to.

As he finished stripping the horses and put the saddles away, he heard voices in the larger camp trailer. It sounded as if the two hunters had finished their nap. Wilf looked at the sun. It was probably about three o'clock. These two fellows would be gone in another hour or so, and then he could see about hunting his deer. In the meantime, he could go on about packing up the camp.

He knew where a little forked-horn had been hanging out in a small valley that ran between two sandstone bluffs. The buck liked to crop grass in the shade on the west side. Wilf and various of his hunters had glassed the animal almost every afternoon, and all the hunters passed him up in favor of something better. Wilf had thought he might do the same, but he knew where the buck was if the time came for him to quit being picky.

He looked at each of the three trailers. He would tow the horse trailer first, then the one with the fifth wheel, then the smaller one. He could even leave the sixteen-footer hitched up if he was going to pull it right on out to Wentworth's place. Still, it was all going to take time, and he had things to do in town as well. He weighed his options. Things weren't looking so good for the little forked-horn buck. That was too bad. Wilf had hoped to take a whole day and hunt for himself, but now it looked as if he might have to wait until some other time to do that.

He walked down and then up a large drainage to make the best approach. Moving toward the shade on his right, he took slow steps up a slickrock path until the valley came into view, half a mile long and a couple of hundred yards across. Sunlight fell on the bluffs along the left side and shone on the dry grass, then ended with the shadows that stretched out from the right. He took a couple of more steps upward to get a better look at the dark slope. When he saw two dusky forms in the rocks ahead, he fell into his cautious mode, lowering himself and moving forward on his knees, then rising into a crouch as he moved further into the shade of the bluff and worked his way around the boulders at the base. The deer came into view again, two and no more. One of them looked as if it had antlers. Wilf held the scope on them for a long moment, and when the animals moved into sunlight that came through a break in the bluffs, the antlers glinted. Wilf crawled upslope, closer to the base of the sandstone wall, with the valley now fifty yards or so downhill to his left. He crept along, peeked through to the west when he came to the break, and then moved forward.

He came to a jumble of rocks, moved in and around them, and settled his rifle on a rock that was chest high. He scoped the two deer again and put horns on the one up ahead and to the left, which grazed, head down in three-quarter profile.

The report of the rifle rang out sharp along the bluff in the cool air, and the buck went down, plunging forward. The doe ran across to the other side of the valley as Wilf moved out from the rocks and walked toward the deer he had shot. He found assurance, as always, in seeing the horns still on the deer when he got close — small, narrow tines, two on each side.

It was an expedient hunt but a well-rounded one all the same, with a good stalk and one clean shot. After that he made a neat job of field dressing the deer on the slope at the base of the bluff. Dusk was falling as he went for the pickup, and the moon was rising as he drove back to camp. He was able to read his watch in the moonlight after he hung up the deer.

Wilf turned the horses into the pasture and closed the gate. The morning frost was melting in the sunny areas, and the sun was starting to climb in the eastern sky. It would have been a good day to hunt for himself, but he told himself again that with the extra work he had picked up, he didn't have that freedom. And even if he had had to go about it in a businesslike way, he felt all right about the way he had hunted his deer. He had gotten away from the vehicle and gone on foot, just a man on the landscape.

He watched the horses graze for a few minutes until he made himself get back to work. As he turned to walk to his pickup, something caught his eye and made him pause.

Tire tracks. Someone had backed onto his garden plot and turned around to pull out of the yard. The vehicle hadn't done any damage, as the plants were dead and dry at the end of the season, but Wilf still wondered why someone would be so careless. Whoever it was, maybe he didn't know a garden when he saw it. Or maybe he didn't think it mattered. It was the type of thing someone from the city would do.

Wilf looked at the tracks and thought back to the conversation with Wentworth. He was pretty sure the man said he had asked around town and was told he could find Wilf at the ranch. Well, he might have come out here first and not bothered to mention it. Wilf shook his head. Whoever it was, he probably hadn't been here before, or he would have known the drive went all the way around.

Wilf closed up the horse trailer, backed it into place, and unhooked it. Among the things he hoped to get done that day, he needed to call Adrienne.

Inside the single-wide, he dialed her work number and asked for her. Her extension rang once, and she answered.

"This is Adrienne Moreau."

"Hi, there. I'm back at my place."

"Oh, are you done?"

"Sort of, but not quite. All the hunters got their deer, but I need to make a couple of more trips to haul in the rest of my stuff. And then I've got another job to go on."

"More hunting?"

"Yeah, guiding. I've got a fellow that wants me to go out to his place and guide some guest hunters for three or four days."

"When is that?"

"Tomorrow morning."

"That doesn't leave you much time before your next trip, then."

"You mean the elk hunters? You're right. It's just a little bit tight. I've got some running around to do today, but I should be done by late afternoon, early evening."

"Oh."

"I know this is kind of short notice, but if you'd like to, I could cook us a couple of steaks tonight."

"At your place?"

"If you want."

A few seconds passed before she answered. "I think

I can do it."

"Well, it would be nice if we could. I don't expect to stay up very late. I need to be out at this guy's ranch real early tomorrow morning."

"What time do you think, then, for this evening? Six o'clock? Seven?"

"Any time in there. I'll pick up a couple of steaks and all the trimmings."

She laughed. "Does that mean a supermarket salad and a bottle of wine?"

"That, and some French bread. I don't want to be too predictable."

"That sounds fine. Some time between six and seven, then?"

"Sure." After a pause he said, "I suppose you need to get back to work."

"I guess I should. And I gather that you have things to do, too. By the way, did you get a deer for yourself?"

"Yes, I did. Nothing spectacular, but I got that taken care of. And that's one of the things I need to do — drop it off at the locker plant. I figure I'd better leave it to hang in a cold place until I can get back and cut it up."

"How about your other job?"

"My day job? Yeah, I need to stop by and talk to them, too."

Wilf had a campfire going and was setting out two lawn chairs when he heard a car door close. After a quick look at the fire, he walked around to the front of the single-wide. The first thing to catch his eye was the maroon-colored Impala, and then he saw Adrienne herself, treading the first step on the little porch of the mobile home.

"Over here," he called out.

As she turned and smiled, he had a vision of what was, for him at that moment, perfect beauty. Against the background of a peach-and-scarlet sunset, she stood shapely and poised with her right foot on the step and the other on the ground. Her long, dark hair cascaded to her shoulders, while her eyes sparkled and her smile made a narrow gleam. She was wearing a red pullover sweater, blue jeans, and a trim pair of lace-up leather shoes.

"I brought dessert," she said, "but it's in the car." She moved her left hand in the direction of the Impala.

"Will it keep?"

She stepped back from the porch and faced him. "It should. It's just a pie I picked up. No time to make anything."

"Oh, I know. I'm glad we could find the time at all." He felt uncomfortable about scheduling in another set of hunters and cutting the time short with her, but he didn't want to apologize any more. "Shall we go around back? I've got a fire going, and we should have coals in a little while."

"Let me get the pie. And I brought you something else."

He followed her to the passenger side of the car, where she stopped and turned. They moved toward each other and met with a kiss.

"We're not in a hurry, are we?" she asked.

"I hope not."

"Good."

He smiled as he stood back. "Do I have to close my eyes?"

"Oh, no. It's not that much of a surprise." She opened the car door, took out the pie in its clear plastic package, and set it on top of the car. Then she reached in again and brought out two dark jars. "Chokecherry jelly," she said, as she handed them to him.

He took the two pint jars and looked at their contents, dark as deer blood. The scene came back, standing in her kitchen and smelling the musty scent of the juice. She mashed the boiled fruit in a conical sieve, using a thick wooden pestle. That was in August, when the air was heavy. Now it was thin and cooling.

"Shall I put these inside? Then we can sit by the fire."

"Sure." She turned for the pie. "I'll wait out here."

When he had her seated near the fire, he went back into the trailer house and brought out the burgundy and two glasses. The bottle had a knob on the end of the cork, so he handed her the two glasses, then peeled off the plastic wrap and twisted the stopper.

"It's nice out here," she said.

"Yeah, it's still kinda stuffy inside. That's a tour home for you."

She laughed. "Did you call it a 'tour home'?"

He smiled as he squeaked the cork out of the neck of the bottle. "Yeah, that's what the real estate guy called it. Makes it sound better, I guess."

She held up one of the glasses for him to pour the wine. "It is rather catchy, isn't it?"

"Oh, yeah. Sets me a cut above trailer parks and—ahem — trailer trash."

"I haven't ever heard you say something like that before." She had an uncertain look on her face as she held up the other glass.

Wilf backtracked. Some of the families she worked

with might live in trailer houses, and he might have sounded snide. "Well, I hope it's all in fun. If you live in a trailer, you live in a trailer, but if someone's trying to sell one, he calls it something nicer, and sometimes it strikes you as funny."

"You mean the language."

"Well, yeah. I'm not making fun of the people who live in the things. I'm one of 'em."

Her face relaxed as they touched their glasses together. "Well, I think your 'tour home' is just fine."

"Thanks. It suits me well enough, for the time being. At least, until I can build something better."

When the fire burned down to coals, Wilf put the grate in place and laid on the two rib-eyes. As he settled into his chair and picked up his wine glass, he squinted.

"Is that a frown?"

"I'm not sure."

"Well, is there something bothering you?"

"I don't know. Oh, I guess maybe one thing."

"Go ahead."

"It looked like someone was out here while I was gone."

"How could you tell?"

"Someone backed a vehicle right onto my garden plot. It's no big deal, but it pisses me off a little."

"I don't blame you. You had a nice garden."

"Well, the season's over, so that part doesn't matter. But it's just inconsiderate."

Adrienne took a sip of her wine, then said with a flourish, "The machine in the garden."

"What's that, a movie?"

"No, it was an idea, from a course I took. We read a couple of poems—one about a toad getting killed by a lawn mower, and one about a deer that was killed by a car. Collateral damage, as they call it now. The idea we got out of it—from the professor, of course—was that man and his machines came in and destroyed nature. Without really intending to, but maybe by being careless."

"Oh, I get it. So the garden is the whole thing."

"Right. Including the deer."

"Sure."

"So, anyway, did they do anything?"

"Not that I could tell. Just came in and turned around."

"Do you have any idea who it might be?"

"I imagine it was the guy who wanted me to work for him. He might have come by here before someone told him he could find me out at the ranch."

"Then it's probably not something you would mention or complain about."

"No, probably not. I'll just go up there and do my job. And actually, I think it's good for me to be able to pick up this other bit of work."

"Oh. Does it look like a pretty normal job to you?"

"I think so. The hunters are probably the type that need to be guided and don't want to get their hands dirty or bloody, so they bring me in. This guy's one of those newcomers from Colorado. His friends are from there, too."

"Did you just meet him?"

"Yeah, but I got a little of the low-down on him from Wilson, the fellow whose place I was just hunting on. I stopped in to square up with him, and he told me about this new guy."

"What's his name?"

"Wentworth. Scott Wentworth."

She shook her head. "Don't know him."

"I hadn't heard of him either, but that doesn't mean anything. He said some people in town recommended me, including Norman Lang." Wilf took a sip of wine.

"Oh, did you buy this place through his agency?"

"No, but I know him. I talked to him not long ago about buying a generator from him, so he might have had me in mind because of that."

"I see. Did your new client buy some property here?"

"According to Wilson, this guy made a ton of money down there in Colorado in real estate, and then he came up here. Bought a pretty good-sized ranch, and now he wants to sell off some of the nice parts for ranchettes—you know, forty-acre parcels for vacation homes or cabins or whatever. I imagine he invited his friends up so he can show it off to them."

Adrienne made a face.

"Yeah, I know. You hate to see it, but there's no law against it. He can bring in a grader and cut roads till hell won't have it, and the county commissioners couldn't do a thing, even if they wanted to." He raised and lowered his eyebrows. "You know, a man has a right to try to make a profit, and all that."

"Oh, I know. There's never any shortage of justification."

"No, and if he's not doing anything illegal, it's hard to condemn him, even if you don't care for what he's up to. I'm not that crazy about the guy myself, but I don't have to like someone just to do some work for him. No more than a backhoe operator, it seems to me. If you're in it for a living, like I'm tryin' to do, you take the work you get."

Adrienne nodded. "I can see that. I guess I just don't always think of hunting as a business...like construction work."

Wilf took another sip of wine. "Well, it is, and it isn't. I love to hunt, when I get to hunt for myself. But when I take other people out to get them hunted, I do it for money. It's work then. And if you're trying to make a living at it, or part of a living, then I guess it's a business. If you're in it for that, then someone like this new guy is a good opportunity."

Adrienne's face showed a trace of tenseness. "If you like it that much, does it ever feel funny to be selling it to someone else?"

Wilf took a moment to answer. "I hate to admit it, but yeah, it takes a lot of the fun out of it. Everyone wants to make a living at something he really enjoys, but maybe the down side of it is that once you try to make a living at it, you can't enjoy it as much."

"Because you have to be concerned about the money?"

"I guess that's it, or part of it. Some of it is just the people you have to deal with. You get lazy ones, and flabby ones, and the kind that don't seem to have any common sense. They're bad enough, and then you get the type that are high and mighty and think that as long as they pay their way, they can do as they please." He stopped and reflected. "Well, yeah. That's the worst part, and it comes from money."

Adrienne's features softened as the firelight played on her glossy hair. "Oh, I don't mean to put a damper on it for you. But I would wonder about the money aspect and whether it might take the enjoyment out of the whole thing. On the other hand, if you want to try to make a living at something you like, you should be able to give it a try."

"Well, thanks. That's the way I look at it. Even if it isn't always fun, it's something to try. You hope the trade-off is worth it. But one way or the other, I just can't see myself working at Pioneer Truss for the rest of my life."

"Oh, did you stop by there?"

"Yes, I did." Wilf recalled his visit—standing in the midst of all the racket of power saws, compressors, nail guns, and drills, and talking to Duane. "The boss said I could go ahead and have these days off. If they get in a bind they might have to put someone on for a while. There's no guarantee I can just step back into my job at the moment I want, but I can go back to work there, sooner or later."

"That's good, I guess."

"Well, it's work. It's humdrum, and it's full of noise. But it's a living, until I can make this other thing work out or I can find something better." He looked at the fire and then at her. "I don't need much, not right now. But you already knew that when you found out I lived in a tour home."

The dusk was gathering now, and the firelight brought a shine to her eyes. "Yes, I knew that. And as far as tour homes go, like I said earlier, I think this one's just fine."

"Thanks." Wilf smiled as he turned the steaks. "It's in a good place, anyway. I can't say I'd enjoy living in one if it was on a rented lot in town."

They sat in silence for a few minutes until Adrienne spoke. "Did you hear about Heather Lea?"

A ripple of worry went through him. "No, I didn't. What's happened with her?"

"Well, you know she's been living in Cheyenne?"

"Oh, yeah. She moved down there a few months ago, didn't she?"

"Yes. About four months ago. Then in the last few days she's turned up missing."

"Hmm. So they put out a missing-persons alert, or

whatever they call it?"

"Right. She didn't come into work for a few days, and since she didn't know very many people there, it took a while until someone thought she might be missing. Once they started looking for her, they sent word up here, too, but she's not anywhere around."

Wilf looked at the coals. "I hope she turns up." In his mind he had a picture of Heather Lea, a dark-haired girl with a nice figure, maybe a little rough around the edges, needing dental work and a hair trim. Waited tables in one place or another. Lived in a mobile home court on the east side of town, where Wilf had gone with her and a twelve-pack when the bars closed. That was a while back.

"I do, too," said Adrienne. "She had her troubles, but I hope nothing's happened to her."

Adrienne's comment gave him a pang. Heather had gone through some of her problems when he had been going through his. She did drink, and she did take men home, and her ex-husband had managed to take the two kids from her. But she was a good-natured girl, in spite of her flaws.

"I hope so, too," he said. "I had the impression that she went to Cheyenne to try to get things straightened out." He had tried not to take or show much interest in other women since he met Adrienne, but he did not feel he had to be careful on this topic. "Where was she working?"

"At the truck stop, or 'travel center' as they call it, on I-25 right after it crosses I-80."

"The one that's south of town, then, as you head towards Colorado?"

"Right."

Wilf nodded. She would have a met a lot of guys there,

but he didn't think she would have just run off with one of them. As he remembered her, she was responsible in that way. She went to work. "Well, I hope she turns up," he said again.

"So do I."

Wilf brought out the salad, bread, plates, and utensils. When the rib-eyes came off the grill, he and Adrienne spent a couple of minutes cutting into their steaks and verifying that everything was fine.

"So you're off on another job," she said, reviving the conversation, "with a friend of Norman Lang's."

"You sound as if you have your doubts."

She smiled. "Well, to tell you the truth, I do. I don't know if you'll be happy working for that kind of clientele, but like I said earlier, you ought to be able to give it a try."

"Since it sort of fell in my lap, I might as well." He recalled his impression of Wentworth, pushy and patronizing at the same time, eager to hire a guide and taking care to flatter him. At some point, all of that might wear thin. Wilf looked at Adrienne and returned her smile.

"You know, you might be right. It looks like a good direction to be taking, but there's plenty I don't know about these guys. If and when I get fed up with them, you can tell me 'I told you so.' "

"Oh, I wouldn't do that. I want you to give it a try, if that's what you want to do. If I were to criticize you, it would be for letting my wine glass go empty."

"Now that's negligence," he said. "Especially for someone who's supposed to know how to run a camp."

"It's my fault," she teased, putting her hand on his leg. "I had you distracted."

2

Wilf pulled over to the side of the road and brought the pickup to a stop. The dim light from the dashboard cast the interior in the familiar tones of half-shadow. As he unscrewed the stopper on the thermos he glanced over the shapes of his gear — the tote bag that held his knives and rifle shells and maps, the canvas jacket that he wore for the early fall season, and the .30-06 in the gun rack. In the drawn-in world of the cab, he had the good feeling of being prepared, of having in order the things that made him capable. Once in his life he had driven off and left his rifle at home, and since then, no amount of double-checking was too much. He poured coffee into the insulated mug, put the thermos away, looked in the left mirror to see the clearance lights on the camper trailer, let out the clutch, and got the pickup rolling again.

He figured he had a good ten miles to go until he would come to Wentworth's turn-off. He hadn't been to the ranch itself since Bonnell started charging a trespass fee, but he had been past the turn-off a hundred times. The road would go over a little bridge where Wilf had seen a huge buck come up out of the creek bed on a dark morning like this one; then it would curve to the right and to the left and straighten out, and there would be the mailbox. A fellow didn't forget any of those things.

It was too bad Bonnell had started charging, but he had just done what others had already decided to do. They made a few hundred dollars that way, and no one could blame them. Wilf didn't care for it at the time. He just hunted for himself then, he and a couple of pals, and it seemed as if some of the better places slipped out of their reach — or out of their legal access, anyway, as it was still sometimes possible to reach across a fence as far as a shot would carry. He remembered resenting the men in the nice outfits with Wisconsin and Iowa plates, the smiling customers who paid good money and tipped as well. Small wonder they edged out the local Joes. But if that was the way things were going to go, there was no stopping it. And now he was on the other side of the fence, getting paid to go onto a ranch where he would have had to pay a year or two earlier. It didn't feel natural yet, but he knew that if he was going to try to make a living out of this sort of thing, he needed to be making connections with landowners like Wentworth and clientele like Wentworth's friends.

Wilf looked in the rear-view mirror again. The trailer was such an easy pull that he had to check from time to time to make sure it was still there. He took a sip of coffee and went through his equipment one more time, remembering each item he had put in the back of the pickup—the hoist, the field box with the game bags and gambrels, the milk crate with six one-gallon jugs of water. Unless one of Wentworth's hunters made a mess of things, it should be a snap to get three nice bucks on the Bonnell ranch. The deer would be there; it would just be a matter of making good kills and then getting everything clean and neat. Some of these guys didn't have the slightest idea of what to do once they knocked down an animal, and lots of them didn't like to get their hands dirty with it. That was all right. As long as they stayed out of the way, Wilf could take care of the carcasses. He liked doing things well and having the right equipment.

The announcer on the radio was going through the statewide news. Wilf turned up the volume at the mention of a missing truck-stop waitress from Cheyenne. The report gave her name, her age, and a brief description, and then the news moved on to a motorhome accident near Rawlins. Heather Lea didn't get much air time—thirty-four, dark hair, dark eyes, medium build, missing since Saturday or Sunday. Wilf could see her now—smiling, tossing her hair over her shoulder, tapping her cigarette in the ashtray as she sat sideways to the bar and let her eyes meet his. There was no room in a newscast to say that she was good-humored, fun to be around, cozy.

Wilf recalled a line he often associated with her. One morning, as he lay in bed with her in the after-glow of an intimate session, he ran a strand of her hair between his fingers and told her how nice-looking it was. She'd smiled and said, "I'm a little Indian on my mother's side." Just for a moment, before he rearranged the sentence and replayed it, Wilf had an image of a small Indian standing next to a grownup. He corrected it soon enough, though, by looking at her dark hair and eyes and then the rest of her. She was a full woman.

Now she was missing.

Wilf turned the radio down and put his attention back on the road. Lots of animals were out at this time in the morning—deer on their way to grass and water, raccoons on the way home from a hard night of stealing corn or chickens.

A small pair of blue-green eyes winked out of sight in the roadside weeds. A cat, probably. Couldn't begrudge cats. They were hunters, too—just a little farther down the chain.

Wilf checked in the mirror and saw the clearance lights again. He remembered the night before, after Adrienne went home, when he was getting his gear together. He had paused at the door of the shed, just before turning off the light, and had looked over his saddles, bridles, halters, scabbards, and ropes, all in place along the wall, beneath the overhead shelf where his panniers and tent bags were stored. For a moment he'd felt a longing, almost a regret, that he was going off to hunt some pudsy greenies in a pickup instead of taking horses and tents and all the necessary minimum for roughing it. Well, that stuff wasn't going anywhere. He should be done with these fellows in a few days, and meanwhile, he was making a good connection.

He crossed the bridge, expecting as he always did to see a deer there. Instead, he saw a "For Sale" sign offering farm and ranch property and giving Norman Lang's name and telephone number. Wilf followed the road to the right and to the left, slowed when the mailbox came shining into view, geared down, and started the slow climb to the ranch.

The lights were on in the house when he pulled into the yard. His headlights swept across the rear end of Wentworth's Navigator with its Wyoming license. It sat next to a light-colored Ford Expedition and a dark Explorer, each with its tell-tale green-and-white license plate from Colorado. Wilf pulled to the edge of the parking area opposite the house and came to a stop. Ahead and to the right sat a grey Ford pickup. It looked fairly new, a model F250 with a cab-and-a-half, plenty of chrome, and running boards. It was parked up on the dirt, off to the side of the graveled yard, and it didn't have a rear license plate. He wondered if it was the ranch pickup and whether they would use it.

Wilf shut off his lights and engine and got out, then reached back in for his jacket. He decided to go ahead and drop the trailer, so he went to the back of his pickup and got started unhooking. He heard the door of the ranch house open, and as he looked around, Wentworth's voice carried across the yard.

"Come on in when you're done there."

Wilf called back an "O.K." and went on with cranking the trailer tongue free of the pickup. When he was done, he walked across the yard, knocked on the front door, and went in.

The door opened into a kind of vestibule with a dim living room straight ahead and a bright kitchen on the right. At the far end of the kitchen, under a hanging shaded lamp, four men sat with coffee cups in front of them. A haze floated around the light fixture, and the blended smell of coffee, bacon grease, and cigarette smoke hung on the air. Wentworth, who sat with his back to the entryway, stood up and turned around as Wilf walked into the kitchen.

"Good morning. I see you made it."

"Sure did." Wilf took off his cap.

"Well, that's just fine. Let me introduce you." Wentworth turned to the men seated at the table. "Fellas, this is Wilf. He's our guide. He's hunted on this place before, so he'll show us how to get it done."

Wilf stepped forward and shook hands as each man rose from his seat. He caught both names of the first man, Jerry Newell, and after that he was able to hang onto just the first names, Larry and Randy. With his left hand like a fin he counted them out. "Jerry, Larry, Randy. Right?"

They all nodded.

Wentworth offered him a cup of coffee and his own chair.

"No, thanks. I just had two cups, and it feels good to be standing up after sitting in the cab for the last while."

Wentworth sat down. The dining area was not very large, and it had only four chairs and a small table. Wilf could tell, from the little he had seen of the house, that it didn't have a great deal of room.

The fellow on his left, Jerry Newell, picked a lit cigarette from the ashtray and tapped it to knock off the ashes.

"Wilf, huh? That's a Canadian name, isn't it? Are you Canadian?"

"My mother is."

Wilf took a look at the man. He had wavy red hair shot with grey, neatly trimmed, and a narrow beard, also red and grey, that ran like a chin strap about an inch wide all the way around. As he took a drag on his cigarette, he wrapped his thumb and fingers around the lower part of his face, covering part of his beard and directing Wilf's view to his shiny red face and round nose. The green eyes looked at Wilf, and the hand holding the cigarette lowered. Newell shot a puff of smoke off to his left.

"You from here, then? A native?"

"That's right."

"Well, good."

Wilf looked at the other two men. The middle one had light brown hair and a rough complexion but was clean-shaven, while the third one had mouse-colored hair and a mustache. In spite of their differences in appearance, they were all peas in a pod, along with their host—somewhere in their forties, obviously well off and self-assured, at ease in this simple little world away from the land of green license plates and whatever men of their caliber made their money at. Wilf needed to get a handle on their names, so he started again.

"Jerry Newell, right?"

"You've got it."

"And Larry—"

"Wight."

"O.K. And Randy—"

"Parker."

"O.K. Jerry Newell, Larry Wight, Randy Parker."

Newell made a waving motion with his right hand, palm open and still holding the cigarette. "You've got it perfect. You could sell cars for me."

Wilf smiled. "You never know when I might need a job."

All four men at the table laughed.

"Well," said Wentworth, "we should probably think about gettin' started." He shifted in his chair but did not get up.

Wilf looked around at the men, figuring there would be five in all. "Shall we take two pickups, or how do you want to work it?"

Wentworth cocked his head and made a half-frown.

"I need to get the brakes fixed on that Ford before I can take it anywhere."

Wilf shrugged. "Well, we could all go in mine."

"Oh, I don't need to go right away. I can stay here, get things cleaned up. I showed Jerry some of the place yesterday, and he said he wouldn't mind going out on the four-wheeler, so to start out, maybe you could go with Larry and Randy."

Wilf looked at the three hunters. "My idea, the way I usually do things, is to get people lined out to hunt on their own if they want, or I can take 'em around one by one until they fill. If you kill something off on your own, just remember where it is, and I'll take care of it."

The three men nodded.

"Everyone's got a license, right?"

They answered in a muttered chorus of "Yeah" and "Oh, yeah."

Wentworth stood up, his height accentuated by the closeness of the overhead lamp. "Everyone's got the same kind, Wilf. For antlered deer. I went with them."

Wilf turned to the three men who were still seated. "The other thing you need is some kind of orange—a cap or a vest or a jacket."

"I've got a cap," said Newell as he reached forward and crushed his cigarette.

"I've got a cap that's orange and a vest that's camouflage and orange," said Wight.

"That's fine." Wilf looked at Parker.

"I don't have anything that's orange."

"That's O.K. I've always got a couple of extra vests. You just want to make sure you're wearing something orange when you're actually hunting." Wilf turned down the corners of his mouth and looked at his own cap, which he held in his left hand. "I don't care for it too much myself, but I keep in the habit. Sometimes it feels dorky, and in a small group like this, no one's going to shoot anyone. But it's the law, and it's in the regulations that come with your license."

"I know," said Parker. "I just forgot."

"No, that's fine. Don't worry. That's why I carry extras."

The men got up from the table and walked through an archway into the living room. Wilf went through the kitchen to stand by the front door as Wentworth rattled some dishes in the sink.

"Do you not care to hunt, Scott?"

"Oh, I'll go along later. I don't want to get in the way to begin with. I want them to get their best shot at something nice, and I trust you to get 'em set up for that."

Wilf smiled. "Well, I'll try. Of course, the deer have to cooperate."

Newell appeared in an orange cap and a dark green pullover fleece jacket, with his rifle slung on his right shoulder. "Every time I miss one," he said, "they tell me it's the jerk on the trigger."

"You hate to think they're right," said Wentworth.

Newell smiled and dipped his head with a motion that made his red face and strip beard look elfish. "Trouble is, they probably are."

Wight showed up as he had said, in an orange cap and in a combination camouflage-orange insulated vest. Beneath the vest he wore a grey wool jacket, and like Newell he had his rifle slung over his shoulder.

Behind him came Parker, wearing a camouflage cap with ear lugs and a dark-blue nylon windbreaker. He had his thumb underneath his sling strap, up by his shoulder. Wilf wondered if the man would hunt enough to find out that a rifle sling rode a lot better on wool or canvas or fleece than on nylon and that a tree branch brushing against one of those synthetic fabrics made a sound as conspicuous as a sneeze.

Well, these were his hunters. Wight was the tallest and looked as if he was in the best shape. Parker looked a little dumpy, with narrow shoulders and a bit of a gut. Newell wasn't much better, but none of them looked like a heart attack waiting to happen at the bottom of the first canyon.

"Well, I guess we're ready," Wilf said.

Wentworth stood in the opening that led to the kitchen. "Good luck," he said. "Take your time and enjoy it. Make good shots."

"Beware of the jerk on the trigger," Newell chirped.

"All of that," said the host, beaming.

Once outside, Wilf led Wight and Parker to the pickup, where he dug a soft netted orange vest out of his field box. He held Parker's rifle as the man put on the vest and secured it with the Velcro tabs. Newell had gone off on his own, and in a couple of minutes Wilf heard the rap-rap-rap of a small engine. He looked around. Between the yard light and the first grey of morning, he could see the other vehicles in the ranch yard, and then he saw an ATV coming around the passenger side of the Ford Explorer. Newell came putt-putting to the spot where the other three men stood. He had his rifle slung on his back with the sling strap running diagonally across his chest.

"What do you think if I go out the road to the big ridge?"

"All the way out?"

"Yeah."

"That sounds fine. I was thinkin' of takin' these two down to the hayfields to begin with, so if you do that, we won't be in each other's way at all. If you kill somethin', just come and get me."

"O.K." Newell kept his right hand on the throttle as he gave a tug to each of his insulated gloves, and then he clicked the four-wheeler into gear, hooked around, and took off. When he got to the edge of the yard he turned on the headlight, then caught a two-track road and headed to the southwest.

Wilf looked at the other hunters. "Well, I guess we can get in. For this first part, we'll pretty much drive around and look for 'em. Whoever wants the first shot can ride on the outside."

He opened the driver's door and set his tote bag on the floorboard, then waited for the men to walk around to the passenger side. When Wight had poked his rifle into the gun rack, Wilf slid in behind the wheel and started the engine. Wight climbed in and sat in the middle, and Parker sat on the passenger side with his gun upright between his knees.

Wilf turned the pickup around, switched on the headlights, and started down the hill. "A couple of things about hunting from the vehicle," he said. "One is, we don't shoot from the cab. Probably just about everyone has done it at one time or another, but we don't on these deals. The other is, I always check and double-check to make sure you don't have a live one in the chamber when you get into the cab or into the back. If I ask you, don't take it personally. It's just one of those things you can never be too careful about."

Wight nodded, and Parker said, "I don't even have it loaded yet."

"Well, I'll stop at the bottom of the hill, before we get to the hayfields, so you can get ready. Just don't put one in the chamber until you get out of the cab and get ready to shoot."

"Have you got shells?" asked Wight.

"Oh, yeah. Whole box full." Parker made a tapping sound, followed by the rattle and ring of rifle shells.

At the bottom of the hill, Wilf stopped the pickup and turned off the headlights. "You can go ahead and load up if you want. Just don't put a live one in the spout."

Parker twisted around, set a green-and-yellow box of cartridges on the dashboard, and then leaned forward to work with his rifle.

"You might want to get out of the cab," said Wilf. He looked at the printing on the end of the cartridge box and noted that Parker shot a .270; then he looked at the rifle.

"It's got a clip, if I can just get it out. So I can load it right where it is."

"Why don't you get out of the cab? I think the two of us would feel better."

"I know I would," said Wight. "That's an automatic, isn't it?"

"Yeah. Semi-automatic, to be precise." Parker opened the door, grabbed the box of shells, and slid out of the cab with the rifle in his hand.

Wilf heard the click of releasing the magazine, the snicking sound of loading four shells, and then the clack of fitting the magazine back into the gun. He didn't like semi-automatics to begin with, but he said nothing. He would just have to be even more careful with this fellow.

Parker got back into the cab, set the cartridge box on the dashboard, and let out a heavy breath. "All ready."

"O.K." Wilf put the pickup in gear and got it moving. "I don't know if any of these deer have been shot at," he said, "but if we get close to some and they don't take off running, try not to get excited, you know. Take your time, get set, and try to concentrate on making a good shot."

"Right."

"Have you hunted much?"

"A little bit."

"Well, if you're not hurried, try for a good clean shot. Try not to shoot if he's in the middle of a bunch of 'em. Wait till he gets in the clear, and then let him have it."

"All right."

"You hear too many stories about shootin' the one standin' next to it, or the bullet goin' all the way through and hittin' the one on the other side. We want to avoid that if we can."

"O.K."

Wilf pulled out onto the paved road and turned right. "There's three hayfields along here. The last one's a little farther back in, and the road hunters don't bother it so much. But they can be anywhere—the deer, you know."

"Yeah. Do you mind if I smoke?"

Wilf felt his spirits sink. It was an aggravation to hunt with someone who had to smoke. If the smell didn't chase the deer off, then the trashy cough did. Or if the guy killed a deer, he got so winded trying to drag it that anyone helping him would get fed up. But Parker was probably the type that wouldn't get very far from the pickup, and when it came right down to it, Wilf couldn't worry about how much the man put himself into the hunt.

"No, go ahead. Just roll down the window."

"Sure."

"And don't throw any matches or live butts out in the dry grass."

"I won't." Parker's lighter flared, and he lit his cigarette with a puff.

"The first hayfield is just up here on the right. One of

you will probably have to get out and open the gate."

At the corner of the field, Wilf turned off the road and stopped at the barbed-wire gate. Parker handed his rifle to Wight, and with his cigarette in his mouth he wrestled with the gate until he slipped the wire loop off the pole. Then he dragged the gate out of the way on Wilf's side to let the pickup go through.

"What's that?" Wight was pointing across with his right hand, almost in front of Wilf's nose.

"Shit." Wilf stepped on the brake by reflex as he recognized the dark, husky shapes strung out in a line to his left. He could not tell if any of them had antlers.

Parker, who had his back to the deer, gave a questioning look. The cigarette bobbed in his mouth as he said, "What is it?"

Wilf shut off the engine. The deer were moving at a slow walk. If they had taken any notice, they were not spooked. "Deer," he said in a low voice. "Set that gate down nice and soft, and walk around the back of the pickup. Come around to your door, but don't open it." He turned to Wight sitting next to him. "Larry, how about you scoot over and hand him the rifle out the window? Don't open the door, or it'll make a noise." Wilf looked across the cab until Parker appeared in the window. "Randy, Larry's goin' to hand you your gun. You can take a rest across the hood. Look 'em all over with the scope, and see if there's any with a good rack." Wilf took a deep breath and let it out. "They're not worried about anything, so take your time. Try not to make any noise to spook 'em."

Parker nodded.

"Where's your cigarette?"

"I stepped on it."

"O.K. Go ahead."

Parker tipped his head back as he took the rifle that Wight handed him. Then he swung the gun around and brought it to a rest across the corner of the hood.

Wilf fidgeted. This was always the hard part, waiting to see if someone was going to get it together to take a shot and then seeing if the shot was any good. He could see the tip of the rifle wavering as Parker tried to pick up the deer in the scope. The animals at the head of the line had already disappeared over a rise.

Parker shifted position, then pulled back on the spring-loaded bolt that flicked a shell into the chamber. He rotated the gun, followed the deer for a few more paces, and straightened up.

"I don't see any horns," he said, in a voice that sounded way too loud. Then he came to the window on his side of the cab.

"How many did you see?" Wilf asked.

"I'm not sure. I think about six."

"I counted eight." Wilf tapped on the steering wheel with his thumb, thinking. "We need to get a better look at 'em, but let's not rush 'em. Go ahead and unload your rifle, and give it to Larry. I'll pull on through, and you can close the gate."

"O.K." Parker held the gun straight up, pulled back the sliding bolt, and caught the live shell as it ejected.

"Did you pop another one in there while you did that?"

"I don't think so. It didn't look like it."

Wilf took a deliberate breath. "Why don't you make sure? We're in no hurry. Take out the clip, and work that catch again."

Parker looked at Wilf as if he didn't like being told what to do with his own gun, but he went ahead and did it. No other shells came out of the chamber, which surprised Wilf.

From the little he had seen of semi-automatics, a fellow usually had to take out the magazine to keep from putting another shell into the chamber when he worked that sliding bolt. Wilf kept his eye on things as Parker thumbed the loose shell back into the clip, put the clip into the rifle, and handed the gun through the window. It would have been easier and safer to open the door and hand the gun in that way, but he figured Parker was doing what he thought he was supposed to do. Wilf started the pickup and pulled ahead so the man on the ground could close the gate.

When Parker was back in the cab, Wilf let off on the clutch pedal and eased the pickup forward.

Parker cleared his throat. "You think there was a buck in that bunch?"

"I don't know. But I think we can get a better look."

Wight spoke up as he turned toward his friend. "Did you get nervous at all?"

"I got a little shaky, but I can bear down. I know that."

Wilf let the pickup idle along and crawl to the top of the rise, where he saw the deer again off to the left about a quarter of a mile. He stopped the pickup and shut off the engine, then reached back for his own rifle in the gun rack. "I'm just going to take a look through the scope." The other two men tipped their heads forward as he lifted the gun and turned it end for end. As he poked the barrel out the window, he said, "They don't spook nearly as fast if no one gets out of the vehicle."

The gun settled right into place, just like in the old days. With one elbow on the window ledge and the other on the cross-piece of the steering wheel, and the engine shut off to take away all the vibration, Wilf had a rock-steady aim. The day was getting lighter by the minute, and the scope picked up what light there was. Then the deer came into view, still dark and husky but no longer in single file.

"Eight of 'em, sure enough."

"Any horns?" Parker cleared his throat again and spit out the window.

"One of 'em looks like he might do, and a couple of others might have little racks."

"I couldn't put horns on any of 'em."

The deer had stopped and were grazing. Wilf watched through the scope as they raised and lowered their heads. "I don't think I saw that biggest one the first time. Or at least not his headgear. And the others, with little horns, they're hard to tell when there's not much light. But when the ears lay a little different, you look closer on those ones. The horns sort of push the ears down." Now the big buck raised his head, and Wilf caught a dull shine of antlers. "That one fella looks pretty good. Let's think about how we'll go after him." Wilf sat up straight, then put his rifle back in the gun rack.

"How close can we get?" Parker shook out another cigarette but waited to light it.

"Oh, no tellin'. But I think we can do better on foot than if we try to get up on 'em out in the open in this thing."

"You mean just walk?"

"Not right at 'em. I think we can go off and around to the right, stay down and out of sight, and come up on the other side of that haystack."

"What if they're gone when we get there?"

"I guess that's a chance we take. We'll just have to look for 'em some more. But that's better than runnin' 'em off."

Parker stuck his cigarette back in the pack. "O.K.

Whatever you say."

Wilf stepped on the clutch and hit the ignition, and the motor hummed back into life. "Let's back this thing down the hill and out of sight," he said, as he shifted into reverse. "Larry, if you don't mind, you can stay here — either in the cab or up on that rise. If they come back this way, help yourself. If you see us, don't shoot in our direction."

"All right. Are you going to carry a gun, too?"

"Not if I go out on foot. I don't have a license. I just have it along in case I need it for something that goes wrong, or in case someone else's gun fouls up and they need a backup."

Wilf eased the pickup down the slope until he reached a level spot and could no longer see over the rise. With a nod of assurance to Wight, he got out of the cab and reached into his pocket for his gloves. The jacket, which was canvas with a flannel lining, and the gloves, regular cotton, had just the right level of warmth for deer and antelope season, when the temperature usually didn't drop far below freezing. It felt like a few degrees above that right now. Wilf pulled on the gloves as he walked around the back of the pickup.

Parker had gotten out and had put on a pair of wool-and-leather driving gloves. He plucked half a dozen shells out of his box and put them in his right pants pocket. Then he handed the box into the cab, closed the door, patted the pockets of his windbreaker, pulled the orange vest straight, and turned to join the guide.

As they walked away from the pickup, Wilf spoke to Parker in a low voice. "It doesn't look like these deer have been hunted this year, so if we get up on 'em, don't get rattled. Once they've been shot at, they're a hell of a lot harder to do anything with. So we'll try to get a good shot the first time."

"Sounds fine to me." Parker put his thumb under his sling strap and hitched his shoulder, then fell into pace alongside the guide. His rifle stock made a brushing sound against the windbreaker as he walked.

Wilf followed the contour of the land back to the north and around to the west, then cut south to a drainage that ran along the base of the hills. It was full daylight now, but the air was still crisp. Parker was keeping up fine; his breathing sounded a bit labored, but he hadn't gotten winded.

Wilf spoke in a low voice. "The haystack should be a little ways up ahead on the left. We'll take a short breather before we walk up to it. Are you all right?"

"Yeah, I'm fine."

"Good. I just don't like to be out of breath when I get to the top of a hill. If you see something, you don't want your gun to be wobblin' all over."

Parker's chest went up and down as he nodded.

Wilf led the way another quarter of a mile until they could see the top bales of the haystack. He took a deep breath and let it out.

"O.K. Make sure you've got your wind. Put a shell in, and be ready. We'll come up to the haystack and take a look around the right end. If they're anywhere close, get the steadiest aim you can, and give it a try."

"All right." Parker stood still for a long moment, then heaved out a breath and clicked a shell into the chamber. "I'm ready."

"O.K. I'll lead the way. You point that thing off to one side. When we get there, I'll take the first peek, and then I'll let you know."

Wilf took it slow up the little rise to the haystack,

turning to see that Parker was with him. Then he went to the stack. The bales were the large, rectangular kind that had to be moved by machinery, and they were arranged in one long, tall row. Although some of them were lined up crooked, Wilf could find no gaps to see through. He went to the right end of the stack, took off his cap, and edged his head around. The hayfield spread out green and golden in the new daylight, and the sight of several deer, less than a hundred yards away, startled him. He drew back, turned to Parker, and made a pointing gesture to indicate that the deer were right there. Then he put on his cap and walked to the other end of the stack, looking back to see Parker getting the rifle into position. As he peered around the edge, he heard the crash of the rifle shatter the stillness of the morning.

He took a full look and saw deer wheeling and running, and in the midst of them a buck with a three- or four-point rack, hunched and frozen, facing away from the haystack at a three-quarter angle.

Gut-shot. The deer was in too much shock to know where the deep, searing pain had come from.

Then the rifle blasted again, and the deer spilled over.

Wilf went back along the bales and came out behind Parker, who was still aiming his rifle at the animal.

"He's down. I don't think you'll need to shoot again."

"He sure didn't go down the first time."

"You hit him in a better place on the second one."

"You sure he's down for good? He's still kickin'."

"Yeah, I'm sure. We'll walk up to him, and when you see that he's done for, you can unload your rifle."

Parker looked at him. "What for?"

"People forget things. They get all caught up in the

moment, and then they take pictures or whatever, and they pick up the gun again, and maybe it goes off. Do you have a live one in there right now?"

"Um, yeah. A new one goes in when you fire, and I didn't take it out because I didn't know if he was going to get up."

"Well, when you're satisfied that he won't, you'll do the best thing if you unload all the way. Then we won't have to think about that part of it again." Wilf patted the man on the shoulder of the whispering windbreaker. "You got a hell of a nice deer. Congratulations."

Parker smiled and nodded, transferred the rifle to his left hand, and held out his right hand to shake. "Thanks, Wilf. I don't know but what I might have screwed it up on my own."

"Well, you didn't. You got a nice deer." And to himself, Wilf said, *One down*.

3

Wilf walked across the open hayfield in the warming sun. There was never any telling where the complications might come from, but he had the first of his three tasks in a good place. The deer was dead, with its tongue hanging out and its eyes clouded over, and he had left Parker sitting next to it with an empty rifle in his lap and plenty of cigarettes.

Wilf recalled the better features of the deer. Parker had gotten a nice one, all right. It had four points on each side, symmetrical, with sharp tips on all the tines. It had looked pretty good in the scope when Wilf saw the first flash of antlers, and it looked fine when he and Parker walked up on it where it lay stretched out on the alfalfa stubble.

Wilf could move at an open stride now that he wasn't planning a sneak up on a herd of deer, and he felt free and easy as he crossed the field. Warmer now, he unbuttoned his jacket and took off his gloves. He felt good.

Adrienne came to mind for the first time since he had started out with these hunters. She would understand this part, at least—the sky above and the land stretching out in all directions, not a vehicle or building in sight, and nothing louder than a meadowlark. This would be the garden, as she had stated it. Right now he was the man in the garden, on foot. That was the best way to do it, like creeping along in the shadow of a sandstone bluff, finding the glint of antlers, then hearing the echoing shot as the deer pitched forward. Even if it wasn't a trophy deer, he had gotten it on the best terms—on foot, on his own.

His thoughts came back to Adrienne. If he blocked out the hunter behind him and the one up ahead, this moment, being alone in the landscape, would appeal to her. Something in the air at this time of year, a fleeting quality, gave it an energy she would appreciate. Adrienne liked being outside, he knew that, and she didn't seem to have any trouble with hunting itself. He could see her point about the commercial aspect, though; he could feel it after having led a tenderfoot up to a haystack and having pointed out the deer for him to ambush. That part didn't feel like the garden. It felt like work for pay.

He didn't like to think of his work as tourism, but from the figures he heard, more and more of the state's income came from dude ranches, bed-and-breakfast ranches, and the like. Guiding fit in there somewhere. There was a bit of money to be made at it, and if he didn't, someone else would, so he might as well give it a try. And Adrienne understood that part, too.

He angled over to his left, to the faint road that was pressed into the edge of the field. He found the tracks and followed them on a slow uphill grade until he came to the rise. There below him sat the familiar shape of his pickup, the faded scarlet in contrast with the frost-burned yellow-and-green alfalfa. He looked around for the other hunter and saw him well off to the right, just below the crest of the slope and walking toward the pickup, with his rifle slung on his shoulder. Wilf raised his hand and waved, and Wight returned the gesture.

When they were within speaking distance, Wight spoke. "Looks like Randy got one."

Wilf realized Wight had probably watched in the scope. From this point he would have a good view of the field and the haystack. "He sure did. A nice one."

"Well, I hope he's happy."

"He seems to be pleased with it."

"Did you do anything to it?"

"Um, no. Not yet. From the way he shot it, I'd rather hang it on the hoist off my pickup and clean it that way, where I've got the water and all."

Wight glanced at the vehicle as they walked toward it. "You've got a way of hanging it up out here?"

"Yeah. You'll see it when I get set up. It's worth the little time it takes me to come back and get the pickup."

When they got to the vehicle, Wilf waited until the hunter put his rifle in the rack. Then he got into the cab, started the engine, checked to see that everything was in order, and set off toward the haystack.

"Two shots, huh?"

"Yeah. The first one was a little too much in the middle,

so he needed a second one."

"Gut-shot, uh?"

"Uh, yeah. It'll be a little messy, but I'll get it cleaned up all right."

"Well, this'll be good for Randy."

Wilf thought of the mess he would have once he opened up the deer. Well, that was part of what he was paid for. If pulling the trigger was good for the other fellow, that was the other half. "Oh, I imagine," he said.

Parker was standing by the deer when Wilf brought the pickup to a stop alongside. Wight rolled down the window and craned to look out.

"Looks pretty nice, Randy."

"Yeah, he does. You think you could take some pictures?"

"Sure. You've got your camera?"

"Right here." Parker gave a pat to the left pocket of his windbreaker. He had the netted orange vest balled up in his right hand.

Wilf got out, dropped the tailgate, and started setting up the frame for his hoist. He slid the base, which was made of square tubing, into the receiver pocket that was mounted on the end of his bumper, so that the frame stuck out perpendicular to the tail end of the pickup. Then he dragged the field box to the tailgate, got out the winch, and hooked it up.

Meanwhile, the two hunters had gotten the deer propped up in front of Parker and his rifle, with the haystack in the background, and Wight was snapping photos with a little point-and-shoot camera that made whirring sounds. He took a few shots from one angle, then a few from another. The picture-taking reminded Wilf of a man he met one time, a fellow who wrote articles for hunting magazines. He called pictures like these "dead duck" photos, and he said editors were bored to death by them and by "me-and-Joe" stories. That was about all Wilf remembered of him, except that he was big and bearded, drank cheap bar Scotch, and said he wished he could afford better.

When the hunters were done taking pictures, Wilf took the deer by the antlers with both hands and dragged it beneath the hoist.

"Would you like some help?" Wight asked.

"No, thanks. From this point on it goes just as well if I do it myself. That way I don't have anyone jostling the deer and making me slip with my knife."

No one spoke as he skinned the hocks of the animal and poked a tip of the gambrel into the space between the hamstring and shank on each side. Then Parker, who had run his hand up and down the shaft of the frame, cleared his throat.

"That's a pretty nifty apparatus you've got there."

"Yeah, it works pretty good. Another guy I know has one, and he skins more than a dozen animals a year on it. I took a good look at his and had one made just like it. You get your animals done quicker and cleaner, and they cool better, too."

Parker took what looked like a thoughtful puff on his cigarette. "I imagine."

As Wilf turned to start winching, he heard the tight whine and flutter of an engine. It sounded like a four-wheeler. When he looked around, he was not surprised to see Newell at the helm.

"Well, here comes Jerry," said Parker. "I wonder if he got anything."

Wilf took a closer look. "He might have. He's not carrying his rifle."

Parker and Wight took a couple of steps back and waited as Newell came sputtering and then coasting into the scene of the kill.

"Got one, huh?" He shut off the engine, and the noise died away.

Parker's voice sounded clear. "Sure did. From right over there. How about you?"

Newell shook his head as he reached up under his pullover jacket and brought out a pack of cigarettes.

"Why'd you leave your gun up at the house? Or did you lose it?"

"I got tired of it bangin' on my back, and I figured there wouldn't be much left over by the time I got here anyway."

Wilf started ratcheting the winch to lift the deer off the ground.

"It was cool as hell," said Parker. "Wilf brought me right up behind the haystack here, and there they were."

"Really."

Wilf glanced around and saw Newell lighting a cigarette with a lighter. Then he went back to winching the deer.

"Isn't that a nice gizmo he's got?"

"It sure is," said Newell. "You know, Wilf, I could get you an electric motor for that. You could run it off your battery."

Wilf raised and lowered his eyebrows, then turned to look at Newell. "Oh, this works just fine. I can set it all up in a minute, and I can take it down and stow it away. Those winches you're talkin' about, they usually mount permanent on the front bumper."

"You could mount that thing there, too, as far as that goes."

"I guess I could. But I like having everything here on the tail end." Wilf went back to his work.

Newell's voice changed tone. "Where'd you hit him?"

Wight spoke up. "He gut-shot him."

Newell made a "Tut-tut" sound with his tongue.

"Well, I got my deer," said Parker. "And he's a nice-looking one."

"That he is," said Newell. "We're just jealous, that's all."

The hunters went on with their chatter as Wilf skinned the hind legs down to the haunches. The deer was still warm to the touch, so he knew he hadn't lost much time. He set his knife on the bumper and pulled down on the hide with his hands, then took up the knife and went back to trimming. He was cutting through the fat around the tail when he heard the rumble of a vehicle coming across open ground.

He looked up, and coming from the direction of the other hayfields to the south was a ranch outfit. It was an older Chevy, brown and cream-colored, with round headlights like Wilf's, and a flat bed with a dog box up against the cab. It looked like Tommy Tice.

As the vehicle came closer, Wilf saw the familiar glasses and narrow features, framed by the hair sticking down out of the cap and over the ears. The pickup came to a stop about ten yards away, and as the engine died, Tommy's cheerful voice came floating out.

"Hey, ya little Indian. What are you doin' here?"

"A little bit of honest work. And what's a rabbit-choker like yourself doin' here?"

"The same. Puttin' up the last of the hay, and thought I'd come over here and gawk. I thought the boss was lookin' for a housekeeper, but you don't look like her."

"Oh, are you workin' for this guy?" Wilf took a quick look at the hunters, hoping he hadn't sounded too flippant about their friend.

"That I am." Tommy raised a cigarette to his lips. "Looks like someone got one."

"That's right. Randy did."

Parker nodded, and Tommy looked at him but said nothing as he tapped his ashes onto the floorboard of the cab.

"Have you seen many good ones down here?" Wilf asked.

"One four-pointer, runnin' with a bunch of others. Looks like you might have got him."

Wilf nodded.

"And last week, just once, I seen one up there on the last field that had his horns all growing down on one side. Don't know if he's any good."

Wilf looked over at him. "I killed one, one time a few years back, that had a droopy horn. He was fine."

"Oh, yeah? Where was that? Or should I ask?"

"Up north, in Niobrara County, back when I used to hunt up there. It's been several years, actually. Seems like yesterday."

"I guess it was, for him."

A ripple of laughter came from the hunters, and Wilf looked over to see Parker smiling.

"Anyway, Randy got the first one here, and we'd like to see if there's a couple more out there."

"This your first day, isn't it?"

"Yeah."

"Well, you oughta be able to find a couple more. I'd try up on top. Nobody's been back there that I know of."

"That's good. What else do you know?"

Tommy shook his head. "Nothin'."

"Just work an' sleep, huh?"

"Work all day, thinkin' about beer and pussy, and it don't do me no good."

"Go out at night, and all you can find is the beer, uh?"

"That's it."

"I thought you had a date once."

"Blind date. With the one-eyed lizard."

Wilf laughed and looked at the hunters, for whose benefit he imagined Tommy was holding forth. Two of them were smoking cigarettes, and all three were smiling. Maybe they knew they were supposed to.

Tommy cranked up his engine. "Well, I guess I'd better get back to work. I just thought I'd come over an' see what kind of violators we had here. When I seen your outfit, I knew." He smiled, waved, turned his pickup to the right, and went bouncing away with the latch on his dog box rattling.

Wilf went back to work on the deer, skinning it all the way down to the neck and then cutting through so that the head and hide came off in one piece. Grabbing the antlers, he gave a shake and then dragged the head and cape to one side. He glanced at the hunters, who were still in their group around the four-wheeler, smoking cigarettes and chatting. Then he went back to the deer, which had begun to swell in the abdomen, and opened it up.

He found the mess he expected, a bloody soup of half-digested forage in and around the intestines and clinging to the wall of the body cavity. As he cut and trimmed and pulled out the bulk of the insides, he saw that the bullet had gone straight through the ribs, clipping the stomach and making pulp of the liver but not forcing the gutshot particles into any gashes in the meat. It had helped, also, that the deer hadn't run. Wilf had blood and stench up to his elbows, but he saw that he could get things cleaned up all right.

After a gallon and a half of water and quite a bit of scraping with his knife, Wilf had the carcass about as clean as he was going to get it. Satisfied with that part, he walked over to the head and hide and looked down, assessing whether the head was worth mounting. Then he looked at Parker, who was giving him a curious look.

"What do you think, Randy? Do you want to take the head to a taxidermist, or do you just want to keep the horns?"

"Probably just the horns. I'd want something a little bigger if I was going to have it mounted. And I've got pictures."

"Good enough. It'll just take me a minute to cut 'em off."

The hunters went back to talking, as Wilf imagined they would do at a two-martini lunch while an invisible waiter cleared the table. Wilf knelt by the deer head and with his knife he peeled the skin away from the top of the skull, on down to the eyes and ears. Going to the field box again, he took out the meat saw and checked the tightness of the blade. Returning to his work, he bent over, steadied the antlers with one hand, and sawed with the other. He made two laborious cuts, gave a twist to the antlers as he stepped on one ear, and pulled the skull plate loose from the plundered head. He turned the antlers around and held them out to Parker, who stepped forward and took them. As the hunter went back to share the trophy with his pals, the guide dragged the tubular hide over to the gut pile, where he worked the offal into the pouch, then dragged the mess past the haystack and swung it off into the uncut grass beyond the edge of the field, where it dropped out of sight. Back at the pickup he noticed the front forelegs and rear hocks he had cut off and tossed aside in the early part of the process. He picked them up, carried them halfway to the haystack, and threw them one by one into the grass beyond the field.

The hunters were still making their merry talk. Parker was holding the antlers out and above him, and one of the others made an animated comment. Wilf took a bar of soap from the field box, poured more water, and washed his hands.

"Say, Randy," he said. "Now would be a good time to tag that deer."

"Oh, O.K."

Parker came over to the pickup and set the antlers inside the cab, then took out his wallet and produced the license. Wilf looked on and answered questions as the hunter cut out the date, signed the license, and detached the carcass coupon. Wilf cut off a piece of string from the spool in his field box and tied the coupon onto the deer's left shank. As Parker went back to his friends, Wilf shook out a deer bag, slipped it up and over the body, lifted the carcass from the gambrel, and gave it a heave so that it landed with a flop in the back of the pickup. Then he took down the winch and gambrel, put them in the field box and closed it, put the water away, pulled the skinning frame from its bracket and slid it into the pickup bed, and lifted the tailgate.

"All ready?" said Wight, as if the lunch had ended.

"Any time."

Wilf heard the whir of the engine as Newell pushed the starter button. Then the engine revved up, the machine clicked into gear, and Newell was putt-putting away. Parker came over to the pickup, where he took the antlers out of the cab and set them in back. Then still holding his rifle, he climbed in to sit in the middle. Wight took the place where Parker had sat earlier.

As Wilf put the pickup into gear, Wight spoke up.

"Are we going back up on top, then?"

"I think so. We can cruise through these other two fields just to make sure we don't miss anything, but we don't want to get in Tommy's way if he's runnin' equipment."

"It doesn't look like there's much more to offer down here, but I was just wondering whether I should get my gun down."

"It wouldn't hurt." Wilf stopped the pickup and leaned forward as Wight got out and made the switch with the rifles. Wilf let out a low breath. *Now for the next one,* he thought.

Wilf left the deer carcass, cloaked in the white game bag, hanging in the shadowed interior of the tractor shed. Parker took his antlers into the house, and Newell went along in the pickup with Wight. Wilf set them out to hunt a ridge on the north end of the ranch. It ran west and led down into a grassy bottom where Wilf had agreed to pick up the two hunters. He'd advised them to take it slow, and after sitting in the cab for about forty-five minutes, he drove around to the bottom and picked them up. By the time they all got back up on top, it was almost lunchtime. Wilf drove back to the yard and parked near his trailer.

He told the hunters he had his own lunch, so they went into the house while he opened up the trailer. It was still cool and dark inside. He rummaged in his ice chest for bread and lunch meat, which he carried to the tailgate. The metal had been cold to the touch earlier, but it was comfortable now as he sat with the sun warming his back. He appreciated having a few minutes to himself again, just eating his lunch and dangling his legs off the tailgate and wondering how Adrienne was doing. She would be on lunch break now, too. Sometimes he had to remind himself, on outings like this, that it wasn't the weekend.

When he was done eating, he sat in the cab and listened to the radio. As a general rule he didn't mind leaving the rest of the world at a distance, but today he was curious to know if there was any news about Heather Lea. When the statewide report came on, he heard the same piece he had heard earlier in the morning. That was too bad. No news would have been better.

After the lunch hour, Wight and Newell came out of the house and said they were ready to go. Wilf decided to take them to the northwest corner of the ranch, where he could drive from point to point along the edge of a mesa. As he did, he let the hunters get out and poke around, looking into the canyons and sometimes walking down in a ways and climbing out. The afternoon dragged along slow and dull, as Wilf spent most of the time in the cab of the pickup.

Late in the afternoon the hunters said they were ready to go back, so Wilf turned the pickup around and headed for the house. Newell and Wight didn't talk much, so it was a quiet ride. Back at the yard, Parker was standing with his hands in his pockets, leaning against the Ford pickup that Wentworth had said was out of commission. Parker, who looked idle and listless, seemed like a good match for the pickup that sat with its windows rolled up and its doors locked. He stood up straight as he asked his friends how they had done, and then the three of them headed for the house. After a couple of steps,

Newell turned and told Wilf to be sure to come to the house for a couple of drinks after dinner. Wilf said he would.

The sun **was** just slipping behind the hills and the air was starting to cool. When Wilf stepped into the trailer, he found that it had warmed up in the afternoon and was comfortable. After lighting the propane lamp that was fixed on the wall above the table, he slid onto the bench seat to rest a few minutes. It was tiring to sit in a pickup all day, bouncing along on rutted roads and trying not to bump into the fellow sitting in the middle. He had hoped to get two deer the first day, but at least they had one hanging.

By and by he got up, lit the right burner on the stove, and dug out a pan. This was a no-frills excursion, not a real camping trip, so he had brought canned goods for the evening meals. Whatever he used was fine, and whatever he had left over would come in handy later. He opened a can of beef stew, emptied it into the pan, and set the pan on the fire. From his ice chest he brought out a loaf of bread and a tub of margarine. It didn't look like much of a meal, so he went through his canned goods and took out a can of pears. He shrugged. At least it was better than driving all the way home and then back out in the morning.

When he had finished dinner and had his kitchen cleaned up, he put on his jacket and cap, turned off the light, and stepped outside. The moon was round and bright, still low in the east—probably one night away from a full moon. He thought about Heather Lea and wondered if she was in some place where she could see this moon. For all he knew, she could be in a hotel room in Rawlins or farther west in a night club in Rock Springs, while in this part of the state, the moon was rising in the thin, cool air of evening. He looked around. The yard light had come on as well, so the area was well lit as he walked across to the house.

His knock on the door was answered from within, so he opened the door and stepped inside. Wilf could hear music coming from the living room as he looked into the kitchen and dining area. The men were seated at the table as before, with a haze of cigarette smoke hanging in the air. Wilf recognized the smell of sizzled beef, and from the mess on the table it looked as if the men had had T-bones. Now they were sitting around relaxed, each with a mixed drink in front of him. All but Wight had a cigarette lit.

Wentworth offered Wilf a drink and ran through the choices. Wilf said he would drink a beer, and a moment later he had a bottle of Michelob in his hand. The other three men were talking about golf, so Wilf let his gaze wander around. Then Wentworth, who had not sat back down, pointed at the empty chair.

"Sit down and be comfortable, damn it, and let me straighten out a few things."

During the day, Wilf had gathered that Wentworth and Parker were both divorced, and now as he sat down he could sense that Wentworth took pride in being master of the castle. The others seemed to have an established line of humor about Wentworth's role as host. When the music ended, Newell flung a barb.

"What is that, the third time we've heard that Neil Diamond album?"

"It might be the third CD by him that I've played."

"Sure, we know," Newell went on. "You play this Neil Diamond because you think it'll impress us. But we know." He gave Wilf a confidential nod.

Wentworth leaned forward to wipe the table. "What do you know?"

Newell sat back and held his cigarette up in front of him, his face beaming. "We know you've got some Barry Manilow records hid. Probably a dozen of 'em."

"You'll have a hell of a time findin' 'em."

Newell winked at Wilf. "What do you think? Has he got some hid somewhere?"

Wilf smiled and took a sip on his beer. "I don't know. I just got here." He realized the CD player had started another disc, but he didn't place it right away.

Newell looked around at his two pals. "You see? We ask for Barry Manilow, and Scott holds out on us." He turned and said, "What kind of music do you like, Wilf?"

"Oh, the regular stuff—Randy Travis, Sammy Kershaw, Ian Tyson."

Parker spoke up. "Who's he?"

"Ian Tyson?"

"Yeah. I never heard of him. I've heard of those other two."

"Oh, he sings Western songs."

"Sure, I've heard of him," Newell said. "The cowboys all listen to him. I think he's Canadian, isn't he?"

"Yeah," Wilf said. "Some of his songs are about Alberta, and up Montana."

"I thought he was. But you say you're not."

"No."

"No reason you should be, just to like him, if all these other guys do."

Wight finished taking a sip and set down his drink. With his bland expression he said, "How do you come to know about him, Jerry?"

Newell lifted his eyebrows and put on a grave look. "I make it my business to know things." Then he relaxed. "I sell pickups to guys like that—you know, hats and boots, and a rope hangin' in the gun rack."

"What kind of pickups do you sell?" asked Wilf.

"Fords. I'm a senior salesman at a Ford-Lincoln-Mercury dealership. When you get ready to upgrade, let me know."

Wilf nodded.

"Of course I noticed you drive a Chevy. Nothin' wrong with that."

"I hope not."

"Maybe he doesn't want a Ford," said Wight. "This morning you offer him a job, and now you try to sell him a pickup."

Newell tipped his head to the left. "Can't help it. Just ask any of the cowboys. Ask 'em, 'What kind of deal does Jerry Newell give you?' And they'll say, 'Mighty fine.' Ask 'em."

"Jerry Newell, friend of the cowboy," said Parker.

"That's me. You won't hear me playin' any Barry Manilow. Or what the hell's this that came on?"

"Billy Joel," said Wentworth. "You ought to remember him. He sang *Uptown Girl* ten or fifteen years ago. Your kind of stuff. The girl, I mean."

"Oh, yeah. He sang it at my high-school graduation."

Wight rattled the cubes in his glass. "More like your twenty-year reunion."

"Oh, he's all right," said Newell. Then, "Who else did you say you liked, Wilf?"

"I think I said Randy Travis and Sammy Kershaw."

"Kershaw," said Wight. "Friend of the car salesman."

Newell tapped his cigarette in the ashtray. "How's that?"

"He does a song about 'Cadillac Style.' "

"I thought that was 'Doggie Style.' "

"No, that's someone else. Your dark brother. This one is *Cadillac Style*. You know it, Wilf?"

"Yeah, I've got a few of his."

"See?" said Parker. "You'd better get with it, Jerry. They play it at all the GM agencies."

"The hell they do. I know who you're talkin' about. They play him at all the mobile home lots. Don't they, Wilf?"

He laughed. "Yeah, I like that song."

"Which one?" asked Parker.

Wilf smiled as he recited the line. "I made her the queen of my double-wide trailer."

"See?" said Newell. "I'll stick with what's-his-name. The one that the Ford cowboys listen to." Glancing at Wilf, he said, "Not that there's anything wrong with this Kershaw fellow. He's funny, and he beats the hell out of Garth Brooks. Now there's a phony-ass sonofabitch for you." He turned toward the kitchen. "What the hell's wrong with you, Scott? Why don't you have any native music?"

"I haven't had time to go to the store. Been spendin' all my time over a hot stove."

Newell gave a dip with his bearded chin. "Well, take off your apron. Get a maid like you talked about before. If you're goin' to turn this place into a vacation villa, you'd better get some native music."

Wentworth stood in front of the table with an arch look on his face. "If you want to sell mobile homes, you can get the mobile home music yourself. You know, I read the other day that some auto agencies are bringing in gay and lesbian sales people, to try to get more of that market. Maybe you should hire one of them and get the Barry Manilow music for yourself. Do you want another beer, Wilf?"

"Not quite yet, thanks."

"I love my friends, you understand, or I wouldn't have brought us all together for a happy time like this."

Newell's face was shiny as ever. "Don't let him ply you with liquor, Wilf. He really brought us here to sell us all a vacation parcel. He gave Larry the full pitch before we got here, and now he's workin' on us."

Wilf thought he felt some tension in the air, something in addition to the general feeling he had of being on the outside of a joke they were pretending to let him in on.

"Actually," he said, "we did see some nice country today. And we'll see more tomorrow." He looked at Parker. "Have you seen much of the ranch?"

"No, but I think I might get to. Scott said we could all ride out together in the morning."

"Should be all right." As Wilf nodded, he realized Parker was wearing glasses, which he hadn't worn earlier in the day. Maybe the man wore contact lenses most of the time.

"The thing that gets me," said Parker, "is how easy it is to build here. You don't have to take out a permit to build, or hook up electricity, or put in a sewer, or anything."

"Not out here in the country, no."

Parker adjusted his glasses. "You can do as you damn well please. This is a hell of a place. And I don't mean just for a vacation home. Hell, I could *live* here."

"I could too," said Newell. "If I could find work."

The talk went on from there, and at one point Parker made reference to Wentworth being a country gentleman.

Wentworth sniffed. "I don't think 'gentleman' means what it used to."

"Nah," said Newell. "It doesn't. Nowadays it just means someone who acts nice around women. You know—let her go through the door first, light her cigarette, give her the first beer out of the six-pack. Or like the Ford cowboys say, open the door of the cab so she can see to put her clothes back on."

Parker laughed. "That's where they were drinking the six-pack."

"Oh, yeah." Newell palmed his face as he took a drag on his cigarette. "By the way, Wilf, I noticed your interior light doesn't work. That might be a sign that it's time to upgrade."

"Might be."

"Always on the job," said Wight. "Trying to sell him a Ford."

Newell tipped his ash. "Just lookin' out for the amenities." Looking around at his pals, he added, "Nothing wrong with sex in the car. Keeps you feeling young, and the price is right." He wagged his eyebrows. "Of course, it's better if you're not all by yourself."

No one said anything in response.

Wilf finished his beer, and Wentworth offered him a second one. He accepted.

Newell picked up the thread about sex in the car. He told a story he had read on the Internet news about two funeral home employees in Mexico, a young man and woman. They went into the garage where the hearse was and started it up, for the air conditioning, and then climbed in back to play. They got asphyxiated.

"What gets me," said Newell, "is the part about the air

conditioning. Like, did they want to be makin' it in a hearse, or did they just go in there for the climate control? I guess it gets hotter'n hell down there, especially in a garage."

"Do you remember what part of the country it was?" asked Parker.

"I think it was Mexico City. And it was during the summer. I remember that."

Parker tipped his head to one side. "There's other parts of the country that are a lot hotter than that, I think."

Newell laughed. "Depends on what you're doing."

"Well, it's too bad," said Parker. "If the girl was that adventurous, she might have done more good to more people."

Newell shrugged. "Yeah, she might have been a good natural resource, and for all we know, the two of them might have been good employees. Just gettin' a nooner." He looked at Wilf. "Take warnin', boy. Stay away from the Cadillacs. You get asphyxiated."

Wight, who had not spoken much in the last little while, said, "Give him your card, Jerry."

"By God, I *will* give him my card. Do you want my card, Wilf?"

"It wouldn't hurt. At the very least, I might need a job."

Everyone laughed again, and Jerry gave Wilf his card.

Later that night, when Wilf had shut off his light and had settled into his sleeping bag, he saw the moonlight on the curtains as he thought about the running line of humor in the ranch house. At one moment or another it seemed as if someone had said more than he realized, or as if not everyone had the same knowledge about something, but for the most part it had all been wisecracks. A guide like himself was a native. A gentleman offered the first beer and turned on the dome light. A working girl was a good natural resource. These fellows with the green license plates would like to live here, just for the liberty.

He could live here, too, he thought, if he could find work. This was one kind of work, sleeping in a trailer in somebody's yard. It wasn't the tent and horses like he thought a good hunting trip could have, but maybe he would get there yet. That would be Cadillac Style for him. How was it that song went?

> *I make Chevrolet pay but I got a big smile,*
> *'Cause my little baby loves me — Cadillac style.*
> Yeah, that was it.

4

Wilf had a carload of greenies the next morning. He did not find it odd that the four of them had piled into his old beater, as he had known hunters who had nice clean vehicles and preferred not to carry around bloody animal carcasses. He imagined Wentworth was not so finicky about the Ford, but if it was out of service, then Wilf's outfit was the only real option. And here they were, a happy bunch, rolling along in the pre-dawn.

From all of the genial insults the evening before, plus a shorter version as the men finished their cigarettes and coffee after breakfast, Wilf derived the impression that some uneasiness, if not tension, existed between the various members of the quartet. Newell made fun of everyone and got it back in full doses, but the ridicule was uneven in the other groupings. Parker did not make fun of the other two, and they showed similar restraint with him, as if he were a little more delicate than Newell. Wilf thought it might have something to do with his being divorced. Wentworth made fun of Wight, but Wight did not reciprocate very much. Wilf had no theory on that.

In spite of any reserve that might exist in the geometry of the four men, the seating arrangements implied a top-down pecking order. Wentworth sat in the cab on the passenger side, with a camera and a thermos of coffee taking up the middle of the seat. Parker sat in back on the field box with his shoulders against the rear window of the cab. Up on the sides of the bed, with their rifles upright, rode Wight and Newell. They seemed to have bounced back from the doldrums of the afternoon before, ready now to blast away at any deer that presented itself.

As the pickup rumbled out of the yard, Wentworth looked over at Wilf.

"Well, did you expect to have done better by now?"

"You mean the number of deer we killed?"

"Right."

"Oh, it's hard to say what you can really expect. You can hope, but in the end you get what you get. You can't determine what's going to come along. What you actually bring down, of course, is the next part."

"I see you carry a gun. I've heard that some guides shoot the animals for their clients."

Wilf shook his head. "I haven't ever done it. I've done some cleaning up on a couple of occasions, but I haven't just outright shot one for someone who couldn't, if that's what you mean. Not that I haven't felt like it a time or two, especially with antelope, when you scare up one buck after another and the guy just keeps makin' bad shots." He looked at Wentworth. "Of course, that's when you're liable to make a bad shot yourself, you know."

"I wouldn't know. I'm not really a hunter myself. I don't even own a deer rifle."

"Oh." Wilf remembered that golfing and pheasant hunting sometimes went together, both of them having an element of leisure and sport, so he asked, "How about birds? Have you hunted them?"

"Just a time or two, when I lived in Kansas. Everyone else did, so I gave it a try. I don't even remember where my shotgun is."

Wilf glanced at the case on the seat. "Do you hunt with your camera, then, as they say?"

"Not really. I carry it along now and then, but I don't take pictures of just any old thing. If one of the guys gets something really nice, I could get a picture then."

They rode on for a couple of minutes without saying anything, and then Wentworth spoke again.

"I was wondering if I could ask you to do me a favor."

Wilf looked over and met his gaze. "Depends on what it is. But it won't do any harm to ask."

"I'd like you to shoot a coyote if you see one."

Wilf nodded. "I could give it a try. There's not a season on 'em or anything. You don't need a license." He thought for a second. He had had other ranchers make a general request, that he shoot any and all coyotes he cared to when he was out on his own, but he wasn't sure of what this landowner was asking for. "Do you mean you want one for a particular purpose, or do you want to dust as many as you can, just to be getting rid of 'em? Because if that's what you mean, your hired man Tommy can kill more with his dogs than I could ever think of touching with a rifle."

"I want one for the house. I'd like to get one mounted."

"A full body mount, standing there?"

"Yeah."

"They look pretty nice. I could give it a try. There's better guns than mine for that business, but if we see one I'll see what I can do."

"How are the other guns better?"

"They shoot flatter, and they don't tear up the animal as much."

"Oh, does yours put a big hole in it?"

"Maybe as big as your fist." Wilf held up his. "But that's nothin' compared to what Tommy Tice's dogs will do to one. Guys who use dogs kill a lot of coyotes but don't sell very many hides."

"That's what I thought."

"But I bet Tommy's got a hell of a good varmint gun, too—probably more than one. He could probably shoot you a coyote nice and clean if you wanted him to."

"Well, if we don't get one ourselves, maybe I will."

Wilf thought about the fleas, and he hoped he didn't have to skin any coyotes. "We'll give it a try," he said. "If we get one, I think the best thing to do would be to stick him in the freezer whole, and let the taxidermist decide how to skin it and flesh it out and all that. Wrap it in a garbage bag first, of course, and then don't leave it in the freezer too long. The taxidermists will take long enough to get at it themselves."

"Just put him in with the ice cream. Like in the murder mysteries."

"Do they do that?"

"They did once in a Perry Mason book I read. Actually, they took the ice cream out and put the body in for a while, to speed up the rigor mortis so it would look like the murder got committed earlier. That's how they caught the guy — they could tell that the ice cream had thawed out and then re-frozen."

"Oh."

"Made a good story, for the moment."

"Yeah. Well, I guess in real life it's pretty common — to put dead animals in a freezer. I don't know about people, but I guess mortuaries have to have some way of putting a body on ice. I do know that these taxidermy places have to keep everything frozen until they can get to it. And wildlife biologists, they've always got stuff in the freezer to disgust their wives. The sheriff's office, too — I don't know where they keep 'em, but sometimes they freeze a whole deer for evidence."

"I thought they gave it to the jail or the fire department."

"Most of the time they do, but I've heard of cases where they bring in a whole frozen deer to prove their case."

"That seems extravagant. They can prove everything with DNA now."

"Yeah, this was a while back, I guess. But even then, sometimes they went to a lot of trouble to bust a poacher." Wilf paused and then went on. "Anyway, you can freeze a whole animal."

"And if he's not too big, you can put him in with the ice cream."

"Right. Wrap him in a plastic bag."

Wilf drove out to the west, with the idea of hunting south of the area where they had gone the afternoon before.

It was easier to drive around to the bottom there, also, so he could send the hunters all the way down and not put them through the exertion of climbing back up. The first grey light of morning was beginning to show now, and he could see fence posts at a distance.

"I'll need someone to open the gates."

Wentworth rolled down his window and told Wight to ask Parker what he would think about taking care of the gates, as he wasn't carrying a gun. Then he turned to Wilf and asked, "All right if I smoke?"

"Sure. It's a little better if you keep the window down."

Wilf stopped for the gate and heard clambering in back as Parker climbed down. Wentworth shook out a cigarette, produced his chrome-plated lighter, and went through his technique of packing the cigarette by rapping the filter end against the lighter in his palm. After lighting the cigarette and blowing the smoke out the window, he spoke.

"Were you ever in the service, Wilf?"

"No, I wasn't. Were you?"

"No. Vietnam and the draft were over by the time I was old enough, and then I was married with kids when Desert Storm came along."

"Oh."

"Have you been married?"

"Um, yeah. For a little while."

Parker stood aside with the gate, and Wilf drove through.

"It's too bad."

"You mean that things don't work out?"

Wentworth nodded as he blew smoke out the side. "You give 'em everything, and it's not enough."

"That happens, all right."

"They want this, and they want that. The woman I was married to, she was never satisfied."

"Huh." Wilf watched in the mirror as Parker dragged the gate back into place.

"That would have been bad enough if it was just things to pay for. I could deal with that. But she always had to be messin' around with other men."

"Oh."

"A guy shouldn't have to put up with that, you know?"

"That's true." The pickup shifted on its springs as Parker climbed back into the bed.

"I think that's probably the biggest reason for divorce."

"Could be." A lot of divorces Wilf knew of came about because of the man getting restless — men like the ones he had with him, he imagined. He put the pickup into motion.

"But there's a twist to everything."

"Oh, what's that?"

"From what I've read, that's one reason the housing industry is still so strong. More single heads of household. Half the families that started out living in one house now live in two."

"Some of them re-combine, don't they?"

"Yeah, but some women don't re-marry just so they can keep leeching money. Like in my case, I have to pay her rent. This other jerk can sleep over there all he wants, but as long as they don't get married and he's got his own place, I pay the bills." He took a puff on his cigarette. "That's why I came up here. Get the hell away from it and mind my own business." Then, as if to patch things up, he took on a more amiable tone. "You live by yourself?"

"Yeah."

"It's better that way, if you can afford it."

Wilf thought that was a curious thing to say. He couldn't imagine how it would apply to Wentworth himself or even to the paramour of Wentworth's ex-wife, and he didn't think the boss would be stepping so far into the affairs of the hired help. Nevertheless, he answered from his own point of view.

"Well," he said, "sometimes you think it would be better to have help paying the rent, but I guess it's worth the little more that it costs to have the place to yourself."

Wentworth gave him a surprised look that lasted but a second. "Actually, I meant it was worth paying someone else's rent just to have things to yourself. I was thinking of my own case. But I guess it comes to the same thing. You look at the price, you see what you're paying for, and you figure whether it's worth it."

Wilf was driving through a pasture of high grass and was heading for a rim where he thought he could set the men out to hunt the ridges down to the bottom. He saw a flash of pale color off to the right and recognized the forms of three antelope bolting away. It gave him something to say.

"They're up early."

Wentworth made a noise that sounded like "Hmh."

"They're fun to hunt, too. Different, but fun."

"I suppose."

Daylight was coming on. As Wilf shut off his lights, it occurred to him that he had never had a group of hunters who talked so little about hunting. Maybe they weren't really hunters but were just going through the motions because they thought they were supposed to or because they thought they were privileged to.

The antelope kept angling to the northwest and faded

from view. Seeing animals, even those that a fellow wasn't hunting, could help him keep up his spirits in spite of the freight he was hauling around.

"I think we'll let these guys out up ahead here, and then we can take our time driving around to the bottom to pick 'em up."

"Sounds good."

Wilf got the hunters lined out and walked back to the pickup, where Parker was standing on the passenger's side of the cab and talking to Wentworth. They were both smoking cigarettes and not making any effort to keep their voices down. Wilf walked up to them and in a low voice asked Parker if he would like to ride in the cab. Parker said no, he could ride in back and hop in and out to open the gates.

When Wilf was back in the cab and had the engine started, Wentworth said that if they had time, there was a spot back over on the left, sort of a lookout, where he had seen coyotes down below. Wilf said they could give it a try, and instead of going back toward the gate, he headed south along the rim and looked out where the land fell away to the west. Following Wentworth's directions, he stopped at the head of a wide draw.

He got out of the cab, pulled his rifle from the gun rack, and stepped away from the pickup before he jacked a shell into the chamber. He heard the pickup door open and Wentworth say something to Parker, so he waited for them in front of the pickup. He imagined they wanted to watch. When they caught up with him, he started a slow walk to the rim of the draw. As the breaks below him came into view, he saw a broad, bare area of slickrock that looked like an island in the middle of the draw. It had a dull shine in the morning light.

"I've seen 'em come out and play there," said Wentworth.

Wilf nodded. "They may have a den somewhere nearby."

"Do you want to wait and see if they come out?"

Wilf glanced back in the direction where he had left the hunters. "I don't know. If something came out and I touched off a shot, I might mess things up for those other guys. At the very least, I think it would distract them."

"Well, whatever you think."

They walked back to the pickup, where Wilf paused to slide back the bolt and press the shell down into the magazine. Then everyone got into the pickup, and they were on their way again.

Wilf drove east, back through the gate, then south until the road forked, where he headed west and began the downhill drive. At the bottom the country opened up into sagebrush and grass, with windmills every mile or so in the distance until the flatlands ended with a row of pale buttes. The bench they had been on top of was now up and to their right, with a long series of draws or breaks fingering their way down to the flat grassland. To a deer hunter, the layout looked as promising as a fellow could hope for.

As the pickup idled along, Wilf saw a shape move out of the bottom of a draw ahead on the right. As he stopped the pickup, he thought the animal was too small to be a deer or antelope.

"That might be one there," he said, shutting off the engine. He gave a soft touch to opening the door, sliding out, and withdrawing the rifle. After jacking in a shell, he laid the rifle across the corner of the hood and got into position.

He picked up the coyote in the scope. The sun had risen, so the yellow-grey dog was not hard to see as it trotted along. For a second it went out of view behind a clump of sagebrush; then it emerged, still headed to Wilf's left as he picked it up again. The coyote stopped and looked back over its right shoulder, a small profile in the center of the crosshairs. Wilf had everything steady, but he did not shoot. He had a feeling he recognized.

He knew it from past moments, when he didn't have confidence in the shot itself or didn't have his heart in it or thought the wrong person might be watching. He had taken shots at moments like that, and he had taught himself that when a fellow, deep down, didn't want to take a shot, for one reason or another, he would be better off not squeezing the trigger. It wouldn't be a good shot. Worse, it would be a bad one, the kind that led a fellow into more bad shots or ruined the whole sense of balance that he needed in order to hunt well.

He relaxed his grip on the rifle, lowering the stock and raising the muzzle so that the coyote went out of view. Again he slid back the bolt and pushed the cartridge down into the magazine. Then he lifted the rifle and went back to the door he had left ajar.

"What's wrong?"

Wilf poked the gun into the rack. "Just didn't have a good shot."

"Too far?"

"I think that was part of it. I couldn't draw down on him fine enough."

"Oh."

As Wilf got settled behind the steering wheel and started the engine, he had the sense that Wentworth was disappointed. He wondered if the man had some motive other than just getting a coyote; he felt as if Wentworth had wanted to be able to get him to do something. It wasn't as simple as just watching him shoot, but rather seeking the satisfaction of having gotten him to do it.

He let the pickup idle along. "You know," he said, "a lot of it has to do with how sure you are of your shot. I think Tommy Tice could make that same shot with one of his varmint guns, and drill him dead center. And as far as that goes, the fur'll probably be a little better as we get farther into the cold weather. So we didn't miss all that much."

"No, it's all right."

Wilf was glad the moment had passed. "Well, at least you know there's no shortage of 'em."

He drove on for almost a mile, then stopped and shut off the engine. Thirty miles in the distance, the sunlight reflected on the line of buttes, while ahead on his right it cast the draws in shadow. He figured he was about a quarter of a mile from where the two hunters should come out at the bottom. If they took it slow, as they had been advised to do, they still had a ways to go. Meanwhile, Wilf and the others would stay out of their way.

Parker got out of the back and loitered by the passenger window. Wentworth poured himself a cup of coffee and drank it, then poured a cup for Parker. Left to his own thoughts, Wilf wondered why his host had asked him about being in the service, being married, or living with someone. He doubted that Wentworth had any reason for prying; it was more likely that it was his style to want to know about someone he was dealing with.

Wilf listened for rifle shots and took in scraps of talk from Wentworth and Parker. They were carrying on a calm conversation about building and development. Wentworth explained that he hadn't done any remodeling on the ranch house because he intended to build a new house in a better location. Parker said Wentworth could probably do better by having building materials and fixtures hauled in from a distance rather than buying them from the local podunk lumberyards and hardware stores, and if he got into a good deal on things he could pass it on to anyone who built on one of the parcels. Wentworth said Norman Lang knew everyone and could get good prices, which might be fine for things like shingles and trusses, but for a lot of the interior stuff, Parker was right, a guy could get better selection and prices elsewhere. Wilf perked up at the mention of trusses, but then he checked out again as he tried to keep his ears tuned for something important.

By and by the shots came, one and then about five seconds later, another. It sounded good. One shot could be a clean kill or a clear miss. A volley of shots usually meant someone was throwing lead at a running animal and not having much luck. But two spaced shots—they could mean a miss, too, but it could well be that the second shot did its work, as Parker's had done.

Wentworth spoke. "Sounds like somebody got something."

"At least he got some shots," Wilf answered, "whoever it is."

"Two shots," Parker added. "I wonder who it is."

Wentworth, who had just taken out a cigarette, rapped it against his lighter. "We'll see soon enough."

Wilf kept his eye on the landscape where the breaks emptied out onto the flat. He didn't know the country well enough to tell which draw was which down here on the bottom, but he knew that either a deer or a hunter would come out up ahead before long.

After about ten minutes, he saw a bead of orange moving. It looked like Newell, who wore only a cap of blaze orange and who wore a darker jacket than Wight did.

"Is that Jerry?" said Parker.

"Looks like it," Wilf answered. "I think we'll drive up and see what's going on."

He started the engine as Parker climbed into the back. The pickup eased into motion and began to close the distance between the men in the vehicle and the hunter on foot.

"It's Jerry, all right," said Wentworth. "I wonder if he did the shooting."

Wilf drove on as Newell stood and waited, looking in the direction of the breaks and then at the oncoming pickup. As Wilf followed the road, he saw that Newell was standing on the driver's side. Before Wilf brought the vehicle to a stop, Parker called out a question.

"Who fired?"

"I think maybe Larry got one," said Newell, as Wilf stopped next to him. "I heard one shot and then another, and that was it. And he hasn't come down yet."

"Is he up that draw there?" asked Wilf.

"Yeah." Newell took the live shell out of the chamber.

"Well, if you want to, you and I can work our way up to meet him."

Newell stepped to his left and looked across the hood of the pickup. "That looks like him now."

"Hop in," said Wentworth, "and we'll go pick him up."

As a general rule, Wilf didn't leave the roads that were already worn into a pasture or field unless he was going to pick up an animal. That was the general code—close the gates and stay on the roads—and he would have waited to see if Wight had meat on the ground, but if the owner wanted him to drive on the grass, he would.

With Newell aboard, Wilf drove across the pasture. He could see Wight coming down the middle of the draw, rifle slung on his shoulder, so the hunt was over in one way or another. Wilf stopped at the edge of the breaks and waited until Wight came up to the cab. The man looked like his usual reserved self as he stopped at Wilf's window. He even had his vest still fastened.

"Well, I got one."

"What's he like?"

"Oh, he's good enough. Legal, anyway. Three on one side and four on another."

"Well, good." Wilf shut off the engine. "We can go up and drag him back down to here. How far up is he?"

"Oh, I don't know. A quarter of the way, I guess."

Newell's voice came from behind as he climbed down to the ground. "You know, that four-wheeler would come in handy now."

Wilf got out of the cab. "We can handle it well enough." He felt in his pocket to make sure he had a knife, and then he leaned across the sidewall of the pickup bed. "Say, Randy," he said, "if I can get into that box, I'll grab a couple of tow-ropes."

Parker got up from the box and opened it. Wilf reached forward and took out two ropes, each wrapped around its wooden handle. He turned and looked at Wight, who was poised to put his rifle in the rack.

"Is it unloaded?"

"Oh, yeah. All the way."

"Go ahead, then, and we can get started." Wilf put a

rope in each pocket of his field jacket. "I think the two of us can drag it down, but if anyone else wants to go, that's fine."

Newell said he would tag along and lend a hand if they needed it, so the three of them headed up the draw. Wight took the lead. At a point where the land began to rise at a sharper angle, he slowed and began looking around to his left. Then he took off in a straight line, angling up the side of the ridge, until he led the others to the spot where the deer had fallen.

It was just as Wight had described it—three points on one side and four on the other. Just behind the shoulder, blood was glistening in a little red hole the size of a fingertip.

"Did you hit him the first time?" Wilf asked, wondering if there was any other damage.

"No, I missed. I kicked up dirt on that little bank in back of him, and he just stood there. Then I made a better shot the second time."

"That's good." Wilf took the rope out of his right pocket and started unraveling it.

"You make those yourself?" asked Newell.

"Yeah."

"Looks like a ski rope."

"Sort of does. I drill two holes and make the triangle like this so I don't have the strand running between two fingers. That can get rough." He handed the loose rope to Wight, then took out the other, undid it, and bent over to tie onto the deer. First he tied the rope around the neck and pulled it snug; next he tied the right front leg up close so that it stuck out along the nose, and then he took another wrap around the neck and tied it off. He held the handle up to Wight, who took it and gave him the other rope. He tied it around the neck, again snug, tied up the other leg like the first one, and wrapped off around the neck with one last knot. Each rope had about four feet of slack.

"You've got him trussed up pretty good," said Newell.

"Oh, yeah. You'd be surprised how much easier it is than draggin' him by the horns. Your hands don't get cramped, you've got a lot less friction on the drag because you've got him up off the ground better, and you don't stumble with the deer bouncin' off your heels." He looked at Wight. "Ready?"

"Sure am."

"Just lean into it with a good, steady pull."

"Damn if it doesn't look like you're chokin' him," said Newell, in his cheerful tone.

"I think he's way past that," said Wight, taking up the slack.

They had an easy job dragging the deer down to the pickup, where Wilf took off his jacket and went to work at hoisting, skinning, and cleaning the carcass. The sun was up higher now, spreading its thin warmth. In less than an hour, Wilf had the animal separated into the usual three parts of body, head and hide, and gut pile. He sawed off the antlers, checked to see how Wight filled out the tag, and tied the coupon onto the shank. Then he made quick work of cleaning up and putting things away.

During the whole operation, the other four men stood around smoking cigarettes and chatting. It occurred to Wilf that Wight didn't seem to be even as appreciative as Parker had been, but that was all right. He had two of these fellows hunted, and he would have this deer hanging in the shed by lunch time. Not bad for a local dummy.

5

Wilf yawned as he sat in the cab, relaxed by the sunlight coming in through the windshield. Newell was down in the breaks alone now, and Wilf was listening, waiting to find out what kind of work, if any, he might have between now and supper.

With only one hunter left, he had his hopes that he might finish this piece of work and get back down to his own place for a couple of days. But as the afternoon stretched out, warm and hazy and dull, he knew he had little control over someone else's hunting. Even when he could lead a fellow right up to a deer or antelope, there was no guarantee that things would go the way he hoped. Any of a number of factors could intervene—not least among them a jerk on the trigger—and the hunter could miss his animal clean, or hit it but not put it down. Until the shot was fired, the guide had to hang back and see how things would go. Then, if a crippled animal got away, he had to know how to go after it on a close search or a long chase. Anything could happen, and the later in the day that it did, the greater the pressure to get things resolved before dark.

The other three men had stayed at the ranch house after lunch, and Newell had seemed to expand, in his own self-assured way, to fill up the occasion of having the run of the ranch and the services of the guide all to himself. Now the man was hunting on his own, and Wilf had no idea of how well. Newell might be stumbling along, running out deer he would never see, or he might be making a good sneak on a legal buck and passing it up in favor of a better one.

As they had ridden out together for the afternoon hunt, Wilf had caught a few sideways glimpses of the ruddy face and trim beard. Now as he pictured Newell, he placed him. The man reminded Wilf of a movie he had seen, a film version of *Macbeth* that Adrienne had seen in the T.V. listings and wanted to watch. Several of the characters had beards, and the whole movie had something of a reddish texture to it. Newell seemed like a composite of some of the characters, the thanes as they were called, who stood around the court or sat around the banquet table, drinking from goblets and laughing at witty speech. Fond though he was of the four-wheeler, Newell would fit in with the leather armor and the torches, a man confident of his rank and privilege, smug perhaps as Macbeth himself as he bossed around the servants.

They were a lively bunch in that movie. It wasn't one of those dry productions, the type that was all set on the stage.

Macbeth and his pals were out riding horses, in a countryside laid to waste, with smoke rising from some sort of pillaging in the background. Wilf remembered a fellow hanging from a gallows, peasants butchering an animal, and the witches with their antics. He and Adrienne had enjoyed that movie.

He got out of the cab and walked over to the rim where the land fell away to the west. Newell had disappeared down in the folds and turns of the many-fingered drainage. There had to be deer out there. The weather was just too nice; that was the problem. The deer shaded up on a warm afternoon like this, especially if there was going to be a bright moon for them to graze at night. That was a funny thing about deer season. A guy might think the best deer had all been hunted, and then with a change in the weather, the country came alive with big deer. Wilf figured that was what they needed, a little snowstorm to blow in. In the meanwhile, it seemed as if the only time he and his hunters saw any deer was in the morning.

Wilf listened for a while longer and still heard nothing. He felt the sun on his face, in an afternoon drowsy with warmth that wouldn't last. In a short while the sun would slip in the west, the shadows would reach out, and the air would cool. That was a good time to get a deer, if a fellow knew how to look in the dusky shade. It was an easier thing to feel than to tell someone about, the whole process of trying to fit in with the elements, looking for slow movement and off-shades of color. He had gotten up on a lot of deer that way, often without firing a shot, and he had led a few hunters to see animals that way as well. This afternoon he had offered to go with Newell, but the man said he would rather go on his own. It was better that way if the person was a real hunter, but in this case he didn't know. If Newell didn't have a deer by noon tomorrow, Wilf might try to take a more active part in getting a deer into the car salesman's sights.

By and by he figured it was time to go, so he fired up the pickup and drove around to the bottom. He had a pretty clear idea of where Newell would come out, and after a short wait he saw the orange cap moving out of the shadows. Newell had his rifle slung on his shoulder as he walked toward the pickup. He did not have the tired, plodding shuffle that some hunters had at the end of the day. With sloping shoulders and a little bit of a gut, Newell was not a robust outdoorsman, but he wasn't a wimp, either. At the very least he was sure of himself. Now he walked across the open area at a steady pace. He shook his head just before he reached the cab; then after opening the door on his side, he took out the live shell, poked his gun in the rack, and climbed in.

Wilf had noticed that none of these hunters carried a fanny pack, a backpack, or an eight-compartment vest, much less all the food and survival doo-dads that some hunters lugged around on a two-hour downhill hunt to the vehicle. He didn't think it was because Wentworth's pals believed in carrying only the minimum of a rifle, shells, a knife, and a license, but rather because they were not interested enough to look through the catalogs. Hunting was not much of a habit with them. Once Newell had his rifle put away, he wasn't any more encumbered than if he had been on the golf course in his cart. As the man reached into his shirt pocket and brought out his cigarettes, Wilf thought he wouldn't be surprised if Newell didn't even carry a knife.

"See anything?"

"Nothing."

"Not discouraged yet, are you?"

"Oh, no." Newell took out his lighter and struck a flare.

"About ready to call it quits for today, though?"

"Oh, yeah. It's happy hour. And Friday at that."

"The mornings have been the best so far, anyway. Maybe we'll get one early tomorrow."

"Sounds good to me." Newell looked out the window as he blew his smoke away. "You can sure go a long time without seeing anything here, can't you?"

"Seems like it."

"Well, this is a nice thing for Scott, but if he had to try to make a living off the place, I don't see how the hell he would do it."

"Some do, some don't. It's harder than it used to be."

"I guess he's gonna get his own cattle."

"Did he have the place leased this year?"

"The last owners did."

"Just the pastures, though, huh?"

"That's how I understand it." Newell tapped his cigarette at the ashtray. "He had to hire that other yokel to do the hay."

Wilf suppressed a laugh, imagining how Tommy would refer to these fellows. "Yeah, he'll be a good one to take care of cattle, too. He's a go-ahead kind of guy. Scott could do a lot worse in that area."

Newell wrinkled his nose. "Well, all he's got to do is keep from losing his ass. Eventually he'll make some money off this place, even if he doesn't do it with breeding cattle."

"You mean the parcels."

"Yeah. This place is a natural for that."

When Wilf knocked on the door that evening and was called at to come in, the men were still in the midst of the evening meal. The kitchen smelled of roasted pork, and a plate in the center of the table was heaped with bare rib bones. Wilf wasn't sure how good Wentworth might be as Macbeth, but the four men together, with their tone of merriment, fit in with Wilf's earlier impression of the thanes at the castle.

Wentworth offered him a drink and invited him to sit down and have some ribs. Wilf accepted a beer but stayed on his feet.

"Sit down and partake," said Newell, with a floating smile.

Wilf looked around the table and smiled back. "No, thanks. I'm fine." He meandered past the table and into the living room.

"Make yourself at home," Wentworth called out.

"Thanks." Wilf glanced around the room. On the mantel above the fireplace he noticed a row of little model cars, so he walked over to look at them. The fireplace itself had been converted into what looked like a gas-log heater with a fan to circulate the heat. The insert unit kept him away from the mantel a ways, but the models were about five inches long, so he could see them well enough. They were classic sports cars of the 1950s and maybe earlier — a Thunderbird, an Austin-Healy, a Morgan, and a Jaguar. They all had shiny wire wheels and trim, and it looked as if the bodies had been hand-painted. The T-bird was an aqua blue, the Austin-Healy a custard yellow, the Morgan an ivory white, and the Jaguar a creamy tan. They made a classy set.

Wilf stepped over to the opening that led to the dining area. "Did you paint those model cars, Scott?"

"Yes, I did."

"They look nice."

"Thanks. It was a long time ago, but I've kept them around, and they still look good."

Newell, who had his back to Wilf, stood up. "Excuse me," he said, glancing over his shoulder. "I'm going to get myself a drink. Do you want one, Scott?"

"No, thanks."

"Anyone else?"

Parker raised his chin. "I could take one. Go ahead and make yours, and I'll be ready."

From the glasses on the table and the bottles on the counter, it looked as if the men were drinking the same as the night before. The Cutty Sark was for Newell and Wentworth, the Seagram's for Parker, and the Absolut for Wight, who drank vodka Collins. Newell poured himself a Scotch and water, then took Parker's glass and poured a Seagram's and water. Parker, meanwhile, leaned over to scratch his ankle, and as he did so, Wilf noticed a bald spot on the back of his head. It seemed like an odd thing not to have noticed before, as it was prominent beneath the overhead lamp.

Wentworth got up. "I'm going to get you a chair, Wilf."

"That's O.K. I'm fine."

"No, I'm going to get you a chair." The host went to the other part of the house and came back with a white cane-bottom chair.

Wilf sat down, away from the table a bit, between Newell and Wentworth. The men were still picking bones and tearing chunks off of dinner rolls, but they were keeping up an animated conversation about a trip they had gone on to Las Vegas and the golfing they had done there. When the topic came to a lull, Newell looked at Wilf.

"We were talking earlier about how careful you are with guns."

Wilf shrugged. "I guess I have to be."

"Larry here, our safety man, was praising you."

Wilf recalled from the night before that Wight worked for a consulting firm on highway safety. It did not surprise him that Wight would notice safety around firearms, but he would not have expected him to go to the trouble of saying anything complimentary. He looked across the table at Wight, whose colorless, clean face had as little expression as usual.

"Yeah. I just said that was one thing I could say about you, that you were careful about guns. I noticed it with Randy and me both."

"Like I say, I have to be. I've just heard too many stories and been around too many incidents." Wilf glanced at Parker. "No offense, but I'm especially touchy around semi-automatics."

"No, that's fine."

"I could tell you why. I've never had one myself, but there was one story I heard that made me leery of 'em."

Parker paused with a half-picked rib in front of him. "Go ahead and tell us. I'd like to hear it."

"Well, it was about a hunter from Ohio, I think. He was out here hunting antelope in a van, and he had his rifle up front with him. He took off across a pasture to go after some antelope, and his gun took a bounce and went off, right through his ribs, and then with the recoil it went off again and again, three or four more times, until it was empty."

"Killed him, no doubt," said Wight, his washed-blue eyes gazing at Wilf.

"Damn sure did. The first shot would have done it,

and then the others were just extra. That was quite a while back, but I remember the story. And there are lots more, not just about automatics."

The others waited for him to go ahead, so he did.

"I was in the same elk camp with a fellow that had his gun leanin' against the seat, pointin' down at the floorboard. I don't know why, because he had a gun rack, but that was where he had it. And at one point, right there in camp, when he was gettin' ready to go somewhere, he slid in behind the wheel and absent-mindedly laid his hand on the gun and put a shot through the firewall. Scared the hell out of him and a couple of others. Who knows why he had the gun loaded, or how cozy he thought it felt to run his hand down the stock and rest on the trigger when he got into the cab. And I'd been ridin' around with him, just a day or two before, and I could remember him drivin' with the gun like that and holdin' it to keep it from slidin' around. You can bet I didn't ride with him any more."

Wight shook his head. "That's just stupid, to have a loaded gun in the cab."

"Sure it is." Wilf took a sip on his beer. "And I don't know how many times I've been around someone—three or four times at least—when they touched one off right outside the cab, fiddling with the gun just before they got in. That's why you always want to point the gun away from the cab, either up in the air or down at the ground, when you take out the live one."

"I notice that's how you do it," said Wentworth.

"Just a habit."

"And I notice you don't take the shell out of the rifle. You just poke it back down in the magazine."

"Just another habit, and again there's reasons. Some

guys put in an extra shell and then take it out each time, but I
don't like to carry loose shells in my pocket. For one thing, I
don't like the jingle, and for another, you don't run the chance
of gettin' another shell, like from someone else's caliber, mixed
in. In my case, if I just hunt with the shells that are in my gun
and not slip that other shell in and out each time, it's a matter
of five shells instead of six. And I rarely take more than one or
two shots anyway."

Newell smiled. "By God, you've got it all figured out."

Wight made a frown. "You mean you don't carry any
more shells than the ones you have in your gun?"

"No, I mean I don't carry any loose shells to be slippin'
in and out. I carry another ten, in one of those little pouches,
nice and quiet. After I shoot at an animal — and like I say, I
usually don't shoot more than once or twice — if I need to
reload, then I get 'em from there, when things cool down and I
can see what I'm doin'."

Parker gave a slow shake to his head. "You've got it
worked out in a hell of a lot more detail than I would."

"I'm just around too many people with guns, and
people I don't know very well. Other guides'll tell you the
same thing. People are careless in just about every way. I know
one guy who's a guide, and he says he's gotten so tired of
people pokin' a rifle barrel in his nose that he wants to do
more and more with archery and black powder, just for that
reason. Another fellow, who also guides, told me about a
hunter that was screwin' around and fell on his rifle —
slipped on some ice, fell down a little slope, twisted his rifle
around ass-end-to, and poked it right through his side, like a
piece of re-bar."

Parker's mouse-colored mustache went down at the

corners. "But it didn't go off?"

"No, he was lucky."

"I guess."

Silence hung in the air for a few seconds, and Wilf had the feeling that he had talked too much. He felt as if he had let these fellows humor him and get him to show off. Maybe not Parker, but the rest of them seemed to play him for the native who was smart about a couple of things. He knew that game, praise a man to his face for something small. It was another version of I'm-smarter-than-you-are.

Newell, who seemed to be practiced at changing the subject, wiped his hands on his napkin and pushed his plate away with a half-eaten roll on it. "Well, here it is Friday night. Down in the settlements, they're puttin' on their glad rags. What have you got planned for us, Scott? A lively game of Bingo?"

Wentworth cocked his left eyebrow and gave a sideways glance. "I know how you like to play Old Maid. I thought we could do that, and I'll serve up some hot toddies."

Newell looked at Wilf. "Do they play poker in the clubs here? I know they do in Montana."

"You mean in the bars?"

"Yeah."

"No, not legally. But they do play cards. In some places they've got a pitch game goin' every afternoon, and tournaments on the weekends."

"Is that legal? I imagine they play for money."

"They do. I don't know how legal it is, but as long as there's no money on the table, nobody does anything about it."

Newell lit a cigarette. "All the same to me, but your state could be makin' some revenue. They don't even have a lottery, do they?"

"No, there's a pretty strong opposition to gambling."

"Unless you keep the money out of sight." Newell made half a smirk as he brought the cigarette up.

Parker rattled the cubes in his drink, which was almost gone. "There's plenty of places to go for all of that."

"Oh, yeah." Newell blew his smoke upward. "What's your game, Wilf?"

"You mean card game, or games in general?"

"Either one. Cards, or shuffleboard, or bowling."

Wilf thought. "I guess I hunt. And you?"

Newell laughed. "Old Maid and Monopoly."

"Jerry's a poker player," said Wight. "He gets some pretty good games going at his place."

Wilf nodded. It wouldn't be a penny-ante dealer's choice game with these fellows. "I don't play much myself," he said. "I guess I'm not that much of a gambler."

"It's actually classified as a game of skill, at least in some places. That's how they get away with playing it in the clubs." Newell gave him a confidential nod. "If you think about it that way, as a game of skill, it's not that much different from your game."

Wight spoke up. "You sound like you're trying to sell something again, Jerry."

"No, I'm not. Just makin' conversation and tryin' to stay out of the gutter, which isn't always easy in this company. But if you guys want, we'll talk about somethin' else. Where do they keep the whorehouses, Wilf?"

"I don't know of any."

Newell gave a broad smile. "Not your game?"

"No, not really." Wilf smiled and took a sip.

Newell picked up his drink glass, which was still half-full. "By God, there's another industry this state is missin' out on."

Wentworth began stacking plates. "We need more guys like you in the legislature. Open up the economy."

"Why not? Make the best of your natural resources."

The comment clicked with the one from the night before about the girl in the hearse, and Wilf expected another remark about natives, but it didn't come. He had a fleeting image of a dark-haired girl—Heather Lea—and then it was gone.

Newell covered his mouth and chin with his open hand as he took a drag on his cigarette. The others waited for him to go on.

"And a renewable resource at that."

"You've got the rationale worked out," said Wight. "Maybe you could sell it to the legislature."

Parker spoke up. "Just the legalization part. Don't let the state sell the permits, or they'll gouge the non-residents."

Newell shook his head. "Do it locally."

The others laughed, and Wentworth said, "In all seriousness, it wouldn't hurt to legalize gambling."

"That's right," said Newell. "Quit pretendin'. Get the money on the table."

The conversation tripped along in that way, and for as long as it took Wilf to drink two beers, it did not come back around to firearms or hunting. It was just as well. He thought he had talked enough. When he was done with his second beer he got up, gave his thanks for the drinks and conversation, and went back to his trailer.

He stood on the far side of the camper, at the edge of the yard, and took a leak before going in. From where he stood, the bulk of the trailer blocked out the yard light. The moon overhead was round and brilliant. He hadn't seen it rise this evening, and he hadn't checked a calendar, but he thought it was a full moon. If it wasn't, it was within a day of it—big and bright, like the horsethief moon in Ian Tyson's song. The moons had names. He didn't know exactly what a planter's moon was, but he had heard of it. There was the harvest moon which, as he heard on the radio, was the last full moon before fall. And he had read once—he couldn't remember where— that there was a hunter's moon, which was like the harvest moon but not quite so big. This moon right now, it could be a rustler's moon or a poacher's moon—whichever was uppermost in someone doin's. It was pretty, that was for sure. Wherever Adrienne was, it was shining down on her, too, just like in the song.

Only Wentworth and Newell were sitting at the kitchen table the next morning. The white chair must have gone back to its quarters, so the dining area did not look very crowded. Wilf sat in Parker's place and waited for Newell to finish his French toast, which was swimming in a pool of syrup. Wentworth was not having breakfast. He said he would eat later, when the others were ready. Wilf supposed the host had gotten up early on a Saturday morning just to fix breakfast for his guest and, in his way, to endorse the morning hunt.

Newell finished his French toast and drank off the rest of his coffee. He pushed his plate back and lit a cigarette, then set it in the ashtray and got up. Wilf heard him go to the back part of the house, where he used the bathroom, opened and closed another door, and clicked a light switch. Meanwhile, the host got up and started putting things away in the kitchen. In a few minutes Newell appeared by his chair again, dressed and armed for the hunt. He leaned over and picked up his cigarette.

He looked at Wentworth, who had just sat down. "I'm gonna leave you in charge here, Scott."

"That's asking a lot. I'm pretty sure I'll be asleep by the time you get out of the yard."

"Any requests?"

"Don't shoot any game wardens."

"Do you expect any out here?"

"No, not really. But as I was sitting here, I remembered a book I read about that guy over in Idaho that shot two of them. I thought maybe it was an irresistible thing to do for some of you."

"Well, I'll try real hard not to."

"Good." Wentworth turned to Wilf and gave a reassuring nod. "I hope everything goes well."

"Thanks. I'm sure it will."

Newell leaned over and crushed his cigarette in the ash tray. "Well, I'm ready. Thanks for breakfast, Scott."

"Sure. Good luck on your hunt."

As Wilf warmed up the pickup, he and Newell agreed to go out to the southwest part of the ranch, where Newell had gone on the four-wheeler the first morning. Wilf asked if he wanted to hunt by himself again and he said yes, so Wilf left it at that, figuring he could re-evaluate things if they hadn't gotten a deer by noontime.

Wilf was driving south along a plateau when the sky began to glow pink in the east. It was a cold, dry morning with a mild wind out of the west. The daylight grew by the minute, and when he looked away from the path of his headlights he could see the grass and sagebrush in good detail. He turned off the lights.

Newell stretched his arms out in front of him and yawned.

"No one else wanted to go along today, uh?"

"Oh, we stayed up pretty late."

"Playin' Old Maid?"

"Yeah. Puckerin' up over our hot toddies."

Wilf drove along and followed the road as it curved to the southwest. The dirt track went down into a dip and came up, then leveled out. A shape moved on the right side of Wilf's vision, and he let off the gas, then touched the brake as the animal came to the road and crossed it. When he saw antlers shining in the early morning light, he brought the pickup to a stop. He looked across the cab at Newell, who was sitting up and blinking his eyes. Then Wilf looked back and found the deer. It was coming to a stop about seventy yards away, ahead and to the left. He shut off the engine.

"Shall I get out?"

"Yeah, slow and quiet. Don't bother to close the door. The interior light doesn't work anyway, as you know. Just take it easy and get a rest across the hood if you can. Don't rush anything. He doesn't look spooked."

Wilf kept his eye on the deer as Newell got out, pulled the gun from the rack, and settled into position against the pickup. The deer flicked its ears when the bolt action went clickety-click, but it stood there in profile. Then the gun blasted and the deer crumpled, falling like an armload of sticks.

Wilf let out a short, deep breath. The deer was down. It wasn't going anywhere, but its front legs were still moving. Wilf heard Newell jack another shell into the chamber.

"I think he's done for, Jerry."

"I'll just cover him for a minute to be sure."

Wilf waited a long moment and then got out of the pickup. The deer was still twitching, but it was down for good. "I think you can put it away now," he said, motioning his head toward the rifle.

"I'd hate like hell to see him get up and run off."

Wilf looked at the deer and then back across the hood at the hunter. "I'll tell you what. If you want to, you can walk over there next to him and wait. I'll pull the pickup around, and we can take care of cleaning him right there."

"O.K."

The deer had gone still by the time Wilf got the pickup alongside, so Newell unloaded his rifle and put it away. As Wilf set up the skinning frame, he listened to the other man talk.

"I kept thinking he was going to get up. I've heard stories about it. Then I thought, he'll get up at about the time we get the ropes around his neck. That could happen, too, couldn't it?"

"Well, yeah. I've actually seen it. With an antelope, not a deer."

"Really?"

"It was a hunter I took out. He knocked it down and it looked done for, like this one. The hunter had a rope set-up he had bought from a catalog and wanted to try out. It was a pull rope, same idea as mine, but it attached to the back of a harness he put over his chest and shoulders. About the time he started pullin', the antelope got up and started fightin' like hell. So the guy slipped out of the harness and hung on, and the antelope sort of froze. The guns were back at the truck, so I just walked up to it real slow, held my knife out at arm's length, and cut its throat with one clean jab."

"The hell. You'd think it would fight more when it started chokin'."

"Well, it did, at first, and then it balked for just that long, and I got to it. It could have been a lot worse, tryin' to get a knife on an animal when it's thrashin' around."

"Well, I was sure expecting something here."

"Never rule it out, I guess. But from the way he fell, I was pretty sure he wasn't goin' to get back up." Wilf walked over and looked down at the deer. It was a fine-looking buck, husky and dark-chested with a good spread of antlers. "A perfect four," he said.

"Yeah. Pretty nice."

"Do you want to have it mounted?"

"Um, nah, I don't think so. Do it like you did the others."

Wilf grabbed the deer by the antlers and pulled it around underneath the hoist. Then he went to work on it. By the time he had the animal skinned and cleaned, the sun had not risen very high in the east, and the air still had a nip. He left the carcass hanging to cool as he went to work on the head. In less than ten minutes he twisted the antlers free. He handed the set to Newell and stood back.

The man who had killed the deer had a cigarette in the left side of his mouth, so he tipped his head back as he held out the antlers and gleaming skull plate. The expression on his face was a mixture of confidence and satisfaction, as if he had expected the trophy and was pleased to have gotten it.

"This is the best deer out of the three," Wilf said.

"That's what I thought, too."

Wilf went back to the hanging carcass and laid his hand on the haunch. The meat had cooled some already.

"We're in no hurry, but if you want to go ahead and get your tag ready, we can pack up here in a little while."

"Um, I don't have my tag with me."

Wilf looked at him. "Where is it? Back at the house?"

"Yeah. I just figured I'd tag it when we hang it in the shed."

"Well, you're supposed to do it before you leave the site of the kill. It says that on the license."

Newell looked at him and nodded. "I'll tag it as soon as we get back."

Wilf shrugged. It wasn't as if he hadn't ever done that sort of thing himself, but that was before he had an outfitter's license to lose. This was a petty thing, and it was all on private property, but he didn't like it. If he was going to take people around and babysit them, the least they could do was follow the rules. He didn't say anything more as he cleaned up and put things away, and he thought Newell showed good sense by not trying to make light talk about other things.

When they got back to the house, Newell took his rifle and antlers into the house as Wilf hung the deer in the shed with the others. It was the kind of job that would go smoother if he had help, but he had hung the first two by himself and he took a somewhat bitter pleasure in not asking these fellows for help with anything. When he had the deer hoisted and tied off, he closed the tailgate and backed up the pickup to the trailer. He was just settling the tongue onto the hitch when Wentworth came out of the house and crossed the yard. He was wearing a charcoal-and-grey parka and a silver-colored corduroy cap.

"Sounds like everything went just fine."

"He got a nice one, all right."

"Good. So you got everything wrapped up in pretty good time."

"As well as I could expect."

With his hands in his coat pockets, Wentworth motioned with his head toward the trailer. "Looks like you're just about ready to go."

Wilf raised his eyebrows. "Unless you've got something else you wanted me to do."

"I don't know what that would be."

"Neither do I."

Wentworth took his hands out of his pockets, and with his left he held out an envelope toward Wilf. "I think this should settle us up."

Wilf took the envelope and looked inside. Then with his thumb and forefinger he counted sixteen cool C-notes. He looked at the boss. "I think it's a little too much. It should only be thirteen-fifty."

Wentworth turned down the corners of his mouth and shook his head. "Nah, it's less than I figured. I expected to pay for all four days, since that's what I spoke for. You saved me money as it is."

"Well..."

"I thought I might have to pay for five days, to begin with. So this is a lot less."

"I don't know. It just seems..."

Wentworth held up his right hand. "This is business for me, and I'm paying what's a fair price to me. If you think it's more, then you can look at the rest of it as a bonus or as tips. I imagine some hunters tip, even if these guys didn't."

"Well, yeah." Wilf had heard more about it than he had seen himself, but he knew it was done. The guide who had complained about having guns pointed at him had also grumbled about low tips.

"It would be my place to do the tipping anyway." Wentworth held out his hand to shake. "You did good work, Wilf. I knew you would, and I'm perfectly satisfied."

Wilf shook his hand. "Thanks. But there is one little thing."

"Oh?"

"I'd like to get the deer bags back when they're done with 'em."

"Oh, no problem. What's a good way to do that? Shall I drop 'em off some place, or have someone give 'em to you? You tell me."

Wilf thought for a second. He didn't care to make a trip back out here, and Wentworth didn't seem to be inviting it. "I guess you could have Tommy Tice drop 'em off. He lives in town and knows where I live, so if he doesn't catch me at one time he can catch me at another."

"Good enough. We'll do it that way."

"O.K."

"Well, is that about it?"

"I guess so. Maybe one other thing. You want to make sure Jerry tags his deer."

"Oh, yeah." Wentworth gave a quick nod. "I think he's lookin' for his license right now."

"Just thought I'd mention it." Wilf held out his hand to shake again. "Tell the others I said so long."

"I'll do that. And thanks again, Wilf. It's been a pleasure."

"All mine."

Newell did not come back out while Wilf was hooking up the trailer and getting things secured inside. He closed the door, checked the safety chain, and climbed into his outfit, wasting no time to start the engine and put the pickup into gear. When he had turned around in the graveled area and had pulled the trailer out straight, he looked in his mirrors. On the left he saw the Ford pickup, and on the right he saw the other three vehicles and the house.

It was a job and he was done, but something didn't feel right. They were a smiling bunch, these guys, but it would be just like them to think it was no big deal to kill a deer without a license up here in Wyoming where the rules were so lax anyway. They had just enough money and just enough of the city-mouse smugness. And it wasn't a matter of someone shooting a deer because he needed the meat. He pictured the four men sitting around the table in the warm house, pleased with themselves at having patronized a native. That was part of it, too, as if he had been paid off. He didn't like what he felt. It was too much like trouble.

As he picked it apart a little more, he could see where some of it was his own fault. He should have asked to see the licenses before he left the house, but he didn't have his procedures worked out well enough, and his previous sets of hunters had all been fine on their word. He could pinpoint it now, though, and he could remember the feeling of losing his authority as he stood in the kitchen of the man who was paying him. He wasn't on his own turf, and he had settled on making sure everyone had orange. He could have checked licenses when the men all went out to the pickup, but the moment had passed, and now that he thought of it, Newell had gone off on his own to start the four-wheeler.

He shook his head. He was done with these guys, and he had other things to do. As the pickup headed down the hill, he looked in the mirror to check the trailer. It was an easy one to pull, uphill or downhill either way, but it was still a monkey on his back. He geared down and followed the road to the bottom, then pulled out onto the paved road and headed back to the tour home.

6

Wilf was happy to see the horses. They were down in the pasture grazing, and when he called out they lifted their heads and looked at him. Then as they broke into a run, he crawled through the fence to meet them. Their movement put him in mind of a song about a fellow riding the rough string. It was winter, and the cowboy's wife was going to have a baby way back in a snowed-in cow camp. A good Ian Tyson song about men, women, and horses—he could hear the guitar strumming, could feel the power of the song in just those few words. Riding the rough string.

Wilf wasn't a bronc rider and didn't expect to turn into one. A fellow had that in his blood early on if he was going to do it, and by the time he got to Wilf's age he might have to give it up. Tommy Tice could shuffle cards and dance the polka, not to mention the two-step, and not let on he had ever had a broken bone; but sometimes when he was shooting pool or just sitting around drinking, he would wince as he put his hand on the back of his neck. "Too many buckin' horses," he would say.

A fellow didn't have to be a bronc rider to feel the bounce of a few words and to know that the melody of a song and the motion of a horse had something to do, deep down, with all the rest of it. The dark horse and the sorrel, galloping up the hill to meet him, as much as carried the whole world with them. When a horse's hooves lifted, all four at once, from the dry ground they had been drumming, the animal seemed to float. A horse had energy, force, control, humor, and affection, all in a package as it braced for a stop and raised a cloud of dust. In the company of his horses, Wilf could feel he was at the center of his world, especially here on his own piece of ground, where he radiated outward to the things that mattered most—the silent land, the laws of plants and animals, and the grace of a woman.

He knew the horses could smell the hunt on him. When they opened their nostrils like that, he wondered what in particular they smelled. Some people said it was the blood, while others said it was the wild animal scent. Wilf thought it might be both, but more the animal than the blood. Take a dog, and it would be different. He smelled the blood and the fat foremost because those things held promise for him. Not so with a horse. A horse might see a deer as something alien, an intruder to be chased out of the pasture or a burden to be loaded on his back. Right now the horses saw nothing, just opened their nostrils with a slow quiver. He scratched the jaw of the dark horse. These fellows trusted him.

He spent a few minutes with the horses, patting them and looking them over. They looked fine, their coats thickening for the cold weather to come, the hair lengthening on their jaws. By the time he got back from the mountains and the last of elk season, it would be time to start feeding them hay. He turned to see how they were doing for water. It looked as if the high-school kid he'd hired had kept the trough full.

Wilf crawled back through the fence and went about checking to see if everything else was in order. Whenever he was gone for a few days he expected to come back to some big change, but it was rare to find anything different at all. He glanced around the yard, peeked into the utility shed, and then mounted the wooden steps that took him into the tour home.

As he turned the doorknob, he thought of how, as a matter of principle, he always kept the front door unlocked, the same way he left the keys in the vehicle, day and night, and did not lock his gun closet unless someone with little kids came to visit. In the code of the country, a fellow trusted others until he knew better. As a practical matter, it wouldn't do much good to lock up a flimsy mobile home anyway. Off the main road like this, anyone who wanted to get in was going to anyway, so it was just as well not to bother with locking the door.

He stood in the living room and glanced around. Everything seemed normal. And even if someone had been there, he would not worry right away. Keeping the front door unlocked was also part of the older code of cow country, to leave the place open in case someone needed it. In the old days, people stayed in one another's cabins or line shacks when they had to. Today, mobile homes on distant ranches were often treated the same way.

A few years back, over in the western part of the state, a couple of fellows got their car stuck in the snow out on a ranch road. It was a small car, not fit for that kind of travel, so a person hearing the story might have wondered what the two guys were doing out there. But the other part of the story made a person wonder as well. One guy froze to death and the other one suffered serious damage from the cold, even though there was a trailer house nearby, unlocked, with blankets and food inside. They must have been outsiders, driving a little car like that with donut tires and not knowing that the owner of the trailer would have wanted them to go inside.

Wilf opened a window for ventilation. A tour home wasn't a very sturdy fortification anyway. This one was a narrow, pre-fabricated carton, offering a thin barrier to the world outside. In good weather, with a window open on each side, he could sit anywhere in a room and never be farther than seven feet from the outdoors. In cold weather, especially when the wind blew, it felt as if the heat got pulled from the center of his body, even when the storm windows were snapped in and the room temperature measured seventy degrees. A minimal shelter, it helped him know what it was like to live on the earth. It was good enough lodging for him, for the time being, and he wouldn't begrudge the use of it to anyone, including the high school kid.

As a matter of course, he checked his gun closet, where he found everything in order. Then he went to stand in the living room again, where the open window was letting in fresh air. Catching sight of the telephone, he thought about calling Adrienne. It was almost noon on a Saturday, so he might be able to catch her at home. He dialed her number and got no answer, but she wouldn't expect him back until later that day anyway.

Outside again, he unhooked the camp trailer and started putting away some of his gear. After dropping the tailgate and pulling the field box toward him, he unlatched the lid and opened it. The smell of deer fat rose from within, where it clung to surfaces such as the gambrel, the meat saw, and the winch handle. The whiff brought back an image of the deer he had cleaned that morning. It was a good one, sleek and muscular with a picture-perfect rack. He should have felt better at having helped get it, but he didn't. It wasn't just a matter of shooting it from the trail. Sometimes that happened after a person had been trudging the ridges and draws, hunting the hard way, and then crossed paths with a big one and took the opportunity. Even if the deer came at an easy moment, a fellow had worked for it. Wilf didn't resent that part. But he had a lingering sense that Newell and Wentworth had compromised him. He felt as if they had paid him first to put a good face on things and second to remember how his bread got buttered.

He closed the field box and lugged it into the utility shed. Next he unloaded the skinning frame and the crate of water jugs, then the ice chests and perishable groceries from the trailer. As he went back and forth putting things away, he brooded on the out-of-staters. Brazen, they seemed to him. If a man wanted to shoot a deer without a license, he should know discreet ways to do it. If he wanted someone to help, it should be someone he was thick with — someone to hold the spotlight, watch for traffic, drop the tailgate, help with dragging, lift one end, or whatever it took. Off the road, back on private property, he had an even better chance to keep it to himself. But someone who did it all for sport anyway and who was smug about bush-league regulations wouldn't know there were unwritten rules all the way up and down.

Wilf shook his head. People in ranch country worked like hell to mind their own business, at least about hunting. When a fellow stopped at a house to hand in the landowner coupons for whatever got killed, it was rare for someone to look at the animals, much less ask who did the shooting. Ranch people in general wanted to assume the rules were followed and didn't want to know when they weren't. And among hunters there was a code as well. If a guy was going to pull a fast one, he made sure anyone else along was agreeable to it. If he did something out of line by accident, he tried not to drag someone else into it. Not everything could be controlled in hunting. Landowners knew it and hunters knew it, and people learned how to look the other way if the offense wasn't blatant. Even game wardens, some of whom had a high level of enthusiasm for writing citations, had a realistic sense of how things happened in the field, even if they didn't let someone off. But these guys with the nice cars and clean hands weren't real hunters or real landowners either one, and the more Wilf thought about it, the more he had half a mind to turn them in just on suspicion.

He tried Adrienne's number again and still got no answer, so he sat down at the kitchen table and ate lunch out of his ice chests. For dessert he had bread and margarine with some of Adrienne's chokecherry jelly. He appreciated the deep red as he spread it across the bread, and he remembered the smell when she had cooked the fruit and mashed the juice out of it.

His memory of the fruit cooking connected to a story she had told him, from an earlier period of her life when she was married. Her husband had a temper, and one time in a tantrum he knocked a kettle of chokecherry juice off the stove, wasting hours of her work and smearing the kitchen with scalding hot, sticky syrup. It looked like a murder scene, she said. The guy stormed out, and when he came home, she told him that was the end of things. Wilf knew she had a tactful way of phrasing criticism and objections, but as she put it, she dealt with women every day who had been abused by overbearing men, and she couldn't let herself take any shit. Wilf liked that.

After lunch he put the camp food away, unpacked his dirty clothes, shaved, and showered. He dialed Adrienne's number, still with no answer. Sitting at the table, fidgeting and thinking of the things he had to do in the next couple of days, he remembered he had to pick up his deer at the meat locker. He looked at the clock. It was a quarter to three. The processing plant closed at noon on Saturdays, like a lot of other businesses in town, but during hunting season if a fellow went around back he could usually find someone well into the evening.

Rudy, the man who ran the place, opened the back door after Wilf had rung the buzzer a couple of times. Rudy was a large, heavy man in his fifties with thinning grey hair slicked back and a bulbous nose. Like most butchers, he wore a bloody apron.

"Hi, Wilf," he said. "What can I do for you?"

"I came to pick up my deer."

"Oh, yeah. For a minute there I thought you came to leave something off, and I was wonderin' how you did it so quick." Rudy let him in and led the way to the walk-in.

"Oh, I've been out, all right."

"I know. They brought in three deer just a little while ago from that fella Wentworth's place. Nice deer, all three—

clean, too. They said you did a good job for 'em."

"Oh, yeah. Everything went smooth. That's a good place for deer, you know." As he spoke, Wilf took in what he had just heard. If the greenies brought in all three deer, then they must have all been tagged. Rudy wouldn't hang a deer, especially from someone he didn't know, if it didn't have a license.

"Yeah, I told 'em they were lucky to have you help 'em. You know what kind of stuff people bring in through my back door. Dirty, stinkin' — you name it." Rudy paused with his hand on the door handle of the walk-in. "Did you bring a bag or anything?"

"Oh, hell, I didn't think of it."

"Wait here." Rudy left and came back with a large clear plastic bag. "We'll slip this over his hind quarters, and he can ride home in the cab with you."

"Won't be the first. By the way, should I pay you before we take him down?"

"Might as well. Then you won't have to come back in."

Wilf paid five dollars for storage, and within a few minutes he had the cold, stiff carcass propped up in his cab and was on his way home. He stopped to pick up some beer, wine, and a few fresh groceries and then drove on out to his place. The high school kid's car was parked in the driveway with a girl sitting in it, and the kid was coming out of the utility shed with a bucket of grain. After a short conversation, Wilf paid the kid and arranged for him to start the routine again on Wednesday.

It was almost four, and Adrienne still didn't answer. Wilf sharpened a butcher knife and the boning knife, got out the cutting board and wrapping paper, and set the deer on the kitchen table. Then he went to work and boned the carcass. When he had it clean, he hauled the skeleton out and tossed it in the gully where the coyotes and magpies could have at it.

Back inside, he looked at the clock. It had taken him a little over an hour to bone the meat, and it would take him two hours or so to cut and wrap it. He washed his hands, called Adrienne and invited her to come out at noon the next day, and went back to work.

His thoughts wandered here and there, staying for a while on the hunters he had just taken out. He imagined their motives were a long ways from his. Some folks hunted for meat, some for a feeling of self-sufficiency. Others hunted for success, which wasn't quite the same as just killing something or getting a trophy, separate motives in themselves. Still others hunted for the mystique of merging with the primitive, connecting with an earlier age and reducing life to its elements. Meat hunters were the most practical, least idealistic of the bunch; some people put them at one end of the spectrum and trophy hunters at the other. Wilf wasn't sure how to place the kind who hunted just to kill something, the ones who gave hunting the image of being a blood sport. Wilf realized he had told Jerry Newell that hunting was his game, but he didn't consider it a sport, much less an adventure in blood lust.

It was hard to say, out of these motives and others, what impelled this most recent bunch to dig rifles out of their closets and take to the field. For them, it seemed to him, going out on a guided hunt had an element of sport to it but was mainly a privilege, a matter of being free from restraint and being able to pull the trigger without having to attend to very many details before and after. Some of it had to do with power, he guessed. These fellows liked to do what they wanted, what they were free to do, and maybe what they could get away with.

The pile of dark red meat went down as the white packages stacked up. When all he had left was the hamburger to grind, he looked at the clock. It was almost seven-thirty. He set up the grinder, thinking he would rather get it all done at once and not have anything left over for the next day. It would be a little later, but then he could relax with a hamburger and a beer.

At mid-morning Wilf was going through his gear in the utility shed when he heard a vehicle rattling up the drive. It was too early for Adrienne, and her car would have more of a hum. He went to the door and looked out to see the dark brown of a two-toned pickup cab. The flat bed and dog box added a further touch of identity, and as the truck came closer he saw the smiling face of Tommy Tice.

The elbow of Tommy's canvas chore coat rested on the ledge of the open window, and as he brought the pickup to a stop he called out. "I was hopin' I'd catch you here."

Wilf took a few steps toward the cab. "I didn't have any place else to go right now."

"Yeah, well you got the boss's little buddies all hunted in good time."

"It turned out O.K."

Tommy just nodded as he looked at Wilf.

"I guess they took their deer to the cooler already."

"Yeah, they did that yesterday. The boss give me the bags to drop by here."

"They don't need 'em to pick up the deer later, I

suppose. They'll have Rudy cut and wrap it all."

"I think they said they were gonna have it all made into salami. He makes it like a summer sausage."

"Yeah." Wilf looked past Tommy into the cab and saw a heap of cloth on the seat. It didn't look as if anyone had washed or folded the bags.

Tommy lifted a cigarette to his lips. "Regular bunch of guys, weren't they?"

"I guess so, for the kind they were. Are they still there?"

"They were gonna leave this mornin', from what I understood."

"That's good enough. I don't suppose you had much to do with 'em anyway."

"No, not really."

Wilf hesitated. He didn't think Tommy was all that stuck on Wentworth or his friends, but he didn't want to ask any questions that would make things uncomfortable. "I'll tell you, though," he said. "It just seemed to me that someone did something."

Tommy took a drag on his cigarette. "Like what?"

"I don't know. Like someone pulled a fast one."

Tommy frowned. "In what way?"

"Well, it seemed like that guy Newell didn't have a license, because he wouldn't tag the deer when I was there. And earlier, when he was down on the hayfield on the four-wheeler, where someone could see him from the road, he didn't carry a rifle. But I don't think Rudy would let 'em hang a deer without a tag."

"Probably not."

"So I don't know. Things just didn't seem right, and I've got an outfitter's license to protect."

"Well, it's out of your hands now."

"I guess so, but if they did something, I'd sure like to know about it if I was part of it."

Tommy took another drag and blew the smoke upward out the window. "I can tell you what I know, which ain't much."

"It would help."

"Well, the boss asked me about two weeks ago, just before the season opened, if I'd like to get a deer license so he could use it there at the ranch. I told him I already had one and was hopin' to use it there myself. He said that was fine, as long as I waited till everyone else was done."

Wilf shook his head. "I wonder why he didn't just get one himself."

Tommy's eyebrows went above the rim of his glasses and then came down. "I guess he hasn't been here long enough to be a resident or to put in for a landowner's permit, and a non-resident license costs too much. Probably just wanted to save money, so he waited to see if he could get mine cheap."

"Huh. I would guess that if he wanted to get a hold of one, it would have been for Newell. He didn't seem to have any interest in hunting for himself while I was there." A thought crossed his mind. "That doesn't leave you much time to get yours, then."

Tommy gave a broad smile. "You don't think I'd go without, now, do you?"

"Well, no, especially if you work right there. Did you get one already?"

"First thing this mornin'. Right at the crack of dawn. I had him hangin' before them other fellas got back to Colorado, if they're even there yet."

"Did you get him on the hayfield?"

"No reason to run all over hell when you know where to go."

Wilf laughed. He had an image of Tommy at first light, taking calm, steady aim from the cab where he sat. Tommy was the practical type. "Gave him a good surprise, uh?"

"Damn sure did."

After a few seconds of silence Wilf said, "What else do you know?"

"Nothin'."

"Me neither." He looked at the bags again. "Am I keepin' you from anything?"

"Not really. I thought I might go up to Douglas a little later on and look at a dog."

Wilf was on the verge of telling how Wentworth wanted someone to shoot a coyote for him, and then he decided not to mention it. If the boss wanted one, he would bring it up himself. "Well, I don't want to keep you if you've got places to go."

Tommy stuck the cigarette in his mouth as he leaned back and handed the bags one by one through the window. As Wilf expected, Wentworth had sent them just as they came off the deer, with smears and patches of dried blood. Now that he thought of it, he hadn't been surprised by what Tommy told him about the boss, either. Trying to use the hired man's deer license was like a bit of dirty laundry, too. Grandstand when you get a chance, and then try to stiff the government for two-and-a-half or three hundred.

Adrienne showed up right at noon, looking trim in blue jeans and a maroon sweater. Her sable hair fell loose to her shoulders and caught the sunlight with a shine. Wilf invited her into the living room, where she accepted a cup of coffee.

"Here's an idea for lunch," he said. "If you don't care for it, I can fix something else. I've got quite a few things on hand—you know, food items."

"Go ahead. Tell me what you've got in mind."

"Well, I cut up my deer yesterday afternoon and evening, and I set aside the tenderloin. It's the nicest part of the deer, and it makes little chops." He formed a circle by almost touching his right forefinger and thumb together.

"That sounds fine. I suppose you have something else on the side."

"Sure. I've got cottage cheese, fresh tomatoes, a bell pepper, and bread."

"At least four colors. That's good."

"Oh. Does a person go by color?"

"Not necessarily, but it's a way of telling whether you've got a balanced meal. You want to avoid the all-brown meals, for example."

"Like meat and gravy and French fries?"

"Right. Hamburgers, hot dogs, pizza, onion rings—you know, all the good stuff that you're supposed to cut down on."

Wilf nodded, feeling a little guilty. "I've got apples and oranges, too. Does that help?"

She laughed. "Don't worry. I'm not criticizing. If anything, I was complimenting you."

"Good, because I'm out of bean sprouts and tofu."

"I thought you might be."

"But seriously, I don't eat hot dogs, pizza, French fries,

or onion rings at home. Or at camp, for that matter, although I do eat things like canned beef stew when I'm out like that."

"Oh, that's O.K. A person doesn't want to worry about it too much, but, you know, as a regular habit it matters."

"I agree with that. One of the reasons I hunt is because the meat is so lean. You'll see as I cut it into pieces. There's not a speck of fat on it."

"Is this the deer you got last week?"

"Yeah."

"And how did things go with the, um, clients you took out?"

"All right, I guess. A regular job."

Adrienne stood in the kitchen and showed interest as he put the frying pan on the stove and unwrapped the package of dark venison. He explained how he liked to cook the meat in an uncovered pan, to let the game flavor escape.

"That's a good skillet," she said.

"Oh, yeah. This cast iron'll last forever. Those Teflon pans are good for a year or two, and then they're ready to go in the camping box."

"And so many of them are aluminum anyway."

"Oh, is that bad?"

She nodded. "Alzheimer's, you know."

"I guess I heard that." Wilf's eyebrows raised as he shook pepper onto the pieces of meat.

She poked him in the ribs. "What's that funny look?"

"Huh? Oh, nothing."

"Wilf, I'm not that finicky. I'm going to eat some of this animal you killed. The blood of the beast."

He turned to her and smiled. "I know."

"Are you uncomfortable about something?"

"I don't know. I think it was just really stupid of me not to kiss you when you first walked in. I mean, how do you drop it into the middle of something like this?"

"Uh, you could put down the spatula and the can of pepper."

He did that and then got back to the skillet before the meat burned. Before long he had the meal served, with a glass of dark red wine for each of them.

"I think I forgot to mention this color to begin with. Does it count as another one?"

"I think so. The meat started out this color, but it changed. This is red, but not like the tomatoes."

"Would beer be in the brown category?"

"I think so. Especially a dark beer." Then she added, "Nothing wrong with it. You just don't want an all-brown meal."

"Right. So you make sure you have some wine, too."

They touched glasses and began the meal. After a few minutes, Wilf spoke.

"I guess there is something bothering me, at least a little."

"Oh, what's that?" She paused with her fork at the side of her plate.

"It's about these guys I just took out hunting."

"I thought you said things went all right."

"Well, I guess they did, in that we got all three deer in a reasonable amount of time and didn't make a mess of anything. You know, sometimes things can go wrong."

"I suppose."

"Anyway, we got the deer all right, but this one fellow didn't tag his."

"Oh. And you think maybe he was illegal?"

"I don't know. They took all three deer to the cold storage, and I don't think Rudy would let anyone hang an untagged animal there. But then I talked to the guy who works for Wentworth. Do you know Tommy Tice?"

"No. I know who he is, but I don't know him."

"Well, I talked to him, and he told me this guy Wentworth had asked about using his license."

"Tommy's license."

"Right. But Tommy said he wanted to use it himself, so nothing else came of that."

"So you don't really know if they did or didn't have the third license."

"Exactly. Like Tommy says, it's out of my hands. But if I got fished into doing something without knowing it, I take that as an offense. On the other hand, I feel dumb because I didn't check their licenses to begin with. I let it slip past me."

Adrienne applied her knife and fork to a piece of meat. "So what do you think you should do?"

"That's the thing. I'm not sure."

"Do you want to find out if you got duped, so you'll know? Or do you want to turn them in?"

"I guess I want to know. But I don't know how to find out on my own without lookin' snoopy."

"You could ask someone else to do it, under the guise of looking out for your own interests. And it wouldn't really be a guise."

"I know. But that's almost the same as snooping. People won't take well to it if everything's on the square."

"And if it isn't, there might be some people who wouldn't take well to it for that reason."

"You mean someone might get ruffled if I turned 'em

in and they got busted?"

"Right."

"Well, I guess there's always that danger. But that in itself isn't a reason not to do anything."

"That's true. Or at least, I agree."

"You know what I think?"

"What?"

"I think, or maybe I should say I feel, that I was paid to look the other way. And I don't like that."

"I don't blame you, but maybe that's one of the hazards."

"You mean of being a guide?"

"I don't know. Maybe I spoke too quickly. But it seems as if that might be one of the hazards of dealing with people who are used to throwing money around. Is that the kind of people you were dealing with?"

"More or less, yeah. I gave you a sketch of this fellow before, didn't I?"

"You said he was a friend of Norman Lang's, which says something, and you said he came up here with a wad of money. So I would imagine his friends are of the same cloth."

"I'd say so. Even if they don't have as much dough at the moment, they've got the same outlook. They've got a little more money than most of us around here, and they look at us like a bunch of bumpkins."

"Then I don't blame you for being offended." She gave him a soft smile as she reached for her wine. "Or for wanting to know if you should feel offended. I already feel that way on your behalf."

"Well, thanks. I appreciate that, really. Especially since I feel kind of dumb about it anyway. As for taking it any further, I just don't know. Maybe it's none of my business."

"Unless they were paying you off, as you say. Then it is."

It was his turn to smile. "You're doing a good job of convincing me both ways. Stay out of trouble, but don't let 'em treat you like a dummy."

"I know. There's the practical voice that says play it safe, and then there's the other one."

"That's it. And it just feels like trouble. I think that's part of why I'm hesitating, to keep from doing something just because I'm mad."

"Well, for what it's worth, you've got my support either way."

"Thanks." He poured each of them another half-glass of wine. "I think for the time being, I'll just leave it alone."

They talked on about other small topics as they finished the meal. Adrienne said she had heard that Heather Lea was still missing, and Wilf said he had heard the same when he was on his way back from the ranch.

"I hope she turns up," he said.

"So do I. When I think about her, I worry. I know she was trying to stay on track to get her kids back."

Wilf decided not to say any more about Heather. As he and Adrienne were putting things away, he looked at the clock. It was almost two.

"I'm not sure what you might like to do next."

She handed him the bread to put in the refrigerator. "What are our choices?"

"Well, I could be horse wrangler. Saddle the horses and take us on a little ride."

"That sounds good. Id like that."

"Or we could sit on the couch and play footsie."

"Do we have to choose between the two?"

"Um, no. It would probably take an hour and a half or so to go for a horseback ride. Would that still leave you enough time for the other part?"

"It would be fine with me if it would be with you."

He winked at her. "Ma'am, ah bleeve a good hand could do both."

Her eyes sparkled as she hooked her finger in his belt loop. "I think so, too."

7

Wilf saw Norman Lang at the service station the next morning. The realtor was driving his shiny Ford pickup, and he had a rope bag hanging in the back window of the cab. Wilf was used to seeing Lang in the Ford Explorer with the Wagon Wheel Realty sign on the door, but the pickup registered with him as well, and when it pulled in, he remembered he wanted to talk to the man driving it.

Wilf saw the black boots, the creased Wranglers, and the grey wool sport coat with suede yoke and elbow patches as Lang got out of the cab and went into the convenience store. Even if he wasn't driving the work vehicle, he looked ready for Monday morning.

As Wilf clicked off the rest of the tankful, he kept an eye on the front door of the store. When he went in to pay for his fuel, Lang was talking to Arnold, the owner. Lang had a styrofoam cup of coffee on the counter in front of him, and he had an air about him as if he and Arnold were discussing something weighty.

Neither Lang nor Arnold took notice of him as he paid, though they were no more than four feet away. Then the woman who took Wilf's money asked Arnold a question about one of the pumps, and Lang was disengaged for a moment. Wilf turned toward him.

"Hello, Norman."

Lang turned and showed surprise. "Oh, hi, Wilf. How are you?"

"Fine, and yourself?"

"Real fine."

As Wilf took him in at a glance, Lang didn't look as good up close as he did from a bit of a distance. His face was running to flesh, with a few veins showing on the cheeks and across the nose. He wasn't full-bellied like Arnold, but he had put on weight in his upper body. He kept his blond hair neat and his face clean-shaven, like most of the local businessmen, and he had a practiced smile with automatic eye contact.

"I didn't mean to interrupt, but since I saw you here, I thought I'd ask about that generator."

A quick frown came and went. "Which one is that?"

"You said you had one that you might want to sell."

"Oh, yeah. I remember now." Lang glanced at Arnold, who had finished with the cashier. "I'll tell you, Wilf, I haven't been thinking about it very much. Are you going to be around later?"

"Well, no. Actually, I'm on my way out of town now. Takin' some hunters out for elk."

Lang gave him a nod of assurance. "Well, just come by the office when you get back."

"Oh, O.K. Thanks."

"Any time."

Outside in the cool morning, Wilf checked the air in the trailer tires. He had to wonder about Lang. The man wasn't talking the same language as he had been at happy hour. Wilf pictured him, standing with his back to the bar and holding his beer bottle by the neck, like some of the regular cowboys did, and giving the nod of confidence. "Good generator. Never been used. Got it for the big millennium power failure, and nothing happened. Just the thing for a camp set-up."

As Wilf pulled out of the service station, he saw the pickup still parked. He wondered if Lang didn't like to discuss personal sales in front of Arnold or if he was giving Wilf the brush-off because he didn't want to sell the generator after all. Wilf shook his head. It seemed so petty, and deep down, he couldn't care less about one of the damned machines. They were as noisy as the compressors at Pioneer Truss, and he didn't like the sound of them coming through the pine trees. But with the extra bit of money he had just picked up, it would add to his equipment, and it was something he could tinker with during the winter.

He looked in the rear-view mirror as he picked up speed on the open highway. The camper was pulling fine, like always. Even with a trailer in tow, it gave him a feeling of freedom to be out on the road on a Monday morning, when other guys he knew were punching in.

At the fuel stop in Laramie, Wilf saw a picture of Heather Lea. It was the typical black-and-white missing person flyer, not a very good image, but Heather all the same. Wilf recognized the flyer for what it was before he read a word. It was a version of one he had seen a few years back at the travel centers and rest stops. The woman's name was Amy something, and she had disappeared when she was jogging. The flyers had hung around for months, and as far as he knew, no one ever found the woman. Now Heather was on the wall.

Wilf noticed her dark hair and recognized her smile, then paused to read her name and description. He felt a pang of worry for her, and he hoped she turned up somewhere. It wasn't just because she was a good resource, as Newell might put it—although her picture brought back some nice associations. More than that, she deserved a chance to get her life straightened out, maybe get her kids back some day. But to keep the cops looking for a missing person, there needed to be a push—family members pressing, foul play suspected, money gone—and not many people would care enough about Heather. As for himself, he didn't know how much he could do, even if he wasn't going off to the mountains for a week or ten days.

At the edge of the campsite, Wilf took a moment to admire his tripod. With ten-foot legs fitting into three sleeves welded together for the cap on top, it was a challenge to set up. He could have asked one of the hunters to help, but they were busy moving into the gooseneck trailer, and he liked doing the job himself. Having almost brained himself with it one time, he knew to use the hand winch to hold the extended leg in the sleeve as he tipped and then pulled the tripod up onto its feet. He settled it in place and looked it over. If any of the hunters got an elk, it would be handier to use the tripod than to rig up a meat pole between two aspens or to try to find a pine tree with a sturdy enough branch. As he released the ratchet and went about putting the hoist away, he wondered if one of the hunters would recommend an electric winch.

The sun was going down behind the mountain west of camp, and the chill came in. Wilf looked at the large trailer, where the lights were on and the hunters moving around inside. He read the name on it: *Château*. That was just about right. Then he looked at the other one, which he would sleep in. This was business, camping in trailers and hunting out of vehicles, while the tents and horses stayed down on the plains. But that was the way these fellows wanted it. He went into the smaller trailer to start fixing supper.

Wilf followed a rule he had learned from another guide: always serve steaks the first night out. A fellow didn't know how long he would have a full crew, so it was best to make a good impression while everyone was present and the count came out all right. Even at that, Wilf had an extra steak. The fourth hunter had not been able to make it. Henderson, the one who had taken care of all the arrangements, said it was something that came up at the last moment, and he made it seem like his own generosity when he told Wilf it would be all right to keep Green's deposit.

Wilf set two skillets on the stove and unwrapped the steaks. He took out one rib-eye for each hunter and one for himself, then wrapped up the fifth one and put it away. He didn't even know Green, but he felt as if someone was missing.

When the steaks were close to ready, Wilf went across the campsite to knock on the Château and sound the call for supper. When he stepped back into the other trailer, he caught the satisfying smell of beefsteak.

A few minutes later, the three hunters showed up with an ice chest of Bud Light. The men squeezed into their places around the little table, with food at arm's length on top of the stove, and the meal got under way in a sociable manner. Wilf learned that the hunters were all employees of state government in Ohio. The three of them were about the same age, somewhere in their early forties, and Wilf imagined they were far enough along in their careers that they could afford an out-of-state hunting expedition. He also interpreted, from their general air of confidence and authority, as well as from their references to other personnel, that they were used to having people work under them. And, like other government employees Wilf had met, they expressed nonchalance and contempt toward the bureaucrats above them.

Wilf didn't take any of their talk personally, not even the part when Henderson asked him if he was Canadian and told him he didn't sound like one. But there came a moment that seemed to define an attitude.

Henderson, who had been quiet for a couple of minutes as he cut and chewed a bite of steak, looked at Wilf and said, "I know you can't guarantee anything on a hunt like this, but our chances ought to be all right."

"It's hard to say. If the elk are here, you've got a good chance. Deer season is just finishing, and when it opens for elk in the morning, there'll be a stream of hunters coming in. You'll hear 'em an hour before daylight, rollin' in in their outfits. If there's elk, the hunters'll move 'em around, and that's where your chance comes."

"Well, I think we ought to be able to knock down something."

"It all depends. But we'll give it our best try, and hope something comes around."

Henderson looked down at his steak, and Wilf noticed the man's jowls.

"I hope it does. I mean, we ought to get something, once we've paid our money."

Silence hung in the air for a moment. Richards and Lundberg, the other two hunters, looked at Henderson until he spoke again.

"To the state of Wyoming, you understand. This part here, it's all clear and straight-across-the-board."

Wilf took a breath and picked his words. "As far as the state goes, they don't sell the animal. Just the opportunity, as they say, to go out and try to get one."

"So it's up to the individual to get his money's worth." Henderson took another bite of steak.

"I guess so, in a way. If a person buys a license and doesn't go out at all, then I suppose he's not getting any of what he paid for."

"Like Green," said Lundberg, in an apparent attempt to lighten the atmosphere. "He's out more than five hundred, between the license and the deposit. He could just as well have given it to me."

"Or me," said Henderson.

"Even at that," Wilf went on, "as far as the state sees it, if a guy buys a license, whether he goes out or not, he gets what he pays for. And that's the opportunity. I didn't invent the idea, but that's the way I've had it explained to me. Ask any game warden, and that's the official line you'll get."

"Oh, I know how bureaucracy thinks," said Henderson, holding his knife with its point up. "We work for one that's a hell of a lot bigger than this one."

"Anyway," said Richards, "at least we've got the chance, like Wilf says. That's more than Green's got."

"Amen," Lundberg chipped in. "All he's got right now is a tit in the wringer. And a pissed-off wife."

Wilf had a blue flame going beneath the coffee pot at five-thirty. The first half-dozen vehicles had already driven past the campground, and one of his own hunters had started the Suburban. He imagined it was Richards, who had gone out the night before and run the engine while he tried to call home on his cell phone. He was probably trying again.

Wilf had told the hunters they could expect breakfast at six and coffee a little before that, so he had the skillets heating when they showed up at ten 'til. As Henderson stepped into the lamplight, Wilf opened his eyes at the bright blaze-orange cap and vest and the dark green camouflage jacket and pants underneath. The man had a compass hanging from a ring on the upper part of his vest, and on his hip he had a toad-stabber knife with two leather thongs hanging from the tip of the scabbard. As he scooted into his place at the little table, his rifle shells rattled in a belt pouch.

Lundberg slid in on the other side. He was wearing cammies and blaze orange also, but he didn't have equipment hanging all over him. After stretching his face and widening his eyes, he fell into a long, deep yawn.

As Wilf set out the cups and poured the coffee, he noticed that Lundberg had a day's worth of blond stubble while Henderson, who had dark hair, was clean-shaven. "You fellas sleep all right in the trailer?"

"Oh, yeah," they both muttered.

"The generator from the other camp didn't bother you?"

"I went out like a light," said Henderson. "I think I'm still on Eastern time."

Wilf put his open hand above the inside surface of the thicker skillet and counted. At five he could feel the heat, so he poured about a half-teaspoon of oil in each pan. Then he gave a few strokes to the batter.

"I'm gonna go ahead and get the pancakes going."

Henderson had put the heel of one hand under his chin and the palm of the other behind his head and was giving himself a twist. "Yeah. Kevin'll be in before long."

Wilf was still waiting for a bubble to show when he heard the Suburban engine shut off. Then he heard the door open and close, and after that the click of the door locks.

As Richards stepped into the trailer and closed the door, Henderson looked up. "Do any good?"

Richards shook his head and slid in beside Lundberg.

Henderson spoke in Wilf's direction. "Is this one of those dead spots?"

"I don't know. I think it depends on what kind of phone you've got and what kind of service. I've heard of guys callin' from deep in the woods, like to report a violation or something like that."

Henderson looked across at Richards. "You'll probably have to go up on top of one of these mountains."

Wilf saw the first bubble rise in the pancake on the

right. "There's roads all the way up," he said. "You can go clear to the fire lookout if you want." He set another cup on the table and poured the coffee.

Richards thanked him and took a sip. Then he looked at his two pals. "Well, today's the big day. Let's hope we do something."

"It would be nice," said Henderson.

The view from the top was the way Wilf remembered it during the rest of the year when he was far away. Through the mountains to the west, the land sloped into foothills and then spread out into plains. In the grey of morning, with the sun not yet up, he could see the lights of Saratoga, some twenty miles away. Off to the southwest he picked up a smaller twinkle of lights that would be Encampment.

This was always the good moment, when he climbed the steep mountainside, resting with his foot against a pine stump or an aspen trunk, then pushing until the next breather, and reaching the top at last, walking past low-lying rocks and juniper bushes and coming out between two pine trees, to see the silent, unchanging world spread out below. The view was always worth more because of the work it took to get there.

Wilf checked his watch. It was ten 'til seven. Along the ridges below him, but still high enough that they would have a downhill walk to camp, his hunters would be poking around, looking for something to shoot. Wilf looked again at the pale expanse of plains, and he wondered if Heather Lea was holed up in one of these out-of-the-way towns. He realized that whenever he speculated about where she might be, he assumed there was a guy in the picture—some unknown fellow next to her as she lay with her dark hair against a pillow. Wilf glanced at the distant lights, then turned and walked toward the trees. He paused beneath a pine branch to put a shell in the chamber and set the safety. Then he stepped between two juniper bushes and moved into the timber.

Time to practice the quiet walk, stepping sideways between dead branches, taking the extra steps to walk around fallen trees. A squirrel chittered, and two trees squeaked high above as they rubbed in the breeze. Wilf shifted his rifle to duck under a branch, then light-footed his way along. He heard the call of a crow from somewhere up ahead, then nothing except his own footsteps on the dry pine needles and twigs on the forest floor.

Through the timber to the east he could see the green of pine branches where the morning sunlight fell. He took out his compass to remind himself of the direction in which the ridge ran, and he pictured the main spots up ahead, the places where he had seen elk. He knew the contours where the trails crossed over the ridge and the elk came from one side or the other, depending on the hunting pressure. He knew the places where the view opened up on the west, where he could walk to the edge of the timber and look out on the sage-covered mountainside—the cleft where a cow elk and her calf had bounced down in faster leaps than he could have imagined, and the rocky slope farther on, where he had seen a cow elk pushing her way up, running from something, pausing with her tongue hanging out as she looked back, then bolting ahead when she saw Wilf.

All of those spots lay a good half-hour and more ahead. In the meanwhile he had to take slow steps, make the least noise he could, and try to get into tune with his surroundings. If he could find elk, or sign of elk, he would have an idea of where to put his hunters. Beyond that, on what seemed a higher level of endeavor, he wanted to blend in.

He came to a slope where a saddle crossed the ridge. From here on out, the prospects got better. He checked the safety, then shifted the rifle for walking downhill.

Tracks ran both ways along the main path, most of them deer tracks but a few larger ones as well. Wilf stepped over the trail, went into the bottom of the saddle, crossed through the dry grass and gopher mounds and deadfall of aspen, then started up the other side. Out of the dark timber now and among scattered aspens, all leafless, he felt the warmth of the sun. He stopped to check his watch — a quarter to nine — and followed the trail up the hillside.

After a sharp climb he paused at a point where he had a good view of the mountainside ahead. There he rested, one foot uphill from the other, his thumb under his rifle strap. Just as he was about to move on, he heard crashing in a patch of aspens downslope on the left. Raising his rifle into position, he moved in back of a tree in time to see two forked-horn mule deer headed in the direction he'd come from. When they had passed, he heard a tramping that sounded like another deer, and after a moment's wait he saw a third buck with antlers a little bigger than the other two. Out of practice, Wilf put the scope on him, holding steady as he swept the antlers and found the front quarters, but keeping his finger outside the trigger guard. Then he relaxed and lowered the rifle, and the deer went on, following the others.

Wilf climbed up the slope and came to a gully that ran down into the aspens where he had seen the deer. He was in the element now, especially as the walking was quieter here, where the path led through low junipers beneath tall pines. When he got out to the other side of the gully, he heard another deer whoofing as it moved through the aspens below. He saw its shape but could not tell if it was a doe or a buck.

He stood still for a moment. These deer had been pushed out by something, probably a human. Wilf felt his spirits sink. As a general rule, meeting another hunter meant that the rest of the hunt was going to be pretty dull and chased out. Wilf took a deep breath, exhaled, and pushed up the mountainside beyond the gully.

As the upper ground came into view, he picked out a dark animal in sagebrush and low, sparse aspens. It gave him a start, and then he registered it as a moose. He hadn't seen moose up this high before. In the past few years, he had seen the dark creatures—darker than deer or elk, and newcomers to this place as he had known it—down below where the land drained into marshy meadows and willow thickets. But this was a moose all right, up on the high, dry ridge.

As he adjusted to it, he saw it was a young moose. A minute later, a larger one appeared, coming up the mountainside. Then a third one came into view, smaller, the size of the first one. A cow and two calves. Wilf watched them for several minutes, not wanting in the least to put them in the scope, just wanting to be part of the trees, sage, rocks, and dirt as the animals passed by. He noted their color, a dark brown running to black, with their legs lighter as the sun cleared the ridge and was shining down into the bare aspens.

The three ran a ways, then walked and poked and paused, and ran some more. For as clumsy as they looked, with their humpbacks and thick heads, they had a smooth run, picking up their feet and bending at the knees. They looked plodding, but they didn't jiggle like a beef cow. Nor did they rock like a horse, lurch like an elk, or bounce like a deer. Their backs stayed almost level as they moved in a lumbering forward momentum and then disappeared into a patch of dark timber.

Wilf came back to himself, standing in the morning sun, high on a mountainside of sage and grass and aspens and rocks. The world fell away wide and open to the west, now in broad sunshine with not a town light to be seen. Miles away, a metal barn glared, and closer in, he saw the white top of a pickup cab. He hitched the sling strap of his rifle onto his shoulder and turned his back on the plains, then climbed up the slope, conscious of walking where the hooved animals had left their tracks.

Wilf found his hunters where he had told them to meet, down in the bottom where the forestry road made a wide turn at the edge of a clearing and where a spur road ambled off to the west into the sagebrush. They were standing in the sunlight, bright in their blaze orange, when he rolled to a stop. Richards and Lundberg climbed in back, and Henderson sat in the cab.

On the way back up the hill, Wilf pulled over at a wide spot to let a couple of ATVs go by. Each one had a rifle cradled on the handlebars, and the second one had a chainsaw tied onto the rear rack.

"I've seen a few of those today," said Henderson.

"Yeah, four-wheelers. They're gettin' more popular all the time. It used to be you'd see a few horses in here, but those things have pretty much taken over. That guy with a chainsaw can go just about anywhere a horse can."

"They look pretty handy."

"I'm sure they are." Wilf wanted to say they helped overweight Americans stay that way, even as they kept up the image of the rugged outdoorsman, but it might be coming a little close to the present company. So he just added, "I don't care for the noise, myself."

Henderson shook out a cigarette. "Oh, there's that."

Wilf geared down to pull around a tight curve. It did seem as if there were two worlds to this business—one where the clients wanted to be isolated with tents and horses in the natural element, and one where they wanted all the toys and comforts. If he did much more with this set, he might have to think about a four-wheeler to go along with the generator.

Henderson rolled down the window, hawked, and spit. "So do you think there are many elk in here?"

"Hard to tell. I didn't see any tracks up on top, and I didn't hear many shots from down here."

"How long do you go without gettin' anything until you decide to go somewhere else?"

"Oh, we can get three or four days out of these spots around here without even having to think about moving camp."

"How far is it to another campground?"

"Assuming that we wanted to go to another improved one, with running water and a shitter, the next one I'd go to is about an hour's drive from here."

"Oh, that's not too bad. Kevin could pull one of the trailers with the Suburban."

"That would be one way. We'll see how it goes."

The guests from the Château brought over their ice chest of Bud Light again as Wilf turned the pork chops for the first time. Henderson and Lundberg carried the beer together, as each of them was holding an open can. Richards was out sitting in his vehicle, running the engine and listening to the radio. In the hour since they had all come back from the afternoon hunt, Wilf had heard the mechanized click half a dozen times as the hunters got into the Suburban for one thing or another.

He wondered what they thought of his habit of leaving the pickup unlocked with the keys in the ignition and his rifle in the rack. Coming from a city, they would have an ingrained caution, and he doubted that they would be quick to adopt the code of trust, which ran as strong in the elk country as in the cow country. It was a simple rule that no one stole anything from an outfit or a camp. Men might argue over who killed an elk or deer, but no hunter so much as touched another man's Coleman lantern.

Henderson and Lundberg slid into their places at the table. Wilf set a small cutting board in front of them and then set on it a knife, a roll of summer sausage, and a block of jack cheese. Lundberg picked up the knife and started slicing sausage.

"Well," said Henderson, "one day gone. I can't say I didn't see anything. Just not anything I had a license for."

Lundberg paused in his cutting and looked up at Wilf. "Bob saw a moose."

"Oh, yeah. They're in here. Have been for a few years." Wilf turned to check on the pork chops.

"Tempting as hell," said Henderson. "He had a nice set of antlers."

Wilf spoke over his shoulder. "Well, you know, those moose are pretty well protected. Just about anyone would turn in a guy for that sort of thing."

Henderson's voice rose in a tone of defense. "I wouldn't actually pull the trigger—not on something like that. I mean, hell, we saw the sign coming in. It's like a billboard."

"People kill 'em all the same. Maybe they get excited, or maybe they don't take the time to tell a moose from an elk. But I heard they lost about eight of 'em in one year, just to hunters."

Lundberg spoke up. "And there's no season on 'em at all?"

"Oh, no. They're barely gettin' 'em introduced here. That's why people don't like to see 'em get killed."

Henderson sniffed. "I think I read somewhere in the paperwork that there was a good reward for tellin'."

"Oh, yeah." Wilf turned toward the table. "I know a fellow who said he reported someone, and I think it was for killing a moose. He said he got five hundred dollars."

Henderson's jowls moved as he nodded. "I bet. In a low-paying state like this one, people would jump at that kind of reward, no matter if they were making a living off the hunters at the same time."

Wilf had an urge to smack Henderson with a hot skillet, but he just tightened his jaw and warned himself not to say too much. "It's not as if the only reason people turned in violators was to get the money."

"Maybe not," said Henderson, "but I'd guess it works as an incentive."

Wilf lay on his back, looking up at the ceiling of the camp trailer. He knew he was letting Henderson's remarks eat on him, but he couldn't help turning over the comments. It seemed as if Henderson saw this whole world in terms of what some people paid for and what others were willing to get paid for. Wilf resented being defined in that way, and it made him wish he hadn't taken a dime from any of these guys—or Wentworth, either. But if he was going to make a business out of this, he had to be practical.

He didn't like the part where Henderson implied that the natives were biting the hand that fed them, but the part about jumping at the reward money cut him even deeper. It made him feel mercenary even as he knew that if he was going to turn someone in—as he had thought of doing with Wentworth and Newell—he sure wouldn't do it for the money. It had never occurred to him, but he still felt the sting of the accusation.

He took a breath and heaved it out. He needed to stick to business and not let this guy get under his skin. To hell with his comments about what a small-time, low-paying state this was.

Wilf rolled onto his side. If this was what he wanted to do, then he needed to keep out the personal element. He didn't have to like a man to get him hunted. Still, it took up some energy to deal with the petty things—energy that he would rather be spending on something constructive, like Adrienne. That was a much better thought to go to sleep on.

8

Wilf stood at the edge of the dark timber, picking out the trail in the first grey light. It wound through tall pines and around deadfall, with patches of snow here and there. For the first stretch it didn't present much of a climb, but before long the going would get steep. With his thumb beneath the rifle strap, he took up the trail.

He had a good start on the day, earlier than the morning before. He imagined the Suburban out on the road now, its headlights sweeping the trunks of pine and fir. Henderson was sizing up as the type that knew everything by the second day. Wilf hoped at least one of the hunters saw elk this morning. He didn't like the prospect of arguing about whether to move camp. Not this soon, anyway.

He came out of the timber in daylight, though the sun had not yet cleared the mountain to the east. Pulling in deep breaths, he rested with his uphill leg bent and his downhill foot lodged against an aspen not two inches thick. He had come out where he expected. The ridge lay a couple of hundred yards above him, a jumble of rocks and juniper brush and then a file of massive pines on the very crest. He watched the top of the mountainside as he let his breathing catch up. Whether he expected to shoot or just take in a good look, he didn't want to be heaving deep when the other side came into view. He worked the bolt of his rifle with a slow twist and pull, then pushed a shell into the chamber, snugged the bolt in place, and set the safety.

The breeze touched his face as he moved forward, one slow half-step at a time, and the shady side of the mountain came into view. He scanned the slopes below him until they fell away so sharp he could not see them. No elk—just the same rocks as always, clustered points on the slope. His gaze settled on the largest clump, out in the middle and a hundred fifty yards downslope, a nice little hideout with the dead snag rising from its base. He made his way there and settled in.

From this vantage point he could see Encampment and Saratoga again, lights winking in the dawn. People down there would be fixing breakfast, drinking coffee, getting ready for work. Some would still be in bed, in houses and motel rooms. As he looked at those towns now, he had a less likely feeling that Heather Lea was somewhere down on those plains. If she was anywhere, it would be farther away.

Closer in, in the middle distance between Saratoga and

here, he could see the foothill ranches. Pale haystacks marked the best places where deer and elk would be feeding on alfalfa stubble. He wondered how many elk were down there. Probably not very many. He hadn't heard the volleys of rifle fire that he sometimes did on opening morning.

He brought his view in closer now, to study again the country that fell away below him. From here he could see most of the mountainside, more than he could when he first cleared the rim. It was all sage and grass and rocks until it disappeared at the bottom. Out from there, visible in daylight but not yet lit by the sun, lay a clearing where the loggers had laid waste to thirty acres or so. Nothing moved there, either, nor at the edge of the timber on either side. Wilf studied the treeline back up the mountain on his left as the trees changed from pine to aspen and back to pine. Then down the right side, pines all the way, until his heart jumped at the sight of something at the edge of the clearcut.

Through the scope he could tell it was an elk, but it was too far away—at least half a mile—to see whether it had antlers. Wilf took out his pocket binoculars, peered as he adjusted them, and zeroed in on the elk. It still looked small in the focus, but he was able to pick out a set of spikes, somewhere in the range of ten inches to a foot, rising above the skull and ears. His pulse settled down as he put the binoculars away. It wasn't a big bull with a full spread of antlers, and there was no way of knowing whether he would be able to find it later in the day or again tomorrow morning. But it was worth a try for hunters who wanted to knock something down.

At the other end of the clearing, though he couldn't see it with his naked eye, ran a road. Sometimes he came back that way on foot, and he knew its course. Any vehicle that came along this morning would send that spike into the timber. If someone spooked him good, he might cross a couple of ridges, but if he didn't get bothered much, he might stay around. Wilf was sure not going to march down the bare mountainside, or even along one of the timbered edges, to try to get close this morning. The best thing to do was to go back up and around the long way, and think about how to get the best chance for his hunters.

He followed the ridge south as the sun rose on his left. He recognized the places where the trail wound through trees and up over a little crest. Then he paused where the ridge sloped downward, bare and grassy, until it leveled out in a grove of aspens. Below him, a gang of crows milled in the air above the leafless aspens, and their cawing lifted on the breeze. After watching for a few minutes, he walked down in the open.

On the other side of the first big aspen he found the gut pile, big enough to be an elk and with wrinkles just dry enough to be yesterday's kill. Most of the bird pecks so far were on the fat. He twitched his nose at a candy bar wrapper and a Pepsi can, scanned the gut pile again, and walked on. He thought of his hunters, moving through the woods and maybe seeing something in the scope. Whether they saw elk or not, at least he could tell them there were a few in here.

After stalking the ridge for about a mile, he followed the contour of a big gully down to the west. Halfway down the mountain he crossed the gully, tramping through dry aspen leaves and unavoidable small branches, and climbed up an intermediate ridge. He wanted to see the salt lick where the rancher with a grazing lease left mineral blocks for his range cattle. When he came out onto the grassy point, he found a pop-up camp trailer. It sat by itself, with no other vehicle in sight. This was farther into the hunting area than he had ever seen a camp before, but if a pickup could climb the grade with salt blocks in back, another could pull up a light trailer like this one.

He doubted that the camper had any relation to the gut pile, unless the hunters had taken their elk into town already. It was more likely that this party hauled the trailer out to here because they had the horsepower to do it, and then drove somewhere else to hunt.

Wilf didn't walk around the pop-up far enough to see the license plate but instead meandered on, trying not to look into someone else's camp. He found the road that led downhill, steep and rutted, and side-stepped his way to the bottom. Although he didn't stare at the camper, he got a good look at it, and it put him in mind of another one he had seen once, also in an unexpected place.

He had come onto it at mid-morning like this, back in a stand of trees, away from the road. Deer season was over, but a headless unskinned deer was hanging from a pine branch. The trailer had an Oklahoma license plate. Wilf didn't like what he saw, but it was back in the days when he might have done something like that himself, so he skirted the camp. As he did, he heard voices and movement inside the trailer, as if a couple of men were just waking up from a late night. He was tempted to turn them in, mainly because they were out-of-staters, but he knew he wouldn't. When he went past the spot a couple of hours later to catch a second glance, the Oklahomans had cleared out.

Wilf stood in the shade of a fir tree and drank from his water bottle. He had a hard climb ahead of him, but it would take no more out of him than following the road around, and it would let him see a part of the mountain he hadn't seen earlier. Satisfied with the thought of not having to meet any vehicles, he put his water bottle away and set off through the woods.

He was following a draw where the climb got steeper through a patch of aspens. Slow, dark shapes—too dark for elk—appeared up ahead. Wilf dropped to a crouch with his rifle across his knee. He picked out three moose—a cow, a young bull with a couple of points poking up in front of his eyes, and a larger bull with a good spread of webbed antlers, four or five points to each side. The sight of antlers quickened Wilf's pulse, even when he had no desire to raise the rifle.

The moose were grazing uphill in the mottled shade, so Wilf followed them in a slow half-crouch. When he came within a hundred yards of them, they paused in clear view and turned to look at him. He lowered himself to a kneeling position and kept still, and the moose seemed unbothered. Wilf noticed their beards, longest on the big bull, and their drawn, droopy faces. He observed their pale legs, then their brown tops from the skull all the way down the back, up and over their humps, to their thin rear ends. The animals were not as big as they looked at first, but they were as big as some elk, and the tines on the bull caught a man's eye. Still, in the main body they were black, or close to it, and they stood around much longer than any elk ever would. That was what made them easy to kill at the same time that it gave a person a chance to tell the difference.

The three moose turned back to face uphill and went

about their grazing. Wilf stayed put, not wanting to stir them out of their natural rhythm. He relaxed and looked at the slopes on either side of the draw. Up on the right, the timber rose tall and thick, but halfway up on the left the ridge ran to bare patches of sagebrush spotted with trees. Looking back at the moose, he saw that they were starting to climb out of the drainage to the left, ever slow. That was all right. Now he could go on up the draw as before, without pushing them.

As he sat waiting for another couple of minutes, movement and color caught his eye. Halfway up the slope on his left, a hunter in an orange vest appeared next to the branchless trunk of a large pine, stood a moment, and then sank back behind the tree. Wilf figured that the hunter, being uphill, could hear the animals treading in the dry aspen leaves and twigs. He was sure it wasn't any of his hunters, as they had driven to a place he had shown them the day before, a place where they wouldn't have to climb either side of a mountain like this.

Wilf did not move. He had no idea what kind of a hunter stood behind that tree, but he knew it was a man with a rifle, someone who was likely to see some antlers in the next few minutes.

He had four choices. His last would be to climb up toward the other man. Wilf didn't like to mix with other hunters in the field, and he wouldn't want someone else to come up and sing out while he was watching moose. As another option, he could walk up the draw as he had planned, but that might push the moose toward the hunter. He could also climb up to his right, where he would stay out of the way of the animals and hunter altogether. Or he could stay where he was and decide later. No matter what he did, he might hear a rifle blast or he might hear nothing.

He stood up and headed to the right side of the draw, picking out the best way to get through the timber. As he climbed the slope, he caught a glimpse now and then of the pine tree on the other side, but he did not see the orange vest again. Although he did not hear a shot, he did not quit fearing for the moose until he crossed the top of the mountain.

Back at camp, he noticed his pickup leaning, and then he saw that the right rear tire had gone flat. He unslung the rifle and let out a long breath as he poked the gun into the cab and settled it in the rack. Now he had a job. He could put on the spare without much trouble, but he couldn't run around that way for the next few days, much less shuttle trailers to another campsite or back down to the plains. He was going to have to take the flat into town and get it fixed.

The hunters pulled into camp in their Suburban as he was tightening the lug nuts on the spare. They took their time getting out of their vehicle, and then Henderson came over to stand by the pickup while the other two went into their trailer.

"Got a flat, huh?"

"Sure did." Wilf shifted his glance from the man's shoes to his face.

"I noticed it when we pulled out this morning."

"Huh. It was good and dark when I left, and I didn't see a thing."

"You must have picked up a nail somewhere yesterday."

"Must have."

As Henderson went into the camper, Wilf stood up and bent over the tire he had pulled off. He lifted it upright and rolled it a few inches at a time. He could not find any nailhead, screw, or other puncture. The tread was a bit worn, as he imagined Newell would have noticed, but he could find no break. Nevertheless, it meant a trip to town. He picked up the tire and swung it into the bed of the pickup.

After lunch, Wilf started the pickup and let it run for a couple of minutes as he thought things out. The hunters said they would be fine for the afternoon hunt, but Wilf didn't like the feeling that he wasn't tending to them. For the kind of hunting they were doing, they shouldn't need a guide, except to get an idea of how to hunt this kind of country and then to have someone take care of a big animal if they got one. The hunters hadn't talked much about what they had seen that morning, and they seemed interested in Wilf's suggestion for tomorrow morning's hunt. They probably wouldn't go out again until about three, and he might even be back by then. There was just one thing he wished he had gotten a better look at. When Henderson had stood by the tail end of the pickup, Wilf thought he saw blood on the man's shoes. Then at lunch Henderson had changed into his hard-soled camp slippers, so Wilf was left wondering. And now he had an errand to run.

The young man at Saratoga Lube and Tire, Jason by the name on his shirt, could not find a leak when he aired up the tire. He squirted soapy water on it, then took it outside and ran a light flow of water from the hose, more than once, all over the tread, on the sides, and on the valve stem. He tried the soapy water again, and still he found no leak.

"I don't know what else to do."

"You think it's all right?"

"It's not leakin'."

"I hate to put it back on and then have it go flat again."

Jason shrugged. "It might do that. I had one like this one time, that it took three times of goin' flat until I found the leak."

Wilf looked at the spare that was still on the hub. It was mismatched with the other three, which was not good for four-wheel-drive, and it was weather-checked. Probably as old as the pickup. "Well, hell, if it's not leaking now, let's put it back on."

Jason wheeled out a floor jack, and then with the help of his impact wrench, he rattled off the lug nuts, changed tires, and snugged the original into place.

"You never know. It might hold up, never go flat again."

"I'll tell you, thinking back about where I drove this thing yesterday, I went through some deep ruts in one place. Do you think the tire could have lost its seal and re-seated itself when you aired it up again?"

Jason looked at the tire as he nodded. "Yeah. That kind of thing can happen."

Wilf smiled. "But then again, maybe it's wishful thinking."

Jason smiled back. "Just gotta wait and find out."

Back on the road, stepping on the gas as he climbed the hill leaving Saratoga, Wilf laid out two things he wanted to do when he got to camp. One was to wrestle the spare tire into the bracket underneath the pickup bed, and the other was to get another look at Henderson's shoes.

The Suburban was gone when he pulled into camp. He got out of the cab and checked the rear tire, and it looked fine. Now for the crummy job. He lifted the spare out of the bed, settled it on the ground, and then scooted under the pickup on his back. He had gotten dirt in his eyes taking the spare down, so he was prepared for it now. From down there, the rear tire looked great. Nice kid at the tire shop, too. He didn't want to charge anything, but Wilf made him take a five. "You can't work for free," he'd told him.

Back on his feet and brushing himself off, Wilf felt the temptation to go into the Château and have a look. After all, the trailer was his — or leased to him, anyway — and he had a right to see if anything was out of line. But he didn't like the feeling. It was their space, and they wouldn't have left a bloody knife in plain view, anyway. If there was something to be found out, he would rather wait until he saw the hunters again.

Even at that, he had to think about what he might do. No one liked a snitch, and he had just gone through the idea with his hunch about Newell and Wentworth. What he didn't know didn't matter. Furthermore, the slur about the reward money still hung in the air. Wilf shook his head. It all depended on what, if anything, had happened. Maybe it was nothing. He would just have to wait and see.

He looked at the tire again and decided to go out where he thought the hunters might be. After checking to make sure he had his own hunting license with him, as he had a rifle in the rack, he fired up the engine and pulled out of camp.

He met the Suburban as it was climbing up out of the bottom where he understood the Ohioans had hunted that morning. He pulled aside as they came up around a bend, and as he waited for them to drive by, he saw another vehicle coming up the hill a ways behind the Suburban. It was a dark green pickup with lights on the bumper, a grilled rack in back of the cab, and the Game and Fish insignia on the door. The dark-haired fellow driving it wore the red shirt of a game warden.

Richards did not stop but just drove past, giving a glance of recognition and pointing forward. The game warden nodded to Wilf as he kept the green pickup close behind the Suburban.

Wilf drove downhill until he found a wide spot, then turned around and took his time driving back to camp. When he got to the campground, the game warden was pulling out. He nodded as before.

Richards, who was standing by his Suburban, gave a small wave and went into the Château. Wilf parked his pickup, went into the smaller trailer, and sat at the table. A few minutes later there came a rap on the metal siding; then the door opened, and Henderson stepped up into the trailer.

Wilf kept himself from looking at the man's shoes right away, trying instead to meet his eyes, which roved.

"Well, we had a little trouble."

"Sort of looked like it. Do you want to sit down?"

Henderson glanced at the bench seat and shook his head. "Nah. I just came to tell you that we're going to have to pull out."

"Oh." Wilf had to look at him for a few seconds until their eyes met. "Is it something you can tell me about?"

"Oh, yeah. It's just one of those stupid-ass things."

Wilf looked at the man's feet and saw a pair of camouflage lace-up boots in place of the tan hiking boots he had seen earlier. Then he glanced up. "Someone shoot something?"

The jowls moved as Henderson nodded. "Steve shot a deer. It was a big one, with a big rack. I think he took it for an elk."

"Is that what he said?"

"Well, yeah. It was a mistake. He didn't do it on purpose."

Wilf tried to hold Henderson's eyes again. "When did it happen?"

"This morning."

"I see. Did you dress it then?"

Henderson looked around the interior of the trailer. "That was the stupid part. Steve was afraid to try to sneak out the whole thing, so we didn't dress it out. We just cut off the head and stashed it."

"Oh. And then you went down this afternoon to do something else with it?"

"Yeah. We were going to move it to a place where we could pick it up later."

"And the game warden was waiting for you?"

"He had us staked out. Someone had seen it and squealed."

Wilf held his tongue for a second. "So he wrote you up for wasting the meat as well as for shooting the deer out of season?"

Henderson cocked his head as if he needed to make a correction. "He wrote Steve up for those things. He just nailed me for helping him."

"Anyone else on the list?"

The lower lip went out as Henderson shook his head. "No. Kevin really didn't have anything to do with it. He just drove us down there. And we kept you in the clear, too, of course. The guy wanted to know who we were with, but we made sure he knew you were nowhere around."

Wilf looked at the table and held his tongue for a second. "So you fellas are all finished hunting, then?"

"Yeah. That's it for this trip."

"Did he take Steve's rifle?"

"Um, yeah. He did that, too."

"Because he shot a trophy animal. That's a separate violation. Did he write him up for that as well?"

Henderson nodded. After a few seconds he said, "I guess we need to square up accounts. If you want to figure it out, I can come back in a little while."

"You're not staying for dinner, then?"

"Nah. We might as well get started back this afternoon."

"O.K. I can figure it up."

"That'll be fine. I'll come back." Henderson seemed to hesitate for a minute and then headed to the door.

"I was wondering about something else, Bob."

Henderson turned back, with an uncomfortable look on his face. "What's that?"

"You don't have any idea of how my tire went flat, do you?"

Henderson looked puzzled as he shook his head. "No. Why?"

Wilf shrugged. "The guy at the tire shop couldn't find a leak, so he just aired it up and put it back on."

"You think someone let the air out of it?"

"No, not really. I think it just broke the seal. That's what it seems like, anyway, after all the trouble I went to."

"That sounds like a pisser. But whatever did it, the thing was flat this morning. I'm surprised you didn't see it."

"Well, it was dark."

"We saw it in the headlights when we backed out. It was sure as hell flat then."

"One of life's little mysteries, I guess."

"I guess so."

Henderson stepped outside, and Wilf was left to figure

the bill. He had been hoping for six or seven days, and the best he was going to get was two. That wasn't much, compared to two days' work of getting camp set up and two more of hauling it back.

These fellows were getting their trip cut short as well. For a moment he felt sorry for Richards, but that was the way things went. When one fellow pulled a stunt like Lundberg's, everyone who hunted with him got to share the consequences. Henderson didn't seem to want to tell any more than he had to, so the three of them must be feeling pretty embarrassed. Then Wilf recalled the comment about leaving him in the clear, as if he had been party to it. Maybe in some way he was, for being the one who brought them here. All the same, he wasn't going to miss this bunch, that was for sure, even if he did end up with a couple of coolers full of lunch meat, soft drinks, and packaged pudding.

Wilf sat at the table in his tour home later that night, drinking a bottle of beer beneath the kitchen light. The small trailer was parked outside, and he could go back for the larger one tomorrow. He could hunt for himself if he wanted, but right now he was disenchanted with the whole mess. He had felt that way all the way back from Laramie, where he had seen Heather Lea's picture again. Whatever feelings of satisfaction he had allowed himself over Lundberg and Henderson getting caught had faded away. He hadn't done anything. True, he hadn't contributed to what they did, but he just hadn't done anything. Up until the moment he saw them driving up the hill ahead of the game warden, he hadn't decided what he would do if he found out they had pulled something. He hadn't gone along with anything, but he hadn't drawn a line when he could have.

Seeing Heather's picture brought back the feeling he had earlier, the sense that there was nothing he could do about her, and he felt it as a reproach.

Maybe there was nothing he could do about helping to find Heather, but maybe there was something he could do about these smug sons of bitches. As it turned out in that case back in the mountains, he didn't have to draw a line, but it burned him that he hadn't done so earlier. Not only with them, but before that.

He still had a picture, all too clear, of Newell's deer laid out, then the man's satisfaction as he admired the antlers, and then his casual assurance about the tag. Wilf could have taken a stand somewhere along the way on that one, but little by little he'd gone along with things, and in the end he'd decided to let it all go. Or so he thought. What he had let go was the little voice that told him he should draw the line. Now he heard the voice again, and he thought he might be able to do something anyway.

9

Wilf sat on the front steps of the tour home, drinking a cup of coffee and studying the Château. It looked pretty good, now that he had the mud washed off, but he doubted that he was going to make an offer on it. He had it rented for the whole month of October, so he had a while to decide, but he hadn't come out of the season as flush as he had hoped.

The big camp trailer would have been a nice piece of equipment. It paid for itself when he was using it, but it wasn't making a dime just sitting there. He had gone through the figures a dozen times on his way to the mountains and back the day before, and they always came out the same. The extra cash he picked up with Wentworth, which had brought little

satisfaction to begin with, had dwindled with the shortfall of
the elk hunting. He wanted to have something to show for this
season, and it looked as if the best he could do was buy
the generator from Norman Lang. Even that idea had a
disagreeable feeling, and he didn't know if Lang wanted to sell the
thing after all, but it was a piece of business he had to tidy up.

At least he had some time to himself for a few days,
and even though the recent fizzle had cost him, he didn't miss
the hunters. They would be well on their way back to Ohio by
now, maybe in Illinois or Indiana. They would have driven in
a straight line while he was going back and forth, stopping in
Laramie each time to fuel up, check the trailer lights, and look
at the right rear tire.

He could see it from where he sat. It didn't look as if it
had lost an ounce of air. Like the kid said, he was just going to
have to wait and see.

Wilf finished his coffee and went inside, where he
poured another cup and sat at the table with the phone
directory. He didn't have the game warden on his sheet of
frequently called names and numbers, and he was in no hurry
to call him. Wilf had not crossed paths with Hopkins since he
had started guiding, but the last time was fresh in his memory.
Hopkins had set up a checkpoint, and Wilf was coming into
town by himself with nothing in the back. When he pulled
over, the warden came up to the cab and went through the
routine—checking Wilf's license, asking where he had
been, glancing in back to confirm the obvious. After he handed
back the deer permit he stayed by the window and looked at
Wilf's cap.

With a friendly tone he asked, "Is that the only orange
you've got?"

"Um, no. I've got a vest in my bag."

"But that cap is what you wear for orange?"

"Well, yeah."

"It's pretty faded. It's really not fluorescent orange any more. Even though it's probably your favorite cap, you ought to treat yourself to a new one." Then a nod and a half-smile, all in the manner of the family doctor.

That was Hopkins, always official. He hadn't changed from the first time Wilf had talked to him, twelve years earlier. Wilf had shot a deer and dressed it, and he noticed a yellowish fluid in the body cavity. But the buck had a good rack, so he tagged it and brought it home. When he skinned it that night, he saw where it had been shot in the haunches with a small-caliber gun, and the meat had gone yellow and purple. He called the game warden and asked if he could get his deer license replaced, and Hopkins gave him the answer he remembered so well.

"What you pay for, Mr. Kasmire, is the opportunity to hunt."

Wilf learned. A couple of years later, he lined up on a deer that was standing in a patch of cattails between two cornfields. When he pulled the trigger, the deer flopped over like a silhouette target at the carnival, and when Wilf started to open it up, green water leaked out. Between that and the smell, he didn't have to go very far to decide that he could leave this one in the reeds. He told the farmer about it and went on his way.

He realized that by the letter of the law, he should have used his license on the rotten deer, as he had used up his opportunity to hunt. As time went on, he counted himself lucky that Hopkins hadn't come across the carcass. The game warden began to make a reputation for himself as an investigator as well as an enforcer. From time to time his picture appeared in the paper in connection with an arrest he had made—in one picture he stood proud with a set of antlers, in another he knelt by a huge mule deer buck still in the flesh, and in another he crouched next to a layout of twenty ducks and geese. Hopkins was a good-looking guy, with broad shoulders, a full head of light blond hair, and a bushy blond mustache, and he struck a good pose in the snapshots. Wilf could see the pride of a man publicizing a dual trophy—the arrest itself and the confiscated game. The pictures were a game warden's version of dead duck photos.

As Wilf read about the big cases and the smaller ones, the fines and the suspended hunting privileges, he decided to clean up his own habits. He had never been a flagrant road hunter, but now he didn't pause long enough to be tempted. He paid attention to stories about the big spotting scopes the game wardens liked to set up, and even when he was far back in the desolate reaches of antelope country, he got all the way out of the cab before he jacked in a shell. In the smaller matters he found it even easier to be conscientious, making sure he had his license signed ahead of time and his animals tagged right away. He didn't want his name in the paper, especially now, and he didn't want to give Hopkins anything to gloat over.

He tapped the end of his pencil on the open page of the phone directory. If he was going to give Hopkins anything now, he had better be prepared for questions. For one, he would have to admit he hadn't checked the licenses on Wentworth's hunters before he took them out. He should have done that, just as a routine, and he should have made sure they all had their licenses signed. With his earlier hunters, just telling them had been enough, but even at that he wasn't as soft as he had been at Wentworth's. The more he thought about how things had taken the turn they did, the more he tracked it back to a moment two days before when he'd made the deal with Wentworth. He hadn't laid out the simple rule that he did things his way. Instead, Wentworth had gotten things onto his own turf and kept them that way. Trying to get Wilf to shoot a coyote was part of the man's normal game.

Wilf dialed the number, and after four rings he got a recording. Unsure of how to phrase a message, he hung up. He tapped the pencil on the directory again, wrote the game warden's number on a slip of paper, and put the phone book back in the drawer. Nine-thirty. He could go to town and run a few errands.

As he turned left at the stoplight, a panel of silver on the right caught his eye. There in the full service lane of the Chevron station he saw Wentworth's Navigator, with the owner standing at the driver's side, his hands in his jacket pockets. Leaning across the windshield, pausing with squeegee in hand as he turned to smile at the customer, was a frog-faced attendant. The sight of him brought up a twitch of dislike Wilf felt every time he saw the man. He knew him from the bars, where, on one Saturday afternoon with a glass of draft in front of him, the man had turned and coughed in Wilf's face. Wilf had come down with a cold the next day and had resented the guy ever since. Now Frog Face seemed to be in the right place, checking the oil and cleaning the windshield, smiling like a kiss-ass at the man with the big new machine.

Wilf drove downtown and made his deposit at the drive-up window. After that he went to the feed store, where he bought six bags of grain for the horses. He swung by Norman

Lang's real estate office and saw a "Back Later" sign with a
clock face showing three-thirty. From there he drove past
Arnold's self-service and mini-mart, but with his gauge at half
a tank he did not stop.

It felt odd to be wandering around town, even on a
Saturday morning. Everyone else seemed to be going about
things in a normal way — the Pepsi man wheeling a loaded
hand truck into Arnold's convenience store, the auto parts girl
not coming to a full stop in her Mazda pickup, a hay truck
parked on the scales at the grain elevator. A man and a woman
had pulled an ambulance out of its bay and were wiping
it with rags, and two old duffers, smiling and talking, rode in
a dark Jeep Cherokee towing a trailer with a golf cart. The
town was like a regular ant colony, with the ants a little slow,
maybe. And yet it gave him an empty feeling, as if something
was missing.

He waited at the crossing as a coal train clacked its
way east. As the cars passed by with their rhythmic racket,
they reminded him of an incident he had seen once at a
roadside bar on the state line. It was a Sunday afternoon, and
the place had a mix of regulars and drop-ins. At the sound of a
whistle somewhere beyond the walls of the bar, one of the
regulars hollered, "Coal train!" The bartender rushed to the
cooler, pulled out a light green bottle of cheap wine, and
handed it over. Three men and a woman ran outside, passed
the bottle around, and chugged it. Then one of the guys took a
running launch and flung the bottle across the highway toward
the train. When the group came in, Wilf learned that the
regulars had a ritual to see if they could hit the coal train with
an empty bottle before it left Wyoming. They were a jolly
bunch, those roadhouse Sunday drinkers, working-class

people or lower, who took their fling at the big wigs and then went back to their barstools. Wilf had met Heather Lea at the state line a couple of times and had gone home with her once, but he didn't know if she was one of the bunch who'd joined in the ritual.

The light quit flashing, the bell stopped clanging, and the arm lifted. Wilf drove on out of town, past the tractors and hay balers and gravel trucks, the rental yard with its forklift mast high in the air, and the old water truck that never moved.

Back home, after unloading the grain, he tried the game warden's number again. This time he got Hopkins, who said he would like to go over the case in person, if there was time. Wilf said that was fine and gave directions for getting out to his place.

The dark green pickup pulled into the driveway twenty minutes later. Hopkins took a couple of minutes to sort through some things on the seat beside him, then set his sunglasses on the dashboard and got out of the cab, carrying a clipboard and a cell phone. He had his head up and his shoulders squared, ready for business. The Game and Fish insignia stood out prominently on the front of his cap, and his brass name tag caught the overhead sun.

Wilf shook hands and invited the warden into the house. After some preliminary conversation about Wilf's new enterprise, Hopkins looked at his clipboard and back at Wilf.

"Of course I'd like to hear about the possible violation you mentioned."

"Well, like I said over the phone, all I have is a hunch, from the way things added up."

Hopkins fixed his blue eyes on Wilf and gave an assuring nod. "That's often where things start."

"I imagine." Wilf paused as he noted the confident look on Hopkins' face. Then he went on. "I don't know if you know this fellow named Scott Wentworth."

A nod of the head. "Sure. He bought the Bonnell ranch."

"Right. He had some friends come up from Colorado a little while back, and he hired me to go out and help them get their deer at his place."

"How many?"

"Hunters? Three. Wentworth didn't hunt, or come anywhere near it. Just the other three. The first two got their deer and tagged them, and everything looked all right. But the third guy, when it came time to tag his, said he left his license back at the house."

"I see."

"And, since I was done at that point, I left not too long after that."

"So you never saw a license on this deer."

"No, I didn't. I realize that's my fault. I should have checked them all to begin with, but I let it get past me. Failing that, I should have followed through on the one I had in doubt. But he went into the house, and Wentworth came out and paid me, and then I was done there."

Hopkins shrugged. "It would have been best to check everything at the beginning, but if you didn't, it's too late to change that part now. Do you know what he did with the deer? At what point did you leave him and the animal?"

"I skinned and dressed the deer in the field, and cut off the antlers for him. Back at the ranch house, I hung up the carcass while he took his gun and the horns inside."

"And that was the end of it?"

"Not quite. When I went to Rudy's to get my own deer,

he told me that all three of those deer from Wentworth's had come into his place."

The blond eyebrows went up. "Oh. Then they must have all had licenses, after all."

"That's what I figured, but then I talked to this fellow who works for Wentworth, Tommy Tice. He told me that Wentworth had hinted around at borrowing his license, but then when he found out Tommy wanted to use his, he left it alone."

Hopkins had begun to make notations and now paused. "So Tommy used his own license?"

"I think so."

Hopkins twisted his mouth. "Sometimes they try to use a license twice."

"I don't think they did in this case. As I understood it, Tommy got his after the others took theirs to the cooler."

"You weren't there for that, though?"

"No."

"Well, that's easy enough to check on." Hopkins drew a little star by Tommy's name. "The main thing to check on, to begin with, is whether they had permits for everything they killed out there. If they did, then it's a matter of when they bought the last one."

"That's the part that seemed fishy to me. I wouldn't be surprised if—"

"I'll check it out." Hopkins wrote down an abbreviation and a question mark.

Wilf backed up and started again. "I didn't like it when it happened, but the way things went, I think I got drawn in and couldn't find an easy way to do something about it at the time. After I thought about it for a while, I decided it was something I should mention. After all, I've got my own interests to look out for."

"Absolutely." Hopkins raised his head and looked down at his notepad. "I can get all three of their names easy enough, but I'd like to know which one was the third one. Do you remember his name?"

"Sure. It's Jerry Newell."

Wilf appreciated Adrienne's figure as she helped him roll out the large canvas bundle.

"This thing's got a lot of ropes." She turned to look at him.

"Yeah. Once you get it up on the frame, you peg it out with them." Then, shifting into an old-timer's voice, he said, "Git 'er tight as a drum."

Her eyes flashed. "Just mighty fine."

They laid out the poles, fitted the joints together to make the roof structure, and dragged the canvas over the top. Wilf lifted the frame while Adrienne slipped the leg poles into place. Then they scooted the side skirts down to the ground and went inside.

"This is cozy as a cabin, isn't it?"

"Oh, yeah. Roomy and snug both. Good heavy canvas. That's why you need such a stout frame." Wilf looked at the ceiling, beige turning to grey in the evening light. "Let's get the bottom pegged down, then stretch out the ropes from the eaves. After that we can roll out the floor."

When they had the floor tied into place, Wilf went to the shed and brought out the four-foot-wide foam pad and a pair of sleeping bags. He handed the rolled-up pad to Adrienne and followed her into the tent. They spread out the curling mattress and knelt on it, then unrolled the sleeping bags, unzipped them, laid one on top of the other, and fitted the zippers together.

Wilf pulled the zipper around on his half and then raised his eyebrows as he waited for her to zip her half. "This is what they call the Adam-and-Eve style in the catalogs."

She smiled. "I don't think they had blankets back in the original garden."

"I don't think so. The weather was milder there. You just had to watch out for snakes."

Dusk was gathering as they stepped out of the tent.

"I can get the fire going if you'd like to go in and get the wine and a couple of glasses," he said. "It's about time for happy hour, isn't it?"

"I'd say so."

Wilf glanced at the tent, then at Adrienne as she walked toward the front steps of the tour home. It was happy hour, all right. After all the run-around this last week, it was not a bad way to spend Saturday night.

The fire crackled as the two of them sat in their chairs and sipped wine. Adrienne was wearing a plum-colored wool jacket, buttoned up, and her dark hair glowed in the firelight.

"It's too bad things didn't work out any better for you."

"With these elk hunters? I guess that's the way things go. I was hoping to get more out of it, but those guys I can do without."

"I'd hate to think everyone who came out to hunt was like that."

"Nah. I think it's just the luck of the draw. I get this bunch of greenies, and then I get the out-and-out violators. But the two bunches I had before that were all right."

Adrienne looked at her glass of wine and then at him. "So you still like the business, anyway?"

Wilf cocked his head. "Oh, fifty-fifty, I guess." He watched the fire for a few seconds. "Maybe less than that."

"Oh?"

"Yeah, there was a guy in this last group that got under my skin. He kept on making his snide comments about the money aspect, and then he made it seem as if that was the main reason anyone would ever report a violation. For the reward, you know."

"But you didn't turn him in, did you? You said you were gone."

"No, I didn't have anything more than a hunch, and they were busted when I got back. But I still felt accused ahead of time."

"Well, if someone else reported it, you couldn't blame them for taking the reward money, if they did."

"Hell, no. More power to 'em. Especially on something like these guys pulled. Shoot a big deer and just plunder the horns." He looked at Adrienne and met her glance. "Don't get me wrong. I don't envy the money itself. And it would have been a crummy way to make up the deficit, especially after what the guy said earlier. But if someone else did, that's fine with me."

Adrienne watched the fire for a long moment. "Are you pretty well done for the season, then?"

"I think I'm done guiding, unless something really unexpected comes up. But I would like to go back and hunt for myself. My permit's good for the rest of the month." Wilf glanced in the direction of the canvas shape in the dusk.

"All the time I was sleeping in the trailer, I wished I was camping in the tent. It just feels better."

"I think you're right. It had a good atmosphere when we were inside getting things set up."

"For one thing, it breathes. And it filters in the light."

"That's true. It has a natural feel to it."

His eyes met hers again. "Well, if you still like it by tomorrow, you're welcome to go to the mountains with me when I go back."

"Oh, I don't know if I could get time off. I thought we were just setting it up to play house."

"That, too. But I thought it would be a nice way to introduce you to the idea. I could go there, get the camp set up, and you could drive up for the weekend."

"It's a thought. It gets colder there than it does here, though, doesn't it?"

"Oh, yeah. You just bundle up."

Adrienne looked at the tent. "It could be fun. Up in the snow and tall trees."

Wilf heard the sound of a car engine, more like a pickup, as the vehicle came up the drive and then stopped. He opened his eyes and saw the canvas wall lit up by the morning sun. He figured it must be seven-thirty or eight. He unzipped his side of the Adam and Eve, rolled out, and reached for his pants.

Adrienne stirred. "Are you getting up?"

"Someone just pulled in. I need to see who it is."

"It's a little nippy, isn't it?"

His pants were cold as he put them on. "Yes, it is. Just

stay put and keep warm." He patted her butt, then turned back to finish dressing.

As he unzipped the tent flap, he heard a vehicle door open, and as he looked out, he saw the bumper and grille lights of a dark green pickup, then blond-headed Hopkins in his red shirt, headed for the wooden steps. Wilf ducked out of the tent into the cool morning.

"Over here."

Hopkins paused with clipboard in hand, then turned and walked back to the front of his pickup and waited there. Wilf moved across the dry grass and then, soles crunching on sand and gravel, came within speaking distance.

"Good morning."

"Same to you." Hopkins gave him a full, steady look with the blue eyes widened. "Sorry to bother you this early, but I was on my way to somewhere else, and I saw your turnoff. I thought I'd drop by and let you know what I found out."

"Oh, really? Already?"

"That's right. It didn't take long." Hopkins glanced at his clipboard, as if getting a prompt. "I talked to Wentworth and then Rudy, and everything matched. The first two hunters, Mr. Parker and Mr. Wight, acquired their permits by way of the Internet. They ordered them from the office in Cheyenne. The third one, Mr. Newell, purchased a license locally, dated the eighth, and the date of harvest was the eleventh. Does that sound right with you?"

"He killed it on the eleventh, all right. A week ago yesterday."

"Then I guess that's it."

It seemed too easy. Wilf didn't have an answer except to say, "I'm sorry for any trouble I put you to."

"None at all. I appreciate the tip. These things are always worth looking into."

"Well, I appreciate your coming by and filling me in on what you found out."

"No problem. That's one thing we like to do, to let people know that some action was taken." Hopkins gave his assuring smile. "That way they know it's worth their effort the next time."

They thanked each other again and shook hands. Then Hopkins got into the dark pickup and drove away, and Wilf went back to the tent.

"That was Hopkins, the game warden," he said as he unlaced his boots.

"What does he want?"

"Nothing, actually. He was checking back with me on something I mentioned to him yesterday."

"Oh?"

"I still had the incident with the greenies eatin' on me, so I told him about it."

"The thing about whether one of them had a license?"

"Yeah. It turns out that all three of them did, and the dates check out."

"So he came out here to tell you that?"

"He said he was passing by and just dropped in. I think he likes the personal touch."

"You mean, dropping in unexpected? What they call in the movies a 'cold call'?"

"Well, that too. But I think he likes to make the informants feel that their efforts went somewhere." Wilf set his cap on top of his boots and crawled into the warm bed.

"Thoughtful of him."

"I'd say." He rested his hand on her waist.

Her dark hair tumbled as she turned toward him in the morning light. "This isn't a cold call, now is it?"

"Not at all."

Wilf answered the phone on the second ring. It was Wilson, the rancher. Wilf thought at first that there might be something unfinished from earlier when he had the deer hunters and horses out there.

"Sorry to bother you on a Sunday evening."

"No bother at all. Is there something up?"

"Not much, really."

"Everything all right out at your place?"

"Oh, yeah. Same with you, I hope."

"Oh, sure."

Silence hung for a few seconds until Wilson spoke again. "Well, I'll tell you. I just thought I'd call to let you know someone asked for a character reference, something like that."

"The game warden?"

"No, more like a customer."

Wilf perked up. Maybe he would get some more work after all. "Someone needs a guide?"

"Didn't seem that way. It was this fellow Wentworth."

"Oh, really? I've already been out to his place, and got 'em all hunted."

"That's what I understood. He said the game warden was out checkin' to see if you did everything right. Said he didn't know for sure what kind of fellow you were, so he thought he'd call me to get an idea."

"Well, it wasn't anything I did. I just had a question

about one of the licenses, and the game warden looked into it. Did Wentworth make it seem like I did something?"

"I wouldn't say so. He mainly just raised the question."

"Huh." It sounded like a little smear job.

"But I told him it was no worry. I said you were a good hand, that you always put the gasoline can back in the pickup before you started the campfire."

Wilf laughed. "Well, I appreciate the good word you put in for me."

"My pleasure."

Wilf sat for a couple of minutes looking at the phone, then walked out onto the porch and glanced around. Down to the left, the horses were grazing in the calm. Off to his right he could see the flattened grass where he and Adrienne had set up the tent. Things shouldn't have to be complicated, but it seemed like the only way to keep them simple was to go on and never peep a word, just look the other way. If a fellow didn't, then right away someone wanted to get even.

For what? Maybe for something the person did after all.

It was as if a little light turned on, and Wilf went from being irritated to being interested. Wentworth had gone out of his way to make a slur, and it seemed like a familiar pattern to Wilf. He had seen it on the news, with public officials accused of wrongdoing, sports celebrities accused of sexual offenses. He had heard it analyzed. The perpetrator, who usually had more power, tried to discredit the person doing the informing, tried to turn the accuser into the offender. It seemed like an odd maneuver in this case, but it made a kind of sense. Maybe Wentworth had something to hide after all.

10

Wilf found Norman Lang in the office of Wagon Wheel Realty at a little after nine on Monday morning. Looking in through the glass door, Wilf saw the realtor sitting at his desk toward the back of his office, so he pushed on the aluminum handle and went in. Lang, who was talking on the phone, made a motion indicating he would be available in a minute.

Wilf waited inside the door. Above him in the center of the room, a light fixture in the form of a dwarf wagon wheel hung down on brass chains. Below the light and to the left, displayed on a dark-stained table with all the subtlety of a coffin in the vestibule of a church, sat a piece of bronze sculpture. A cowboy, lurching halfway out of the saddle on a twisting horse, had just made a catch on a calf that was being yanked back by a rope on its neck.

Trying to keep his distance from the phone conversation, Wilf looked around the room. Along the left wall he saw three tall file cabinets and a work area, dark now, with a computer and a copy machine. Pinned to the paneling on the right was a county map, flanked by two columns of plaques and certificates.

Against the back wall, a small brown refrigerator squatted with a plastic fern on top of it. Above it hung a painting, and next to it, in back of Lang's desk, hung another.

Lang made a wave motioning for Wilf to come sit in one of the two captain's chairs, then half-turned and spoke in a voice louder than before.

"Sure. You bet. I've got someone just walked in the door, so I'll call you when I get a chance."

Wilf passed by the bronze calf roper and pulled back a chair. As he sat down, he got a better look at the two paintings on the wall behind Lang. One showed a deer in a hayfield, with a fenced-in mounded haystack on the left and a sickle-bar mowing machine on the right. The other had a ranch pickup with wooden stock racks, something from the early 1940s, parked next to an old windmill with bluffs in the background.

Lang spoke with a tone of finality. "I sure will." Then he set the phone in its cradle and turned towards Wilf. He rose halfway from his seat as he leaned forward to offer his hand. "Firemen's ball," he said. "They call me every year."

Wilf noticed the little veins on Lang's cheek and then the round turquoise, bordered in silver, that served as the cinch on the man's bolo tie. "I just get the postcard invitation, or request for donation, or whatever you want to call it."

"Oh, they send me that, too. But I get a call as well, to make sure I don't forget." Lang rubbed his nose and then said, "So tell me, Wilf. How are you doing?"

"Just fine, I guess. And yourself?"

"Can't complain."

"You look good."

"I try to fool people." Lang gave a clever smile, then pushed an ashtray forward.

Wilf shook his head. As he did, he noticed that Lang was a clean-desk man.

"And how's the guiding business?"

"Oh, good enough. I got everyone hunted out at Scott Wentworth's place."

"He had some friends in from Colorado, didn't he?"

Wilf's glance, which had slid up to the deer in the hayfield, came back to the realtor. "Yes, he did."

"Well, that's good." Lang raised his eyebrows and gave a salesman's smile of assurance. "And what can I do for you today?"

"I thought I'd check back in with you about the generator."

"Oh?"

"You said you thought you might like to sell it."

"I think I might have said something like that."

Wilf shrugged. "I don't remember exactly how it went, but I was wondering if you were still interested in selling it."

Lang turned in his chair and hiked a boot up onto his knee. "Have you not found any new ones you like the looks of?"

"Well, I haven't shopped around for any. I thought I'd check with you first, since that was where we more or less left it."

"To tell you the truth, Wilf, I haven't decided. You never know when something like that might come in handy. Whatever

I bought it for in the first place might still come around."

"You mean a big power failure?"

"Big or little. We get another blizzard, like the one in '97 when Harry Baumgartner slid in front of the Wal-Mart truck, and I'm sittin' in an icebox for two days. Hell, when the power went out that time, I didn't have a way to keep my tractor plugged in, so I couldn't even clear out my driveway."

"Oh, really?" Wilf found himself looking at the pickup in the other painting.

"You've heard all this stuff on the news, haven't you?"

Wilf shook away an image of Heather Lea. "I've heard different things. Which stuff do you mean?"

"These damn terrorists. They can put us in the dark without any warning. Knock out power plants, relay stations."

Wilf was getting the picture. "Well, then, it sounds like you actually have decided."

Lang's face tightened for a couple of seconds. "What does that mean?"

"Not much, I guess. At one time you said you would sell it, and now it's pretty clear you don't want to. But that's all right. I'm just sorry to put you to the trouble."

The smile came back. "Not at all, Wilf. If anyone put anyone—jeez, there's a babe."

Wilf turned in his chair and followed Lang's motion to a blonde woman who had just walked past the window. Wilf admired the snug skirt as it moved out of his view.

The realtor let out a soft whistling sound. "Don't know that one."

Wilf shook his head. "Me neither."

Lang set his foot back on the floor and turned to sit square at his desk. "So what's next? Goin' to take some fellas out to look for elk?"

"I've already done that. That was where I was headed the last time I saw you." Wilf could see where the conversation had landed, so he just said, "I might go out a little later on for myself."

"Where do you like to go for elk?"

"Well, this year, I'm goin' to the Snowy Range. Up by Lincoln Park and Brush Creek. Even if I don't get any elk, it's nice country."

"Isn't that the truth?"

Lang straightened out the stapler and pen stand on his desk, and as he did so, Wilf noticed a pewter figurine of a cowboy holding a branding iron that looked like a golf club. From Lang's arranging of the objects, Wilf interpreted that the interview was over. He stood up, glancing again at the deer in the print, and held out his hand. Lang rose to meet it.

"Always good to see you, Wilf. If I can do anything else for you, let me know."

"You bet."

As Wilf turned and walked away, he passed the bronze sculpture. It looked absurd to him now. In style it was not that much different from similar sculptures he had seen of Indian buffalo hunters or elk with locked horns, but the action seemed exaggerated. And the twisting calf reminded him of an illustration he had once seen of Lot's wife, eyes wide in frozen terror as she turned.

The fresh air felt good as Wilf stepped outside and walked down the sidewalk. He was relieved to be out of Lang's office, glad to be done with that lingering piece of business and uneasy at having gone through it at all. First the man tried to sell him the machine, then he had someone more important to talk to and said come see me later, and then he treated him as if he was asking for a favor he didn't deserve. Funny stuff. Maybe he had someone important to talk to today as well. The phone conversation didn't sound like someone trying to get a donation for the firemen's ball. No matter. At least he was done with it. And for as much as he cared about a generator or the type of people he would have been buying it for, he didn't think he had lost out on much.

Still, he didn't like the way Lang had dealt with him. The man had a condescending air about him, a way of implying that he moved on one level while Wilf, who was not likely to ever buy or sell a ranch, moved on another. Even when he was being a good old boy, standing in the bar with his thumb hooked in the front pocket of his creased Wranglers as he choked a long-neck Coors Light, he had his posture. Feedlot riders, stockyard cowboys, and hunting guides bought used pickups and used horse trailers, and Norman Lang would offer to sell them a generator that was still brand new. Never been used. Work out just right for you. Huh. Lang wouldn't try to sell a generator to the likes of Wentworth to begin with, much less welch on him later.

Wilf opened the door of his pickup and got in. His thoughts moved from Lang to Wentworth, and he smiled as he imagined the meeting between the landowner, all proper and superior, and the game warden, aggressive in his own way but courteous when he reached his boundary. Too bad Hopkins hadn't rooted around a little more, but it was evident that he preferred to do things his way. Wilf would have bet anything that Newell didn't have a permit the morning he killed the deer, yet he came up with one that was dated three days earlier.

There were ways to check further on something like that, but most of them were out of Wilf's reach. Most but not all—and here he was, at a little after nine on a Monday morning, with nothing else to do.

Wilf sat at the kitchen table with the phone in his left hand, a pencil poised above a notepad on his right, and a business card in front of him. Easy-listening music played in the background as he waited for the call to be transferred. Then he heard a click and a voice.

"Hello?"

"Is this Jerry Newell?"

"It sure is."

"This is Wilf Kasmire, up in Wyoming."

"Well, Wilf. Good to hear from you. What can I do for you today? Ready to upgrade? I'll put you in something you never dreamed of."

Wilf laughed. "No, I don't think I'm ready for that. And I didn't call for a job, either, though I might need that as much as a new pickup. I called about something else. I hope you've got a minute."

"Sure. I haven't made my million yet today, but it can wait a few minutes. What's on your mind?"

"Well, I'll tell you, Jerry. It's about the deer hunting. The game warden had some questions about the licenses, and since I didn't see yours, I couldn't vouch for it."

"Ah, hell, Wilf. There's nothing to worry about. My license was fine, and that game warden knows it."

"Oh?"

"Sure. Scott called me and told me the guy was snooping

around, but everything's above board."

"That's good to hear. I'm just looking' after myself, you know. I've got an outfitter's license, and that's my livelihood right now."

"Oh, I don't blame you."

"And now that the game warden is lookin' into things and askin' questions, I thought I'd check for myself."

"I'd probably do the same thing, Wilf."

"Thanks. I didn't want to put anybody out."

"Nah. And like I said, there's nothing to worry about."

"Right. So there shouldn't be any harm if I talked to the other two, should there?"

"Um, you mean Randy and Larry? Oh, I guess not. They sure had their licenses. You saw that."

"Sure I did. But just to feel better about it myself, I'd like to be able to talk to each of them. Do you think there'd be anything wrong with that?"

"Well, no."

"I hoped not." Wilf paused. "Do you happen to have their work numbers? It would save me some time."

"Um, yeah. Just a minute."

Wilf wrote down the numbers as he heard them. After reading them back to verify them, he gave his thanks.

"Don't mention it, Wilf. I wish I could do more for you today."

"So do I."

"When you're ready, let me know."

"I sure will, Jerry."

"I can always keep an eye out for you. Do you know what you might want to move into, when you do?"

"I was thinking about a hearse with air conditioning,

but I might be satisfied with a pickup with a bench seat and an interior light."

Newell broke out laughing. "I think the second one is easier to find, and it might go better with your line of work."

"I think you're right, Jerry." Wilf thought for a second and then said, "Thanks for everything. I appreciate it."

"Any time, Wilf." Newell still had a laugh in his voice as he hung up.

Wilf called Parker's number and learned that he had not come into the office yet. Next he called Wight's office and got him on the line in a few seconds.

"This is Larry Wight."

"Hi, Larry. This is Wilf Kasmire. From Wyoming."

"Oh. Uh-huh. What can I do for you?"

"Well, it seems that the game warden has been checking on licenses for that hunt we were on, and..."

"Mine was all clear and legal. You saw that. I had it signed ahead of time, and then I filled out the other part and notched out the date, just like it said in the regulations."

"Oh, I know. I didn't mean to suggest otherwise."

"Well, everything should be all right, then."

"It is, with you. I was just wondering if there was anything else I ought to know?"

"What do you mean?"

"I'm just protecting my outfitter's license."

"Well, O.K."

"And I was wondering if you noticed any...um... irregularities in any of the other licenses."

"I made sure mine was in order, and I didn't inspect anyone else's. But I know everyone had one."

"That's what I understand. But I never saw the third

one, and I hope you don't mind my checking for myself."

"Not at all. But I think you'll find everything is legal."

Wilf stared at the phone after he hung up. He hadn't expected Wight to be as cordial as Newell, but the man had been pretty short. Wight was a good one for making sure he did everything right. Wilf remembered that. Mr. Safety Man, looking after his own ass.

After lunch, Wilf called Parker's number again. According to the receptionist, he still hadn't come in and had not given an idea of when he might. Wilf asked for Parker's home phone number, and the receptionist said she couldn't give out that information. Wilf thanked her and hung up.

He didn't want to tip his hand by calling Newell again, but he wanted to talk to Parker. On a hunch he dialed Hopkins, first at the game warden's number and then at the house. A female voice answered, and Wilf had a picture of Mrs. Hopkins—trim and blonde and well-kept, a match for her husband. She forwarded the call to the warden's cell phone. The answer came as a quick and gruff, "Hello."

"Hi. This is Wilf Kasmire. You remember the three hunters you checked on?"

"The ones from Colorado? Yeah."

"I was wondering if you could tell me where they were from."

"I don't have that with me, but I'm pretty sure two of them were from Longmont and one of them was from the metro area—maybe Westminster. Did you have something else on them?"

"Not at the moment. I'm just checking a couple of things on my own."

"It's all right."

The phone clicked off, and Wilf imagined Hopkins far away on a wind-swept hillside, peering through his spotting scope and hoping to see a rifle barrel poke out of a pickup cab.

Next he called Adrienne, who said she could look up all three names in Longmont, Westminster, and Denver in a matter of minutes.

"If you're going to be doing much detective work, though, you might want to get a computer for yourself."

"I might. I saved some money today by not buying Norman Lang's generator, and I've pretty well decided I'm not going to buy the big camp trailer just yet. If I actually had some of the money I'm not spending, who knows what I might buy. Oh, and I saved some more by not buying a new pickup."

Adrienne called back a few minutes later. She found numbers for Wight and Parker in Longmont and for Newell in Westminster, plus a few close matches in the Denver area. Wilf wrote down the numbers and thanked her.

"Anything else?"

"Not along these lines."

"Any others?"

"What time do you get off work?"

"Same time as always, sailor. Buy me a drink?"

"Might could. I'm putting in a hard day, but I should be done with all my money-saving activities by then."

Wilf called Parker's number and got no answer, just a recording with an impersonal voice and message.

Wilf tapped his pencil on the phone directory, which he hadn't put away after looking up Hopkins' home number. He thought back through all the people whose paths he had crossed, and an image came up. He could call Rudy and ask where Newell had bought the license. Hopkins had said it was "purchased locally," and Rudy might remember.

He did, just because it was different from the other two. They were printed out, and this one was handwritten. It came from Chuck Arnold's store. They sold fishing and hunting licenses and who knows what else there. Wilf thanked him and hung up.

That sounded just about right. Arnold was a friend of Lang's, and Lang was a friend of Wentworth's. If Arnold wasn't a pal of Wentworth's before, he might be now. And as far as Wilf knew, Lang might have been talking to either of them on the phone earlier in the day.

Wilf decided not to call Hopkins until the evening. Meanwhile he tried Parker's home number a couple of more times, got the same recording with each call, and dialed his work number in the late afternoon. Parker hadn't come in. The best time to try would be again in the morning.

Knowing that Hopkins worked out of his house, which in turn was owned by the Game and Fish, Wilf dialed the office number at a little after eight. When the recording came on, he hung up. He knew that Hopkins and his wife were fitness enthusiasts who had no kids, so he could imagine the game warden working out on a rowing machine or huffing on a treadmill. Wilf dialed the home number, and the female voice answered on the third ring. A long minute later, Hopkins came to the phone.

"Hello."

"Hi, Todd. This is Wilf Kasmire again. I hope it's not too much trouble."

"None at all." Hopkins sounded as if he was trying to

keep from breathing too hard. "Did you have something else on the deer hunters?"

"I don't know. I just had this feeling that there was something else to it, so I called up a couple of them. I haven't been able to talk to the last one yet, but from talking to the other two, I still have my doubts about this thing."

"But you don't have anything new to go on?"

"I guess not. I talked to Rudy, and he told me where they bought the license, and that didn't make me doubt any less."

"Why is that?" Hopkins sounded sharper now.

"Well, you know who I'm referring to."

"Sure. A local license-selling agent."

Wilf appreciated the discretion. "I have nothing to go on but a hunch, but what with him being a friend of a friend of Wentworth's, I think it's at least possible that somebody did something."

"Anything's possible, that's for sure. But I wish I had something a little more tangible. I'm not saying your gut feeling isn't a good one, but I don't have anything new that I didn't have before."

"I see. Then you don't think it's worth looking into any more."

"I'll make note of it. I've got some long days ahead of me for the next little while, but if I get a chance, I might look into it. Meanwhile, if something else comes up, be sure to give me a call. If I'm not in the office, leave me a message."

Wilf figured there was nothing to lose. "I guess there's one other little thing."

"What's that?"

"Wentworth said he went with them to get their licenses,

but both you and Rudy say that only one of them bought his permit here."

"That's true. The other two applied online."

"That doesn't match perfectly with what he led me to believe, but it doesn't have much to do with the legality, either, I guess."

"Probably not. But I'll make a note of that, too. Anything else?"

"No, that's it. I want to thank you for listening."

"No problem. Have a good evening."

"Thanks. And same to you."

Wilf called Parker's number and again found no one there. He was tempted to call Newell at home, to ask if he knew anything about Parker, but someone like Newell might be easier to talk to when his wife wasn't around.

Wilf took a beer out of the refrigerator and used the flap of his shirt pocket to twist off the cap. Feeling restless inside the house, he went out to the shed and turned on the light. It gave him pleasure to see the saddles, halters, bridles, and ropes all in place. Too bad he didn't have more call to use the stuff. Maybe next year, depending on the kind of clientele that came his way.

The receptionist at the trucking company said that Mr. Parker had not yet come in this morning. Wilf tried the home number again, with the same result as before. After a few minutes of fidgeting, he called the Ford agency. He heard the background music, and then a click.

"Hello."

"Jerry?"

"Wilf. How're you doing? I didn't expect to hear back from you so soon. What can I do for you?"

"I'm sort of following up on what we talked about yesterday."

"The hearse?"

Wilf laughed for Newell's benefit. "No, the other thing. The deer hunting."

"Oh, yeah. Look, Wilf, like I told you, there's nothing to it. Everyone had a legal license."

"I know that. And you've been a help. That's why I felt all right about calling you back."

"Well, what else is there to say about it?"

"I don't know. I called Larry Wight, and he sounded just a little tight about the whole thing."

"Oh, he can get that way."

"And then I tried to call Randy Parker, and I couldn't get a hold of him. He wasn't at work all day yesterday, he didn't answer the phone at home on into the evening, and he hasn't come into work yet this morning."

"That sounds kinda odd. Randy doesn't run around all that much. You know he's divorced."

"Yeah, I'd gathered that."

"But still, he doesn't get off the leash."

"The secretary expected him to come in, so it's not like he was out of town."

"I doubt that he is. I just had lunch with him on Friday, at the Steak and Ale in Westminster, and he didn't say anything about going anywhere."

Wilf thought for a second. "Do you think Larry would know anything about him?"

"Oh, I wouldn't bother Larry with questions like that."

"Why? I thought they were friends."

"Well, they are. We all are, really. We golf together, we play poker, all that sort of thing. But Larry and Randy are kind of on the outs right now."

"Really? Is that why Larry seemed tight-ass yesterday?"

"No tellin'. Did you mention Randy?"

"Not that I remember. I think I just talked about the deer permits. But he seemed to want to cut me off at every point."

"That's him."

"Huh. He didn't do anything out of the ordinary with his license, did he?"

"Oh, no. He wouldn't dream of it."

"Maybe he thought I was going to mention Randy."

"Might be. I don't think he wants to answer very many questions right now. You didn't call him at home, did you?"

"No, I called the number you gave me. Is he in some other kind of a jackpot?"

Newell took a couple of seconds to answer. "Well, it's mostly between them."

"Oh. Then it probably doesn't have much to do with what I called about."

"Probably not."

"But do you think it has anything to do with why I can't get a hold of Randy now?"

"I couldn't tell you, Wilf. I know it was on Randy's mind when we had lunch the other day."

"Then probably the last person I should ask is Mrs. Wight."

Newell gave a half-cough, then said in slow syllables, "I don't think it would be a good idea." After a pause, he spoke again at his normal pace. "She's not all that bad, as far as that goes. He says she's a cold fish, but I don't know one way or the other. If she's pissed now, she's got good reason."

"I'll be careful when I talk to Randy, then. I feel sorry for him."

"So do I. And as if you couldn't tell, I'm a little pissed at Larry. He figures he's not stealin' anyone's peaches if they're divorced, but I don't care for it. And you know, I didn't know a damn thing about it when we were up there at Scott's."

"It doesn't sound good."

"No, it isn't. It goes against being a good Elk."

"How's that?"

"The Elks' Club I used to belong to, a while back, had a sign in their bar. It said, 'What you see here, what you say here, stays here. Be a good Elk.' "

"Oh, O.K. I get it."

"That's for the boys. Among them. But it's also a good rule not to mess around with your wife's friends or your friends' wives. Makes it easier for others to be a good Elk."

"I see. Well, like I said, I'll be careful not to mention anything when I talk to Randy."

"It would be for the best." Newell's voice picked up as he said, "Anything else I can do for you today, Wilf?"

"I don't think so. I'm still a ways off from buying another outfit, but I'm saving money every day."

"Is that right?"

"Yeah, I figure I save fifty to a hundred dollars a day, just by not knowin' where the whorehouses are."

Newell laughed. "I bet you do. You're going to do all right, Wilf."

The phone rang while Wilf was looking through a catalog. He glanced at the clock as he picked up the receiver; it was almost eight-thirty.

"Hello, Wilf? This is Todd Hopkins."

"Oh, hi, Todd. How are you?"

"Just fine." Hopkins cleared his throat. "I was wondering if you've gotten anything new on that third deer permit."

"Not much. I talked to Newell, and he still says everything was according to Hoyle."

"Sure."

"I talked to Wight before I talked to you last. He's not very co-operative. I haven't been able to get a hold of Parker, and there's some kind of a personal squabble between him and Wight."

"Oh. You haven't talked to Scott Wentworth, have you?"

"No, not since this started."

"Well, I think it would be best if you didn't talk to him or Jerry Newell for a while. I can't tell you not to, but I think it would go better for my side of things if you didn't."

"That sounds easy enough. Is there anything you can tell me?"

"I think so. I found some time earlier this evening to check into the issuance of that third permit."

"Oh."

"It'll be in the paper, I imagine, so I don't think I'm doing any damage by telling you."

"I wouldn't have any reason to pass it on ahead of time anyway."

"That's fine." Hopkins paused for a couple of seconds and then spoke again. "I went back and talked to Rudy, and he said the hunters, or Wentworth, called his place and asked what they needed to have on their deer. He told them the carcasses had to be tagged, and they brought in their licenses as well as the carcass coupons. From Rudy's I went to the license selling agent, where I was able to determine that he had pre-dated the sale of the license."

"Oh. Was it out of sequence in his book?"

"It wasn't too hard to find out. I've issued the license agent a citation, and I've filed charges against Mr. Wentworth and Mr. Newell. They should have warrants served on them before long."

"I see. So that's why I shouldn't talk to them."

"That, and for the case in general."

"That sounds fine."

The warden paused again. "So, before we get off the line, Wilf, is there anything else that you can think of that might be germane?"

"No, not really. Just this funny little thing about the missing person."

"Who's that?"

"Parker. He hasn't come into work for two days, and he doesn't answer his phone at home."

"Oh, right. You said there was something between him and the other one."

"They've had a falling out, I guess. Over personal things."

"Nothing to do with hunting?"

"I don't think so."

"Well, if anything comes up, let me know."

"I sure will. Good night."

Wilf set the catalog aside. All the time he had been talking to the game warden, he had been gazing at lawn ornaments. The buck with a sprig of antlers looked like one he had seen on a snowy night in a motel parking lot in Raton, New Mexico. It was standing in the back of a mid-sized pickup, with a rope around its neck. Some things dropped out of the catalog from one year to the next, but the tacky deer didn't. Someone was buying them.

Wilf reached for the telephone and tried Parker's number again, and he imagined the phone ringing in an empty house. When he heard the message click on, he hung up.

Something didn't feel right. He had followed through on his hunch about the license, and he had enjoyed listening to Hopkins as if the warden were practicing his court testimony, but he didn't feel satisfied. Some piece seemed to be out of place.

Even if Parker was worked up about the way his ex-wife was carrying on, he wasn't the type to disappear for two days. He was a responsible office manager for a trucking company, not just a roofer or a sheetrocker coming off a weekend binge. Wilf tried to imagine him holed up somewhere with a chippie, but the image didn't fit. He would at least have called in to work.

Wilf went back to looking at the catalog. As he turned the pages, he couldn't shake the feeling he had about Parker. Maybe the man was curing his blues with a call girl, or wandering through the lights and bells of a casino, but Wilf had the dread feeling that he was in some dark place, cold as a stone.

11

Wilf stood at the kitchen sink with his sleeves rolled up. From where he stood washing the morning dishes he could turn and look out the window to see the horses grazing in the pasture. The line of a song kept playing through his head. *With the dawn, I will gather my horses.* It was an Ian Tyson song, about a guy trying to get his life together after his woman has left him. He says he will follow her to Mexico. The beginning and ending of the song have the sound of horses running and snorting, with a jingle of bits and spurs and a cowboy "yip" or two.

It was a nice song with a wistful tone, a pretty idea of chasing a dream to Mexico. But somewhere along the way, a fellow had to work. The outfitting business hadn't panned out all that well, and there wouldn't be any more work until next summer at best, if he wanted to try taking people on pack trips. No telling when he might be able to go back to Pioneer Truss. Duane said maybe a month. The way things went in this little corner of the world, "a month" could mean after New Year's. And the idea of going back to work there did not inspire him. Just dropping in for the time that he did, with the noise of all the machines, had served as a reminder of what he wanted to get away from.

Funny idea. He wanted to get away from the machine, and there he was, two days earlier, trying to buy a generator so he would be better equipped as an outfitter. That was what he was — an outfitter. He might as well be a cowboy poet. The last one he heard had told a joke: What do you call a cowboy poet who doesn't have a wife or a girlfriend with a good job? Unemployed. He had heard similar jokes about songwriters and rodeo cowboys, delivering pizza and selling fire extinguishers. Even if things were further along with Adrienne, he couldn't imagine himself sitting around and cleaning guns and tack all winter.

He had a hard time picturing the kinds of work he might find this time of year. Fellows like Wilson didn't have much work through the winter. When they did, during the summer, a lot of it entailed running hay equipment. Some of the cowboys he knew worked at feedlots, where they ran front-end loaders to clean out pens. Work was work, but if he wanted to get away from the machines, he was going to have to think of a better escape.

Now that he mulled it over, there might be one thing about him that suited him to doing cowboy work. He smiled as he remembered a cartoon in which one little boy said to another, "I've decided I don't want to be a cowboy because the idea of living in a trailer house is repugnant." Feedlot cowboys and ranch hands sure-enough lived in that kind of company housing. At least this one was his, even if he didn't have a job at the moment.

Maybe it was just another pretty idea that he could make a living at something he loved, like hunting and the outdoors. Then there was the other part, as he had said to Adrienne a little while back—when a person tried to make a living that way, he couldn't enjoy it as much. That seemed to be the case with hunting, and it had been that way with the landscape as well. He had had to get a long ways away from the Suburban and the Château before he was able to empty out, as he thought of it—to lose himself in the dirt and rocks, grass and sagebrush, trees and sky. Standing on a peak at sunrise and seeing the morning lights of town in the distance, hearing the caw of crows as they circled over a gut pile, stopping at the sound of hooved animals tramping in the timber—he might be better off trying to take in those things on his own and not have to worry about getting back in time to fix sandwiches and set out the potato chips.

Maybe there was a line of work he could enjoy. When he had worked for building contractors, it was common wisdom that a fellow wasn't expected to like his job. He remembered a sheetrocker saying one time, "The kid told me he didn't like this kind of work. I told him he wasn't supposed to." The next guy down the bar said, "That's why they pay you."

On the other hand, he had heard people declare that they loved their work—not just country singers being interviewed for the radio, but people in real life, like funeral directors and court clerks. Sometimes he thought they were just saying it because they were supposed to, like insurance agents and car salesmen, but maybe some of them meant it. Adrienne, for example, even if she didn't say it out loud for other people's benefit, seemed to enjoy her work. Wilf wondered what the little boy in the cartoon would turn out to be. At least he didn't seem like the type to kid himself.

Nine o'clock. Wilf sat down at the table with a cup of coffee, thinking about what he might do for the rest of the day. The town paper would be out by late afternoon, and he could look there for help wanted.

The news about Newell and Wentworth, and Arnold, might be in there, too, depending on how soon it was released to the sheriff's department. It wasn't a big news item, like embezzling money, but it would make its way around the coffee shops and bars before long.

Hopkins had made it sound like it was all sewn up, but Wilf still had the feeling it was over too soon. He didn't have a strong hunch, but he felt there might be more to it than the game warden had mentioned to him. Things just didn't seem finished.

Maybe it was because the question about Parker had been left hanging. Loose ends like that were a nag.

Hopkins hadn't said anything to the effect that he shouldn't talk to Parker. It was late enough in the morning to find out if he had come in for work, and if he had, Wilf could make it a courtesy call, to wrap things up. If Parker had caller I.D. at home, which he probably did, he would know Wilf had called a dozen times. At the very least, he deserved to know what for. That was a good enough reason to call him now.

Wilf dialed the number of the trucking company and was greeted by the receptionist's voice.

"Good morning," he answered. "I was wondering if Randy Parker has come in yet today."

Silence hung in the air for a few seconds until the receptionist said, "No, he hasn't."

"Do you have an idea of when it might be best to call back? I've been calling for a couple of days."

Another short silence. Then, "I'm sorry, sir. But Mr. Parker isn't with us any more. Is it something that someone else can help you with?"

"Not really. It's about a personal matter, nothing all that serious. Do you think I can reach him at home? I do have that number."

"I don't think so." Her voice was still hesitant and tense.

"Oh, I see. I think I understand. You mean he went away for good."

"Yes. He passed away."

Wilf felt a thump and drop in his chest, and he searched for something to say. "I'm sorry. This was a friendly call from the beginning. I'm sorry for the trouble."

Automatic language saved her. "That's all right, sir. Thank you for calling, and have a good day."

Wilf let out a long breath as he settled the phone in the cradle. If he thought there was a piece missing before, the puzzle and the gap both just got bigger. He couldn't imagine how Parker's death could be connected to anything that had happened up here in Wyoming. Maybe it was something simple—to an outsider—like a stroke or a heart attack. Probably not a car wreck, or someone would have known about it sooner. Whatever it was, though, Wilf knew he needed to find out. The easiest way would be to call Newell, but that was out of bounds. He sure wasn't going to call Wight. There had to be people who knew, and ways of getting the information, but Wilf couldn't see past the obvious.

Then it occurred to him. Adrienne. She had gotten the phone numbers in no time at all. She might be able to find a news report.

He called her number at work, and after filling her in on the latest from the game warden, he told her about Parker. "I realize it probably doesn't have anything to do with this other business, but it's got me hooked. I'd sure like to know what happened to him. And I can't just call up one of the other guys at this point."

"When do you think someone found out about him?"

"I would say sometime late yesterday. Maybe last night. I doubt that it was a car wreck, or someone would have known about it right away. He's been missing for a couple of days at least, and maybe since the end of last week."

"I can try looking on the Internet. Most newspapers have an online version these days, but they're not all updated right away, and some of them are pretty spotty in what they cover. I can give it a try, though. It's the one named Randy Parker, and he lives in Longmont. Right?"

He wanted to correct her to past tense, but he just said, "Right."

"O.K. I'll give it a try."

Wilf poured himself another cup of coffee and sat down to wait. A few minutes later, the phone rang.

"Hi. I found out something, but not much."

"That's O.K. Go ahead."

"Well, they found him dead in his home, late yesterday

afternoon, but the report didn't say how he died or how long ago. But it does say the case is under investigation."

"That's something, but you don't know how much."

"That's what I was thinking. You don't know if it's suicide, murder, an accident, or natural causes. Probably not the latter, if they're investigating."

"You sound almost cheerful about it."

"Oh, sorry. I didn't mean to. But it's got my curiosity, too, and since I didn't know the guy — well, you know."

"No, that's O.K. I just feel kind of sorry for him. I don't know that he was the most likeable of the four, but he was the least offensive. The others seemed to go easy on him, too. I guess his wife had left him, got a divorce, and from what I gathered recently, she was carrying on with one of the others."

"Not what's-his-bucket?"

"No. The other one that lives in Longmont."

"Oh. Well, you know, there might be some good scandal going on."

"You *do* sound cheerful."

"Sorry again. I was optimistic for your sake. I'll tell you what. I'll ask around the office here and find out if anyone knows anyone down in Longmont or nearby. It's not that big of a town, and if there's gossip going around, there might be a way to tap into it."

"It's worth a try."

"All right. Give me a little while, and I'll see what I can find out."

Wilf put on a jacket and went outside with his coffee. A blue jay landed in the bare young ash tree at the edge of the front yard. Across the driveway, a mound of fresh dirt showed where a gopher had moved into the garden. Wilf meandered over to the pasture gate, watched the horses for a few minutes, then walked back to the driveway. The right rear tire was still holding up. He kicked it, just for good measure, and went into the house.

Adrienne called back at a little after ten. "Well, things got interesting," she said.

"Oh, good. You found out something?"

"I did. Kay's husband is originally from down that way. He's got a nineteen-fifty-something Chevy that he keeps in storage in Longmont, and they go down there to car shows and all of that. I think sometimes they go there just for Ed to see his car, but that's another story. Anyway, they know people in Longmont, so she called a friend who has a laundry. Not as good as a beauty salon, but good enough."

"Go ahead."

"It seems that your friend Randy Parker died of auto-erotic asphyxiation, some time over the weekend but they're not sure yet."

"What kind of asphyxiation?"

"Auto-erotic. It's when a person accidentally strangles himself — or herself — during masturbation."

"Oh, yeah. I think I heard of that. There was a guy up in Gillette, a few years back, and they found him hanging in a doorway in his house. In the kitchen or the bedroom, as I recall. Wasn't there something fishy in the whole thing, and that was why it made the news?"

"Yes. He was the county attorney up there, came from a good family and all. They insisted he wouldn't have done a thing like that."

"That's right. He lived on a ranch way out in the country. One of the older families there, the kind that says,

'No one in our family would do that kind of thing.' " Wilf tipped his coffee cup to verify that it was empty.

"Really. So they managed to get one investigation after another, to see if they could prove there was foul play. I guess he had sent a few guys to jail, and the family had a theory about big-time drug dealers setting it up."

"But they never proved anything."

"No. The most probable theory was that he went a little too far in giving himself pleasure."

Wilf shook off a chill that crept across the back of his neck. "Sounds like a needless way to die, and then to get found that way. Do they do it with a rope?"

"Actually, they more often use a belt. They hold it around their neck, sitting in a chair. It cuts off the flow of blood to the brain, and it's supposed to give a real white-light orgasm. It's just that sometimes it goes wrong when they're alone."

"You hate to think of how people discover things like that to begin with."

"Yes. I think it might have had some sinister beginnings, like men practicing on women with their hands, or people trussing one another up. There was a movie about it several years ago, about the time I got out of college. I didn't see it, but I think some men did it to a woman using a plastic bag. In the last few years it's been a fad for people to practice alone, in the privacy of their own homes."

"That's nice."

"In case you're wondering, I didn't learn any of this first hand, so to speak. I took a few minutes to look it up, and I found a couple of interesting sites. No illustrations, though."

"Well, then, I won't be in any hurry to get a computer, after all."

"There are sites with pictures."

"Uh, I've heard of them."

"Anyway, back to the asphyxiation."

"Right. You were saying it was some kind of a fad."

"Or a trend, if you're in the funeral business. Or law enforcement, I suppose."

"If I've heard of it, then I guess the average cop would know enough to recognize it, even if he didn't know right away whether it was suicide or an accident."

"Or foul play. Don't forget the drug lords."

"Of course." Wilf had a faint image of Larry Wight. "And thinking of my friend Parker, I can see why they have to do an investigation. They really do have to consider all three."

"I suppose so."

"Once they start prying into things, they're bound to find out about the ex-wife and the close friend. They'd have to look into it, at least."

"That makes sense."

"Now that I think of it, I tried calling him a dozen times at home. If he's got caller I.D., I might expect a call myself, if someone is investigating."

"Maybe. Did he have a voice message?"

"Yeah."

"Some people who have an answering machine don't bother with caller I.D."

"That's true. I don't."

"Even in town, where it's cheaper, a lot of people just have one or the other. Of course, some people have both, and burglar alarms, and surveillance cameras."

"Well, who knows what Randy had. Even if the cops picked up my name and number, they could have found out from his pals that I was nobody important."

"Not important enough to drive all the way down there, anyway, and strangle him, just because his friend cheated on a deer license."

"That's nicely put."

"And if they fix the time of death as Saturday night or Sunday morning, you've got a natural alibi with both me and the game warden. You're on the right side of the law in this case."

"That cheers me up."

"Just a little graveyard humor, Wilf. Or gallows humor, if you buy the conspiracy theory in Gillette."

Wilf laughed.

"I don't mean to make light of it, but you've been too morose about some of this."

"Well, this guy Parker wasn't all that bad, and it's kind of pathetic if they find him dead in that sort of a position."

"I mean even before that. A couple of his friends pulled a fast one, and you helped get them caught, and you've just been kind of blah about it."

"Yeah. I guess so. And the elk hunters before that. At least I was pissed then."

"Give it a day or two to go away, and do something to make yourself feel better."

"Like what?"

"Well, what some women would do is go get a facial and a manicure, or go buy a new outfit. What do men do? Buy a new pickup?"

He laughed. "Those that have the money, maybe. The rest of 'em go get drunk and try to get laid."

Adrienne had a smile in her voice as she said, "Why

don't you try to hold out for the rest of the day? Do something small and nice for yourself in the meanwhile. Like a bacon cheeseburger and a tall mug of beer."

"Then have you look at my fingernails later on?"

"That's the idea."

Wilf thanked her for her help on tracking down the news, and they both hung up. He tried to shake off the thought of Parker dying the way he did. There ought to be something else to think about. Adrienne was right about one thing. He was letting things wear on him. He ought to let some of this stuff go away. The business with the elk hunters was all finished, the problem with Newell and Wentworth was wrapped up, as far as he was concerned, and Parker was all done as well.

But there was one thing that would not go away, something that nobody, as far as he knew, was doing anything about. He recalled the black-and-white flyer he had seen on the wall in Laramie. Heather had not been found in the privacy of her home or anywhere else. Wherever she was, Wilf realized he was beginning to fear for her.

Wilf saw Tommy Tice's pickup outside the Lariat and decided to pull over. The sun had not yet crossed the yardarm, and Tommy had come in from the ranch. The box in back of the cab had no dog noses poking out, and the gun rack was empty. It looked as if the door locks were pushed down. Tommy might be settling in, and with happy hour still on the way, he wasn't likely to be in a hurry to go anywhere.

Inside, Tommy was sitting at the bar with his cigarettes and change next to a bottle of Budweiser in front of him.

"Well, damned if it ain't my trouble-makin' pal," he said.

"Oh, did I cause a big stir?"

"Nah, not that much. But I want to thank you for sending the game warden around."

"Ah, you know how he is. Once he thinks an idea is his, he takes off with it." Wilf looked for the bartender and saw that he was busy at the drive-up window. "So what's up? I came into town to get the newspaper, and I saw your outfit. Thought I'd stop and see if you were on your feet."

"I got drunk as an Indian in here the other night, but I'm all right today. Just got here a little while ago." He stretched back the corner of his mouth without smiling. "The boss sent me home early today."

"Is this home?"

Tommy lit a cigarette. "Sometimes."

Wilf sat on the next stool. "So, is there anything new out at the ranch?"

"You might say. The game warden's been out there twice, and I guess he wrote up Arnold for post-dating a license."

"You mean pre-dating."

"Yeah. So that was a bag pinch."

"Really. I imagine Hopkins is pleased."

"I guess so. Especially when he gets to turn over work to the sheriff's office."

"Oh, sending out the warrants?" The bartender appeared, and Wilf ordered a bottle of Budweiser.

"That, too, I guess. But I meant the part about the pickup."

"What's that? I didn't hear anything about a pickup."

"Well, you know that Ford he had parked up by the house?"

"Sure. I saw it when I was there."

"Turns out it was hot."

"The hell it was."

"Damn sure. I guess the game warden didn't like the way some of his questions got answered, so he put a bug in the sheriff's ear to check out a few other things, just out of curiosity."

"Huh."

"Come to find out, the pickup came from Colorado. That was where it was registered last. It got repossessed by a Ford agency and was supposed to be shipped to a wholesale auction. Somewhere in between, it disappeared, and guess where it ended up."

"What a surprise. A fella could almost guess which dealership it came from." Wilf paid for his beer and took a sip. "They must have been trading favors. Newell finds him a pickup, and Wentworth lets him hunt on his place. Then he thinks better of it and decides to get a license."

"Sounds close to the way I heard it."

"Who'd you hear it from?"

"The deppity that drove the pickup to town. That guy named Schultz."

Wilf tried to put a face to the name. "I think I know which one. When did this happen?"

"The game warden yesterday, the sheriff's office today."

"So they had the pickup impounded?"

"Yeah, it turned out to be a bigger to-do than it should have been. They were goin' to haul it off on one of those roll-back wreckers, but the guy couldn't get the hydraulics to work, so one of the deppities just drove it on into town. They searched it and didn't find anything more serious than a box of condoms and an air freshener."

"That's nice."

"Sure is. It's good to know that someone believed in safe sex, even if he left the things where they weren't doing any good."

As Wilf took another drink of beer, he had a picture of the pickup sitting off to the side of the driveway with its window rolled up and its doors locked. He recalled seeing Parker leaning against it and how he had thought they went well together.

"You know," he said, "that pickup was supposed to be out of commission."

"Is that right?"

"Yeah. Wentworth told me we couldn't use it because he needed to get the brakes fixed."

"Hell, he drove it all over the ranch. He just didn't take it out on the oil roads. I figured he didn't want to pay the fees to license it. And insure it, too. You've got to do that to license it, of course."

"Well, there's always more to the story, isn't there?"

"Seems like it." Tommy tapped his cigarette on the ash tray. "You know, I talked to the deppity when he got to the bottom of the hill. If the brakes weren't working, he'd've known it."

"You'd think so."

Tommy got up to go to the men's room. Wilf picked at his beer label as he turned things over. When Hopkins had called—not so much to tell him what he had found out as to keep him from calling Newell or Wentworth—he told Wilf just as much as he felt he needed to. Well, that was all right. Give away cards to get cards back, as they said.

He wondered what Wentworth had said to Hopkins to push him to do more. He might not have said anything in particular, just acted in his high-handed way. Hopkins was no dummy, and he wouldn't like to be treated like one. However it came around, he'd found out that Wentworth had something else to hide.

Tommy came back to the bar singing a song.

"To be plugged in the ass like a two-dollar whore
On the big rock can-dy moun-tain."

"So are you out of a job?" Wilf asked.

"I don't think so. He just sent me home early today because of all the hubbub. I've got another week or two's worth of work, and then I 'magine I'll be lookin' for somethin' else."

"Oh, well. Take it as it comes."

"That's right. I was lookin' for a job when I found this one. And yourself? I thought you'd still be elk huntin'."

"That didn't last long. The hunters got themselves into a mess and had to pull out early."

"Oh." Tommy looked at his beer and then at Wilf. "See any elk?"

"I saw a little of everything. I plan to go back up and hunt for myself here shortly."

"That's what I'd be doin'. Why hang around here if you don't have to work?"

Wilf had an image of dark hair and a maroon sweater. "Yeah, I think I might take off in a day or two if there's nothing going on. I'll take a look in the paper."

"All I ever see ads for is truck drivers and bartenders. They're both too dangerous for me." Tommy called for the dice cups so he could shake for the music. As he slammed his cup on the bar and took a peek, he sang his verse again.

"To be plugged in the ass like a two-dollar whore

On the big rock can-dy moun-tain."

Wilf finished his beer and said goodbye to Tommy, who was still rolling dice.

"No, sir," Tommy said in a faraway voice, "I never have gone to bed with an ugly woman, but I sure have woke up with a few." He looked at the bartender and said, "Three sixes." Then he turned to Wilf. "So long. Hope you kill an elk."

As Wilf backed his pickup out of the parking spot, he saw a Ford 250 go by. It looked like the one he had seen at Wentworth's, but it had Wyoming plates.

Good old Wentworth. That was just like him, thinking he could get a free ranch pickup, let his pal hunt on his ranch, buy a license after the fact—just as he could cut roads and parcel up the land, without having to answer to anyone. Not in this podunk place where no one knew any better.

Wilf felt his stomach tighten. This whole thing seemed crooked, and he had played into it. The greenies might have been able to go out and get their deer without him, and nobody would have known any better. But Wentworth had brought him in to make things look good, and he, Wilf, had been all too glad to take the money. Sold out three nice deer to some guys that didn't care that much about it anyway. Well, maybe Parker did. He seemed to appreciate it. But overall, it was just another game, with Wentworth showing off to his friends what kind of services he could buy.

Take their money and hate their asses. That was what some people said about tourists. It would be better not to take their money to begin with, not to have any truck with any of them. Then he wouldn't have to feel like the two-dollar whore that Tommy sang about.

12

Wilf sat at the kitchen table in Adrienne's townhouse apartment, looking through the sliding glass door. In the corner of the patio sat a pyramid of four pumpkins from his garden. Beyond the patio, half of the backyard lay in shadow while the morning sunlight shone on the other half. The ash tree in the middle of the yard had lost all but its last few yellow leaves, so the branches cast their meager shadows on one another as well as on the carpet below.

Adrienne stood at the counter, her hair dark against the back and shoulders of a lavender-colored blouse. Wilf's gaze took in her charcoal-grey skirt and trim calves. She finished slicing the pumpkin bread and opened the refrigerator door, then bent forward to reach into a lower shelf.

"You want to be careful there. You might start something and be late for work."

She stood up with a jar of chokecherry jelly in her hand. "I thought I took care of you."

"I can't help it."

She picked up the cutting board by its handle and set the half-sliced loaf and the jelly on the table. Then she put her arm around his shoulder and nudged her breast against the side of his face. "You just need to brace yourself up. Get some self-control."

He looked up and matched her smile as she moved away. "That's a hell of a way to do it." Glancing outside again, he said, "When I get back from the mountains, I'll see about raking your leaves."

"That's not one of those figures of speech, is it, like tuning your piano or getting your ashes hauled?"

"Um, no. No extra meaning in that one. Just the humdrum thoughts of the unemployed."

"Oh, you'll get over that," she said as she sat down.

"Being out of work, or worrying about it?"

"Both, I hope. Meanwhile, relax. And enjoy some time off."

He could picture the high country, with timbered slopes and snow-covered clearings. "It should be all right. From what I've seen on the weather channel, there ought to be more snow."

"And that's supposed to be good for the hunting?"

"Supposed to be. Unless it gets too deep." He scooted two slices of pumpkin bread onto his plate, then spread the wine-dark jelly onto them.

"What if I can't get in in my car?"

"You ought to be able to. The campground is less than five miles from the highway, and it's a good road coming in— wide, well-graveled, mostly flat. It gets a lot of traffic. If it doesn't look good, I'll drive to the highway and meet you. Otherwise, I'll wait for you at the campground and we'll go in my pickup from there."

"Just follow the map."

"Yep. One right turn off the highway. That is, if you're coming from Laramie. If you go around the other way, from Saratoga, you'll turn left. But there's only one way to turn anyway. From there it's a straight shot into the campground." With his fork he took a bite of the bread and jelly. "Hey, this is good."

"Good punkins," she said.

Neither of them spoke for the next few minutes. Wilf finished his first piece of bread with jelly, took a sip of coffee, and set down his cup. "Too bad nothing came out in the paper about these guys and their maneuvers."

Adrienne looked up. "It might have been too close to press time when they got the charges filed. The paper comes out again tomorrow for the weekend edition, so there might be something in it then."

"I'll be interested to see how it gets treated. You know, I wasn't surprised at any of it."

"I don't know the Colorado bunch, but I was surprised that Chuck Arnold would do something petty like that. I doubt that he could have made much on it."

"Maybe he didn't. He might have done it more as a favor. He's friends with Norman Lang, and so is Wentworth. But even if Norman had something to do with it, you can bet he'll stay in the clear."

"Oh, I'm sure of that. He doesn't mind giving or receiving tips on foreclosures, bankruptcies, divorce settlements, and the like, but I don't think he'd get his hands dirty."

"Nah, not him. Even when the Hildebrands got talked into selling the old man's ranch, he waited until the bank and the lawyer were done convincing them it would cost too much to divide it up. He let it drop into his lap, with their help of course, and then he sold it in parcels himself."

"Nice guy."

"He had help. And that's the way they do things. They get a little collusion going, and then they feel smart as hell about it."

"Well, I'm glad someone gets caught once in a while."

"Oh, yeah. I'm glad it went as far as it did. It doesn't hurt my feelings to see Wentworth or Arnold, either one, get his ass in the sling. And the same would go for Norman Lang if they brought him up on something."

Adrienne smiled. "You're mad at the whole bunch of them, aren't you?"

He smiled back. "I'm gettin' over it. And a little newspaper coverage will help."

At the fuel stop in Laramie, Wilf checked the right rear tire. It was still holding up. Everything under the hood was O.K. as well. This was the way to go, with no monkey on his back. Now that he wasn't towing the gooseneck, he had the camper shell bolted on, and even with the tent and chairs, he could haul a full camp in the back of his pickup. Food, water, a little wine and beer, plenty of clothes and bedding, and three bottles of propane. He was good for eight or nine days at least, including a couple of days with Adrienne.

He looked at the sky as he felt the cold trigger on the fuel nozzle. It was always chilly here at this time of the year, as the change in climate came on faster in the higher elevations. Grey clouds hung overhead, and a few hard pellets, somewhere between snow and sleet, swirled down in the wind. He couldn't waste any time if he wanted to get the tent set up before dark. He knew the temperature could drop fast after nightfall, and he didn't want to be handling metal poles and stretching thick canvas in the cold glare of the headlights.

Inside the store, he saw Heather's picture again. He took a moment to look at her. It was just a black-and-white photocopy, grainy from being enlarged, but it touched him as much as if it had been a snapshot in his own album. He noted her dark eyes, shadowed cheekbones, and half-smile. Although most of the expression had been washed out with the reproduction, he saw her as he knew her, sad and troubled but hoping to be happy again. Some of her weaknesses he had recognized in himself.

It must be the way other people felt when they saw a flyer for someone they knew. Beyond the flat image and the blank stare, they could see the person while everyone else just walked by and saw a poster. That was the way he imagined it with the jogger, Amy something. Her picture had been papered all over the state, and there would have been a lot of people — more than in Heather's case — who cared about her and who felt pangs of fear when they saw her on the wall. Maybe Heather's disappearance would be similar to that other girl's, a case that never got solved.

Wilf had to shovel away a foot of snow to make a bare spot on the ground, but he got the tent pitched and tied down before night fell. The sky had cleared out, which meant that the temperature could plummet. Dusk drew in as he unloaded the gear, stowed most of it inside the tent, and set up the propane bottles outside with the hoses running under the tent wall. Then, after taking off his snow-caked boots and putting on his camp slippers, he set up housekeeping. The lantern sent out a bright glow, and the heater broke the chill in the air. He stayed warm as he moved around, laying out the bed and setting up the kitchen.

This was camp. To hell with Wentworth, the greenies, Norman Lang, and the guys from Ohio. He didn't need their money, and he didn't need their noise. He appreciated the quiet here, with only the faint rushing sound of the two propane appliances. He unzipped the door and peeked out through the flap. The moon was just a sliver, which should be good for hunting. He liked to camp in a tent when the moon was full, the way it had been when he'd camped at Wentworth's. With the light out, he could lie in his sleeping bag and see the clear shadows of the pines on the canvas roof and walls. Maybe he would get some good moonlight by the end of his stay.

When he went to bed later that night, the world went dark as he had expected. Dark and cold. As he snuggled in his nest on the ground, he thought of other nights, in a smaller tent, when he had heard the crunch of horse hooves on snow just a few yards from where he lay. That was the best. He needed to work it back into his yearly rhythm, hunt with the right people so that all the trouble of hauling horses would be worthwhile. He couldn't put a face on any of the people, but they weren't any of the ones he had been hunting with lately.

Morning broke clear and cold. Wilf fired up the lamp, the heater, and the stove. According to his thermometer, the temperature inside the tent was at four degrees. He set out the coffee pot and the red can of Folger's. When he pulled a plastic quart bottle of water out of the insulated bag, he felt the give of frozen crystals around the inside of the bottle. For as much as he enjoyed keeping things basic, he had to admit that a trailer like the Château had some things going for it.

He sat in a chair, wrapped in his overcoat and with a stocking cap pulled down over his ears. The country was different than it had been a week and a half earlier. A thick blanket of snow now covered everything. The bloodstains where Lundberg had killed the deer would be layered over, as would the earlier tracks of animals and men. Wilf recalled the blood on Henderson's shoes, the shifting glance and the sullen jowls.

He didn't miss those fellows, and he was glad not to have to camp in the same place. With everything in the back of his pickup, he had been able to come up to this spot, where he could hunt out of camp on foot every day. Traffic still came through, but he didn't have to drive anywhere unless he had an animal on the ground and had to go fetch it.

The coffee took a long time to perk. When it was ready, he mixed it half-and-half with milk in a large blue enamel mug, then cut into the loaf of pumpkin bread that Adrienne had set aside for him. As he ate the bread and washed it down with the coffee and milk, he began to feel warm inside. When he finished eating he poured another cup of coffee, mixed in enough milk to color it, and huddled back into his chair. The thermometer on the tent wall read thirty degrees. It took a while to warm a good-sized tent like this, and the air was always much warmer by the ceiling than down lower where he sat.

When he finished his coffee he turned off the stove, the heater, and the lantern, then unzipped the door flap and stepped outside. Cold and dark and quiet. His insulated boots made soft pushing sounds in the snow as he walked to the pickup. Still in the dark when he opened the door, he took out his rifle. After patting all his pockets to make sure he had license, shells, knife, and granola bars, he slung the rifle on his shoulder and set off on the morning hunt.

The snow was not packed or crusted, but it was deep enough to make for slow going. His first climb followed an old logging road, now closed and with eight-foot pine trees growing out of the middle. Uphill on his left and downhill on his right, slash piles from old logging operations jutted out of the snow, irregular figures in the dim light. The trail did not rise in a steep grade, but he labored enough that he took a breather after about ten minutes. He did not want to get winded.

As he stood there, still in the dark of pre-dawn, with no sound except his own breathing, he felt as if he was already going out of himself, flowing through the barriers of clothing, and fitting in with the trees and rocks and snow. His breathing evened out, and after a few minutes he moved on.

When he came to the top of the first ridge, the sky was beginning to turn grey. He could make out the snow-covered shapes of deadfall in the timber, and in a few more minutes he would be able to see what tracks, if any, indicated animals passing through. He brought the rifle up to his shoulder a couple of times to get the feel of clearing the bulky coat and getting the butt in place against his shoulder. He repeated the action a few more times, to practice finding the crosshairs in the scope. Then he jacked a shell into the chamber, flicked the safety, and pushed forward through the snow.

At a little after sunrise he heard the first snowmobile, a drone-like whine that carried in the cold mountain air. Up on the high ridges he didn't have to cross paths with snowmobiles or their cousins the four-wheelers, but he could hear them from a long way off.

He walked the ridge for a couple of miles, keeping in the timber most of the time but every once in a while walking to the edge when he saw open sky. For a stretch of half a mile he followed an elk track, not expecting to find the animal but wanting to walk where it had walked. It gave him a deep, narrow feeling to be cut off from everything else as he moved through the timber. A tune was running through his head, the tune of a song about silver spurs. He fitted words to it, words he had never heard in a song. *To follow the track of the elk.* He could hear the guitar music, and the new song lifted his heart. He played the words over and over, and he could still hear them after the elk track had gone off over the side of the mountain into thick brush and timber.

At the end of the ridge, he sidestepped down a shaley slope and came out where a four-wheel-drive road crossed a creek. No vehicles had come this way since the snow, so the road lay under a blanket of white fluff. The creek chuckled westward, toward the plains and Saratoga. At this spot it leveled out over a stretch of gravel, with larger rocks sticking out here and there and lining the edges. Ice had formed along both sides of the stream, and snow had piled unbothered on the rocks.

Wilf set his rifle aside, took off his cap and coat and vest, rolled up his sleeves, and knelt at the edge of the creek. Reaching across the shore ice, he scooped double handfuls of water and washed his face. The bracing cold brought him more awake than ever, more alert, more in tune with the gravel, the water, the ice, the snow-mounded rocks, the uprooted tree that lay across the clear, dark creek. Words occurred to him. *A mountain stream is like a pretty girl.* He splashed his face one last time, then dried his chilled hands and got covered up again.

He decided to follow the road back up to camp, as he would have easier going. With his rifle slung on his shoulder and his spirits raised, he set off. After a half-mile climb out of the bottom, he came to a cattle guard where a Forest Service fence crossed the road. The fence posts had mounds of snow the size of cantaloupes, and the cross braces had puffy ridges of snow along their length. So did the rails on the cattle guard. Off to the left on the other side of the gate, where vehicles turned out, he saw a stump about a foot across and three feet high, with a cap of snow taller than it was wide. By grabbing a post and swing-stepping around, he went through the gateway without disturbing the snow along the rails.

Downhill and leveling out, he came to a spot where the road forked back to his right, to the northwest. It looked as if a pickup with chains had come down the road in front of him and had headed out that way. He thumbed his sling strap and headed onward. He passed the first beaver ponds, then the meadow where he had seen a coyote magnified in full morning sun the year before, then another series of beaver ponds sheeted with dull ice.

About half a mile from camp, he heard snowmobiles. He stepped to the side of the road and continued walking. The sounds were coming up out of a wooded area on his right, where in recent years the four-wheelers had worn a path through the timber. Now with the snowfall, the snowmobiles had taken to the trail. Two men with ski masks covering their faces came gliding through the trees. They turned right on the Forest Service road, and Wilf noted the rifles across their backs as they moved on up the hill.

Back at camp, he extracted the shell from the chamber and pushed it down into the magazine. Then he hung the rifle in the cab of the pickup and unzipped the tent. The sun hadn't warmed things very much. Condensation from the morning coffee had turned to frost along the ceiling of the tent, and the thermometer had gone back down to twenty. Wilf got the stove and heater going again, and he took out a towel to wipe off moisture as the frost melted and dripped.

Although his feet had stayed mostly dry in the snow-packs, his jeans had gotten wet up to his knees. He took off his pants and hung them on a coat hanger at a safe distance from the heater, then put on a pair of thermal underwear and a pair of herringbone wool pants. As he toasted a cheese sandwich in a skillet and heated leftover coffee with milk, his legs warmed up and the interior of the tent took on the comfort of a cabin.

He had a short afternoon hunt, as he had to drive down to meet Adrienne. The road to the campground had been well packed with vehicle traffic, though there were no trailers or tents in the campground itself. Wilf parked on the road across from the split-rail fence and waited. Adrienne was supposed to get away from work at noon, so even if she chose to go around the long way through Saratoga instead of over the top, she shouldn't have to travel in the dark. If she didn't show up by dusk, he would drive out to the highway and wait for her. Meanwhile, he sat in his pickup and waited as an occasional vehicle rumbled by. Most of them were headed out this time of the day, but some were coming in. Friday afternooners. Two big Dodge pickups pulled into the campground, one pulling a gooseneck camper and the other towing a trailer with four snowmobiles. Four men got out, each with a blue can in his hand, and with the engines of both trucks running, the men stood around drinking their beer and talking in loud voices. Then the two with the snowmobile trailer got into their outfit, backed out of the campground, and parked alongside the road while the other two pulled the camper around and backed it into a numbered site.

A few minutes later, a pair of narrower headlights came around the curve, and Wilf's pulse quickened at the sight of a maroon-colored Impala. Within a few minutes they had her car parked on the side of the road and her bag in the back of his pickup.

"That's the place where you stayed with the poachers?" she asked as he turned into the entry and put the vehicle in reverse.

"Yeah, that's it. Four other guys just came in, and I imagine a few others'll show up later on."

"It's supposed to snow more."

"That's all right." He shifted into second gear and let

out the clutch. "Just makes things cozy."

She looked back at her car, then turned to him and smiled. "How long could we hold out, with the food you've got?"

"Maybe a week." He gave a broad smile. "But we could live off the fat of the land."

She laughed. "Shoot a deer, like your elk hunters did?"

"Nah. Get a nice plump snowmobiler."

Wilf lit the lantern and stood next to Adrienne as the glow lit up the inside of the tent.

"This thing looks about the same as it did at your place, but it sure is colder."

"We'll get it warmed up." He put his arm around her waist and then released it. "Have a seat. I'll light the stove and the heater."

Within a few minutes, the air began to warm up around them. Wilf took out a couple of plastic glasses and poured wine. They touched their glasses and drank.

Adrienne looked around the tent again. "This is pretty nice. Nothing fake or fancy."

"I'll tell you, the ideal thing is to do the tent and the horses together. That's a good match. But I just haven't gotten to do it much."

"It sounds down-to-earth and basic."

"It is. It's my idea of a 'quality outdoor experience.' That's what they call it in the business."

"That's the term, huh?"

"Yeah. It's how they describe the product they offer. You know, they have their lingo. Then a guy like me is supposed to safeguard the quality."

"Get your clients off and away from civilization?"

"Either that or the opposite, depending on where you are and what they want. So far, with most of the business I've done, I've ended up working out of the pickup and sleeping in camp trailers."

"You don't think you could match the higher-quality experience with the kind of people you've been working with?"

"Not these last two bunches. They want everything out of the can."

"They don't care to have things more basic?"

"I think their main idea of the 'experience' is the part where they pull the trigger."

Adrienne flicked her eyebrows. "Just pop off and pull out?"

"Really."

She held out her hand to indicate the tent. "So, do you think you need to re-focus, and just specialize in this kind of 'product,' as they say, and hope for a better kind of clientele, or try to keep a broad range of products for whatever kind comes your way?"

Wilf gave her a steady look. "To be honest, sometimes I think, to hell with the product. Just give me the experience, and to hell with trying to sell it."

"Sounds like you've come a ways on this."

"I'm still thinking it through, but it sure seems like there's something missing."

"You mean, like you've lost some of the enjoyment?"

"That and more. I don't know if I could say exactly what. It's not my pride, I don't think, because that helps me get pissed. But it's something like that." He took a sip on his wine. "I tell you, it's a feeling that I sold out on someone or something. I mean, I felt used by Wentworth and his pals, but it's more than that, more than just selling out on myself, although that would be bad enough."

Adrienne nodded, her hair shining in the glow of the lantern.

Wilf went on. "When I was up here before, with those hunters from Ohio, this one guy made some remarks about getting his money's worth. Well, I told him that what you paid for was the opportunity to hunt—that's game warden language—and in my mind, that's what we were putting a price on. The activity. But somewhere along the way, it seems you cross over into putting a price on the animal itself."

Adrienne frowned.

"You know, I've read articles by the Game and Fish that tell how much an animal is worth in terms of how much income it generates. They figure the amount the average hunter spends on gas, food, lodging, and all that, and they figure that a mule deer buck, let's say, brings in four hundred dollars to a community. Now what do you think of that?"

"Well, it sounds kind of cold to me."

"It does to me, too. Now that's from the tourism point of view. Then from the tourist's point of view, which is like this guy from Ohio, there's a similar way of putting a value on it, which is in terms of how much it costs him. He figures he spends five hundred or a thousand dollars, and he thinks he should get something at least as big as a mule deer."

"But you don't have any of it priced like that."

"No, I don't. Not by individual animal. I told myself I could charge for helping the person with his opportunity, and that was as far as I went. I said, I'll go this far, and that's it."

"And that's all you've done, isn't it?"

"Yeah. In my mind, that's as far as I went. I didn't help

these guys up here kill a deer, not any more than I helped Wentworth's pal shoot one without a license. If I was selling anything, it was a product—the hunting experience, or the opportunity to have the experience. But when it comes down to it, even though I don't feel like I sold the deer, I feel like I sold out on them."

"You mean by helping these guys?"

"Right. By helping them get into that position to begin with. By putting an animal into their sights." Wilf took a measured breath. "And I don't mean just these two violators. I feel that I did the same thing, in a lesser way, with the guys that had legal permits. I sold out on the deer because I put some kind of price on some part of it to begin with."

"So what do you think you'll do?"

"I'm not sure. I don't want to say that the whole business is rotten just because of a couple of guys, but I know I don't like the money aspect of it. I feel like I'm selling something that's not mine. I know other guides don't feel that way, so maybe I should leave it to them. Meanwhile, I'll just take comfort in knowing that the guys who pulled something got caught." Wilf looked at his wine glass for a moment before he spoke again. "But that's enough of the downside for the time being. I've got plenty of time to think about it."

"Oh, yeah."

"I was wondering, though..."

"What?"

"On the cheerier side of things."

"Which is?"

"I was wondering if the shysters made it into the paper."

"Oh, Wentworth and Arnold? The paper hadn't come

out yet when I left, but the gossip had gone around."

"Oh. Anything new or strange about it?"

"Nothing major. I think the one new detail I heard was that the pickup had been repossessed from someone who had gone bankrupt in the floor-covering business."

"Huh. I heard they found a package of condoms in the glovebox. I wonder if they were his."

She laughed. "I heard that, too, but nothing about whose they were."

"Yeah, funny stuff. There was something bogus about that pickup all along. At first I thought we might use it, but Wentworth said it needed brake work. Then I found out it was running fine. The deputy drove it down the hill."

"He didn't want you to drive it, then?"

"I don't know. He could have driven it himself, but he didn't. I don't think he wanted anybody to touch it. That's what it seemed like. Him and his little secrets."

Adrienne's face beamed in the lantern light. "You don't think it was because he didn't want anyone to find his condoms, do you?"

Wilf laughed. "I hadn't thought of that. But I would hope he could think of an easier way to hide 'em."

"I should think so. He might have made a couple of blunders, but I think he's at least that clever."

They went to bed early, with a quilt and a top sheet of canvas spread over the Adam-and-Eve bag. In the course of events, a metallic clunk sounded outside the tent.

A few minutes later, Adrienne spoke. "Did you hear a noise a little while ago?"

"Yeah. It sounded like it came from the pickup."

"What do you think it was?"

"Sometimes, when it gets real cold, the fenders or the hood make a popping or a thumping sound. These old pickups have other funny sounds, too, like when the weight settles. You get a pop or a creak."

"You don't have a couple of large tattooed women rolling around in back, do you?"

"No, I checked real close when I got your bag out."

"Well, that's good. I did hear something, but because of the other things going on, I wasn't sure what it was."

"I heard it, too. One of those things that goes *clunk* in the night."

"As opposed to things that go *bump*?"

"Well, there are those, too. They make it hard to hear other things."

13

Wilf stood in his long johns and looked through the tent flap at the darkness outside. About eight inches of snow had fallen overnight, and white flakes were still falling thick. He zipped the door closed and with his flashlight found the matches. When he lit the lantern, he saw where the roof sagged between the metal rafter poles.

Adrienne stirred in the bed.

"Snowed quite a bit," he said. "And it's still coming down."

"Are you going out to hunt?"

"Not 'til it lets up. I think I'll go back to bed for a while."

He turned off the lantern and crawled under the warm covers.

When he woke again, grey light was filtering into the

tent. As he glanced around he decided he had better clear the snow off the roof and away from the entrance. He had the feeling of being closed in.

The atmosphere cheered up when he got the lantern lit and the stove and heater going. The thermometer read fourteen degrees, and the water for coffee had frozen crystals in it again.

"Is it still snowing?" came Adrienne's voice.

"I'll take a look and see."

He unzipped the flap and looked out upon a world of white. Another two or three inches had fallen, and a few flakes drifted in the air. About ten inches of unmarred snow covered the hood, cab, and camper shell of the pickup, and a peak sat on the rear view mirror on this side. His camp shovel, which he had left leaning against a young spruce tree, had a ridge of snow on the crosspiece of the D-shaped handle, and the head of it was buried in the white drift.

He closed the flap and sat down on the edge of the mattress, scooting the snow packs close at hand. As he turned the first one upside down and shook it, Adrienne stirred again.

"Do you always shake out your boots?"

"Old habit."

"In case something got into them in the night?"

"Well, that, too. But I don't always wear the same pair from one day to the next. One pair gets wet, or the weather changes." He looked into the second boot, then turned it up and shook it. "One time I got a real surprise. I was camping by myself in the back of the pickup, in pretty close quarters, and I shook out a pile of rat poison."

"Really? What was it doing in there?"

"Oh, a few years back I had trouble with mice in the shed, a real infestation. I set out two kinds of poison, little pellets and big ones—the blue kind, you know."

"Sure."

"And the mice were storing it, especially the larger pellets. I found a whole bunch of it in a bag of grain. When I emptied out the boot on the floor of my pickup bed, I figured it out real quick."

"You had the boots stored in the shed, then?"

"Yeah. I didn't have that much room in the house. I changed that, of course, and I try to remember to shake 'em all out before I leave home, but I still do it again when I put 'em on."

"Good idea. I bet you were careful cleaning up all the blue pellets in that tight little space."

"You can bet I was. Me and my little whisk broom." He pulled on the boots, tightened the laces, and tied them. "I wish I had a long-handled broom now, for all the snow."

Outside, he used the shovel and the whisk broom to uncover the doors to the pickup. With his folding camp saw he cut a pine branch about four feet long and bushy. He used it to clear off the hood and windshield of the pickup and the roof of the tent. After that he brushed off the propane bottles and tightened the guy ropes on the tent. Then with the shovel he cleared walkways from the entrance to the bushes and to the pickup.

Adrienne's voice came through the wall of the tent. "Coffee's ready."

Warmth and the rich smell of coffee greeted him as he ducked inside. Adrienne was sitting in a chair, bundled up in a cranberry-colored parka, a brown fur cap, and grey wool gloves. He smiled at the sight of her.

"Do I look like Natasha of the Ukraine? Or the squaws

along the Yukon?"

"You look great."

"How are things out there?"

"The snow's kinda deep. About a foot of it to push through."

"Do you think you'll go out to hunt?"

"I might give it a try. How about you?"

"I think I'll stay here and read. I didn't come equipped to go through that much snow."

"Yeah, it might be tough going. But I'll give it a try for a little while."

By the time he got to the top of the ridge, his pants were soaked above his knees. He could picture the long johns and the dark wool trousers hanging in the tent, getting warm and dry for him. Meanwhile, he was beginning to wonder how good an idea it was to be hunting in snow that was up to his hip pockets in places. He had never killed elk in deep snow, but he had heard stories from hunters who had, and he assumed it was possible. So far this morning, though, he had not seen a track of anything.

To the northeast he could see the ridge he had hunted the day before, dark timber powdered in white. Overhead, the cloud cover had stayed the same, so that the still, white world lay in dull light.

He unslung the rifle from his shoulder and began brushing it off. This was a tough go, floundering knee-deep, not knowing where the drifts got deeper, dislodging heaps of snow overhead with the mere touch of a branch. He didn't like getting moisture on the scope and down around the bolt.

Too much could even warp the stock. But he was giving it a try. A couple of hours at least. With the tip of his gloved finger he wiped the bolt clean, then worked a shell into the chamber.

Half a mile further, he came to an old buck and rail fence. He walked downhill to find a spot where the fence had broken down and had sunk in the snow. Imagining how the fallen rails, hidden in the drift, might trip him up, he extracted the shell from the chamber and pushed it down into the magazine. When he crossed the fence, he decided to leave the shell where it was.

Back in the timber again, he moved through tall pines. From up ahead on the right came the deep soft thump of hooves. His pulse quickened at the flash of yellowish tan as two shapes lurched through the open spots between tree trunks. Wilf jacked in a shell and got the scope up to his eye. The heart-shaped rump of an elk moved through his field of vision, and then the animals were gone, thudding into the timber. Wilf set the safety and moved on.

He had to fight the snow one way or the other. In the open spots and in the aspens he had deeper trudging, but in the pines he got dumped on whenever a breath of wind came up. He didn't mind getting his jeans wet, or even his socks and the liners of his boots, but he didn't like getting moisture on his rifle. When snowflakes began to fall again, he decided to go back to camp. He found a bare slope that looked as if it would take him down the mountainside, and with slow, careful sidesteps he picked his way to the bottom.

From time to time he had heard snowmobiles, but the road this far down had not been traveled yet today. One of those machines could cover in a few minutes what it took him an hour to push through. He wondered if he would accept a ride if one came by.

As it turned out, he did not have to decide. After a long solitary trek, he saw the ivory-colored tent and the faded red pickup appear against the white background of the campsite. He left the road to push through the last two hundred yards, with rocks and dead branches underfoot and snow-capped stumps poking up all around him. When he got to the pickup, he opened the driver's door. Resting the butt of the rifle on his right thigh, he clicked the live shell back, pushed it down, and slid the bolt forward. Then he hung the gun in the rack.

"Is that you?" came Adrienne's voice from inside the tent.

"It sure is. Wilf of the dragging ass." He noticed icicles along the edge of the tent and on the guy ropes; then beyond the tent he saw what looked like snowmobile tracks.

He unzipped the tent and stepped into a warm, thick atmosphere. Adrienne was still wearing her coat but had taken off her cap and gloves. She was sitting in a chair at a right angle to the heater. Wilf kissed her and then sank into the empty chair. He looked at the thermometer. A little over fifty degrees.

"Did someone come by?"

"Yeah. A guy on a snowmobile. I didn't get a good look at him. He was all covered up."

"Oh, yeah?" Wilf started to unlace his boots.

"He stopped outside here and called out. I unzipped the window and talked to him from there."

"What did he have to say?"

"He said the road was closed."

Wilf paused at the laces. "Oh, really? Which one?"

"The one we came in on. He said the other one out to the highway was still open."

Wilf pulled off his boots and wiggled his feet in the

damp socks. "Well, as Tommy Tice would say, that's a bag pinch. We'll have to think about what we're going to do about it." He stood up. "But first I'm going to get out of these wet pants and into something dry and warm. Then I'm going to bring my rifle in and wipe it dry, put some oil on it."

Wilf sat in the camp chair with the rifle across his lap. His pants were warm, his upper body was warm, even his hand that held the cold cartridges was warm. But a chill ran through him. "Son of a bitch," he said.

"What's wrong?"

"Look at these shells." He held out his hand with the five cartridges.

She raised her eyebrows. "It looks like they got a little water on them."

"Yeah, they did. But that's not what's got me surprised."

"What does?"

"One of 'em doesn't match."

"What do you mean?"

"You see this one?" He pointed with his left index finger. "It's a different caliber."

"You mean it doesn't belong with the others. It doesn't look much different, but I can see it's a little narrower."

"You're sure right it doesn't belong. It's a .270, and all the others are .30-06."

"Did you get them mixed up?"

"*I* didn't. I don't even have a .270, so I don't have any of them on hand."

"Well, how did it get there, then?"

"Good question." He looked at her. "Someone else

had to put it there."

"You're sure."

"Damn sure. That shell was on top of the other four in the magazine. I don't know how many times I worked it in and out of that chamber. I don't even like having 'em together in my hand." He took the .270 shell with his left hand, rubbed and rolled it on the charcoal-black herringbone, put it in his shirt pocket, and buttoned the flap. He shook his head as he looked at Adrienne. "Someone did this on purpose."

"What for?"

"To cause trouble. That shell would probably fire in my gun, but it would cause all kinds of hell. If it didn't blow up the rifle to begin with, it would leave little fragments of casing in there, and then the next shot would blow things up."

"You think someone wanted to get you?"

"I'll tell you, it's more than just a little prank. People get killed with things like that. You've got your head right down there when you fire. Hell, I heard of it happening to a shotgun, and it got the guy's son standing next to him."

"Who do you think did it?"

"I don't know. It could have been that sound we heard last night. All the new snow would have covered up any footprints. But it could have been earlier. I haven't fired that gun since before I went up to Wentworth's. One of those guys—the one that died, in fact—had a .270, but, hell, it's a common caliber and you can buy the shells anywhere."

"You think one of them did it?"

He shook his head. "I don't know. I don't think they would have done it at the time, but they've had reason to get pissed at me since then."

"Do you think someone could have known to

follow you up here?"

"Oh, hell. I don't know that, either. Probably so. I don't make a big secret of where I go to hunt. I could have mentioned it to those guys. I know I did to Tommy Tice and Norman Lang. If Wentworth wanted to get even with me, he could have gotten it from either of them. And there's other guys in town who know I come up here. It's a big country, but it's not that hard to find someone. Just ask people if they've seen thus-and-such kind of outfit with whatever plates, and you can find someone. I've done it."

"But someone else did this? You're sure of that?"

He nodded slowly. "I'm sure. I just don't know when. God, just the thought of it gives me the chills. I don't know how many times I worked that shell in and out of that chamber." A wave of recognition washed through him. "You know, we talked about all kinds of firearms stuff one night up at Wentworth's, including how I handle my rifle. For all I know, I've had it in there all along, but I'd bet someone did it since the shit hit the fan on that deer license."

"Someone in that group?"

"Maybe they didn't do it themselves, but they would know enough to have someone else do it while they kept their hands clean."

"I don't know, Wilf. It sounds like a pretty strong measure to get even with someone for squealing."

"I agree. But it just depends on how much they have to hide. That stolen pickup was more than I expected to begin with."

"That's true."

"You think of Wyoming as a low-crime state, especially up here in the elk country, where no one touches anything.

Then something like this, and you're not sure who or when. But I know one thing. I didn't put that shell there."

They sat for a couple of minutes without talking until Wilf spoke again.

"You didn't get a good look at the fellow who came by?"

"No. He was wearing a ski mask."

"Yeah, they all do. He could have been anybody. But I still don't like the idea that someone could have gotten into the cab last night. And now we're all snowed in."

Adrienne laughed. "Just like the Donner party. But I don't think he'd be a good one to cook. He looked kind of thin."

"Well, we'll wait for a fat one. He said the road to the highway was still open, huh?"

"Right."

"Did you tell him where your car was, or anything like that?"

"No, nothing. He didn't stay around very long."

"Good. He might have been a harmless sort. Did he have a rifle?"

"He had some kind of gun strapped on his back."

"Standard issue, it seems." Wilf was quiet for a minute and then said, "I'll tell you what. I think we should get you down to your car before it snows any more. If you go out by Saratoga, it should be all right. Once you get out of the mountains it gets better. I pulled out of here when it was like this one time, and there wasn't any snow on the ground by the time I got to Saratoga."

"How do we get to my car, though?"

"It's not too hard. There's a trail that the snowmobilers and four-wheelers use. We'll have to walk through deep snow, but it's all downhill, and I'll go first."

"Just carry my stuff?"

"I've got a frame pack that I bring along in case I need to quarter an elk. We can tie your stuff onto that."

"I could leave my bag here, and you could bring it."

"You might like to have the extra clothes and all."

Adrienne waited a moment until she spoke. "How about you?"

"I think the main thing to do is to get you on the road before dark. I can come back up here, spend the night, and see about getting out tomorrow. If the Forest Service doesn't open the road, I can go ask some loggers to get me out. We passed a camp of theirs when we came in last night."

"You're not worried?"

"Not much. Whoever it is has already made their move. I sort of feel like a sitting duck, but I don't think anyone'll do anything out in the open."

"And you don't want to hunt any more?"

"This stuff has kind of ruined the mood for me."

"That's too bad."

"It could have been a lot worse if I'd fired at the two elk I saw this morning."

Wilf stood at the edge of the road and waved as the Impala drove away, its maroon hull making a contrast with the white road and landscape. As he had hoped, the snow on the main road was packed well enough that the car could navigate, and it didn't swerve as it picked up speed. When the car disappeared around the bend, he hitched the empty pack on his back and set out on his uphill climb. He followed the trail he had broken on the way down. No snowmobilers came along, but he heard one whining farther up.

When he got back to camp, dusk was drawing in. The roof of the tent had about an inch of snow on it, as did the windshield of the pickup. It wasn't enough to worry about. He went into the tent and lit the lantern and the heater. His rifle was lying on top of the bed cover where he had left it. This would be one night when he didn't leave it in the cab.

He opened his eyes to grey light again. The roof did not sag very far, so he imagined it hadn't snowed much more. Thinking it might be a long day, he rolled out of bed and got things fired up. He unzipped the door and looked out on an overcast world of grey and cold. He still hadn't decided whether to pack up camp first or to go ask for help. It didn't look as if the day was going to get any better right away, so he thought it was less likely that the Forest Service would clear the road. If he went to find the loggers, it would be better to have everything ready to go in case they had to tow him out.

With that in mind, he packed up most of the gear while the coffee came around. When he was finished with breakfast, he shut off the propane appliances to let them cool while he wiped up and packed away his kitchen. He stacked everything by the door of the tent, then put on his boots and stowed the gear in the back of the pickup.

Down came the tent, with water-beaded poles and muddy stakes and stiff, wet ropes. Everything would have to be set up or at least laid out to dry when he got home. For now, he concentrated on getting the canvas folded so that he could roll it into a manageable bundle.

The whine of a snowmobile came from the road he had

driven in on. A minute later, a machine came into view. It came around the curve, turned right into the clearing, and came sliding to a stop next to where Wilf knelt on the canvas. The rider looked big, and his voice had a commanding tone.

"This is no time for a summer camp, buddy."

Wilf turned and got a full look at the man. Like the others, he was wearing a ski mask. It was dark with white stripes in the shape of thunderbolts. Over that he wore a camouflage cap that matched his quilted vest. Beneath the vest he wore a field jacket with a different pattern of camo, and the vest was parted at the bottom where the man's girth spread out. Below the part in the vest he had a camouflage shell pouch that rattled when he shifted in his seat. Wilf noted the machine itself, green and yellow, and the black plastic rifle boot that angled up on the man's right side. As a game warden might have been quick to notice, there wasn't a speck of blaze orange in sight.

Wilf didn't say anything as he tried to get a fix on the man. The engine had been shut off, and silence hung in the cold air until the stranger spoke.

"Don't you know the road's closed?"

"I think I might have heard something like that."

"How do you think you're going to get out?"

"Suppose you let me worry about that."

"You're kind of smart to be here all by yourself."

"Who says I am?"

"If you weren't, you'd have that thing rolled up a hell of a lot better."

"Suppose you let me worry about that, too."

"Worry all you want." The man shifted with his gloved hands against the handlebars, and his pouch rattled again.

Wilf wondered what caliber of shells the man carried, but he said nothing.

The big man pushed against the handlebars and squared his shoulders. Brown eyes glared through the eye holes of the ski mask. "I'll tell you, I was going to offer to help you get out of here, but now I think you can just go to hell."

Wilf looked him square in the eyes. "I don't need your help, or your advice. If you came here looking for trouble, you might get more than you bargained for. If you didn't, we've got even less to talk about."

The man pushed a button, and the engine came to life. "You ought to be someone's girlfriend," he said. The snowmobile lurched forward, then skidded away in a curve to the left.

Wilf took calming breaths and made his fists relax as he watched the machine sweep away. He had a good hunch the man carried .270 shells with R-P on the head of each casing, but it wasn't worth a fistfight to try to find out. The man had come to harass him, but he hadn't seemed to be looking for an actual fight. Anyone who would arrange that much would be tipping his hand too far. Maybe someone had sent the guy to intimidate or to check up, but maybe he was just taking it upon himself to be a jerk. Wilf decided he would have to put this one in the category of things he wasn't going to know for sure.

As he trudged up the hill to look for the loggers, Wilf carried his rifle slung on his shoulder. He didn't think the snowmobiler would try anything, but it was still elk season, and Wilf had a license.

He paused at a curve in the road and took a breather. Below him lay the campsite, with his pickup all packed and ready to go, and a bare spot in the snow where he had pulled up his stakes. Raising his glance, he took in the snow-covered ridges with patches of dark timber and leafless aspens. It was a wonderful country, and he hated to have it ruined, even for a weekend, by the likes of that guy on the snowmobile.

When it came right down to it, though, he knew it was up to him to figure out who was harassing him and why. He had made the choice to try to make a living off of other people's leisure—and off of all of this. He had been willing to put a price on wildlife and the experience of going after it, something that should be above price, and he had been willing to do it with those who could afford to pay. He had shrugged off another guide's comments about poor tippers, but he hadn't turned down any pay himself. He could track his troubles back to that.

There would always be someone else willing to take the money and rationalize it, but he wasn't going to pimp nature any more. He could see himself as he had been— serving flapjacks, leading his hunters up to one animal after another, doing all the skinning and gutting and cleanup. He had thought he could make an honest living at it, and maybe he had been honest, but there had been no honor. Instead, there had been some kind of a bug or virus in him, some malignant little thing that had urged him to exploit the thing he loved.

He looked at his pickup again, an old beater that he was supposed to upgrade so he could look better to his clients. As if that was what it was all about—make more to spend more, spend more to make more. None of that was going to get him the love of a woman like Adrienne or the grand view from on top of a high ridge, where he could follow the track of the elk.

He turned and headed uphill again. He would find the loggers or someone else to dig him out. Being snowed in was the kind of problem he liked to deal with. But he knew that when he got it solved, he had another problem to consider. The .270 shell had come from somewhere, and maybe the bully on the snowmobile had, too. Things like that didn't grow out of a forged license or even a stolen pickup. Something else was at stake. He had only a hazy idea of who was in it and who wasn't, but he had a good hunch that it all flowed through Wentworth.

14

Wilf called Tommy Tice at 6:30 in the morning. When Tommy answered on the second ring, Wilf heard what sounded like a television voice in the background.

"Tommy? This is Wilf."

"Well, what the hell. I thought you'd be elk hunting."

"I went up, but the snow got too deep, so I came back. I got in late yesterday afternoon. Had to set up my tent all over again to dry it out."

"Sounds like fun."

"I've had more." Wilf glanced out the window at the tent rippling in the morning breeze. "Say, there was something I wanted to check on at the ranch, and I was wondering if

I could get you to help me. Something I've got a hunch about and would like to take a look at if I had a chance."

"Well, the boss is sure gone right now. It wouldn't be a bad time."

"Are you going out there this morning?"

"That was my idea. If you want, you can meet me at the bottom of the hill."

"O.K. I'll see you there."

As Wilf hung up, a phrase ran through his mind. *Call for the gate.* That was what a rough-stock rider did when he was on the animal in the chute, settled in place, and had his hat pulled down. It was the last thing he did before things broke open. No need to tell Tommy Tice what was up quite yet, and for all he knew, there might not even be a rodeo.

Tommy was waiting in his flatbed pickup, smoking a cigarette, when Wilf pulled up. A rifle hung in the gun rack as usual, and two dogs were pushing their thin noses out through the open space at the top of their box. Wilf rolled down his window while Tommy, who had his window down about an inch, rolled it the rest of the way.

"Whatcha got in mind?"

"Something up by the house."

"You can go ahead and get in with me if you want, then."

On the way up the hill, Wilf said, "Well, I'll tell you, I keep thinkin' something's not right with that pickup he had here. It doesn't make sense."

"Just thought he'd get away with somethin'."

"I keep thinkin' there's more to it. Like why he had it all locked up and parked off to the side. Earlier I thought maybe he didn't want anybody to touch it, and I couldn't figure out why, and now I think he didn't want anybody to move it."

"Well, someone damn sure did. And the deppity got his ass in trouble. He said that once he took the keys, he didn't want it out of his sight. But he should've sat and waited for another tow truck. That's what they told him when they chewed him out." As the ranch house and empty yard came into view, he added, "Why do you think he didn't want it moved? There wasn't anything in it except the rubbers."

Wilf gave him a direct look. "I think there might have been something underneath it."

Tommy parked the pickup in the driveway, and the two of them got out. Tommy took a last drag on his cigarette, dropped the stub, and ground it out with his boot sole. Then he led the way across the grassy area. "Here's where it was parked," he said.

An area of bare dirt, about three feet by three, lay exposed. It had been packed down, and a few scraps of dry grass had blown onto it, but no attempt had been made to hide it.

Tommy looked at Wilf. "Think somethin's down there?"

"I would guess there either is or has been. No tellin' what, though."

"Hole's not big enough to have a body in it. And I don't think he'd have buried a set of deer horns."

Wilf shook his head. "Whatever it is, I think we should have someone here before we dig it up."

"I've got my cell phone. Let's go ahead and do it."

Back in the cab of the pickup, Tommy placed a call to the sheriff's office. He shut off the phone and set it on the seat next to him, then reached into the pocket of his canvas chore coat. He pulled out a pack of Camels and a book of matches, shook out a cigarette, and lit it.

He rolled the window down another inch and blew out a stream of smoke. Then he looked at Wilf and said, "No elk, huh?"

"Nope. Too much snow, though I did see some. I walked past this one spot where I helped two guys load an elk a couple of years ago. They didn't seem to be all that proud of it, and I thought it was just because it was a spike. But then they showed me where he had an eye missing on one side and sunken in on the other."

"Blind."

"Yep. I told 'em I'd like to find his brother, but they didn't laugh. When I was up there this time, I thought I'd settle for his brother well enough, but I didn't get a shot."

"Oh, well. There's always another time."

"Yeah."

Tommy motioned with his head. "If we get snow, it might bring out the coyotes."

Wilf looked out at the grey cloud cover. "We might get some." He glanced through the back window toward the box. "Got a new dog?"

"Nah. These are the same two I had before. But I thought I might give 'em a run, what with the boss bein' gone."

"Oh." Wilf resisted the temptation of asking where the boss was or how long he would be away. "Are you gettin' close to the end of your work?"

"Pretty close." Tommy took another drag and flicked his ashes out the window. "Not much more." He stared out the windshield for a moment, showing his untrimmed sideburn to advantage, and then turned to Wilf. "Who do you think shot him?"

Wilf gave a start. "Who?"

"Why, the boss." Tommy's brown eyes had a calm look through the glasses.

"What do you mean?"

"I thought that's why we were here. I got a call from what's-his-name, Newell, this morning, a little while before you called. He says the boss is in the hospital. Someone put a bullet through him in a parkin' lot last night down in Loveland. Shot him through the gizzard as he sat in his outfit."

"The hell." Wilf imagined blood spreading out over the clean leather upholstery of the Navigator. "No, I didn't know a thing about it. I've just had someone harassing me, and I thought there was something funny about that Ford pickup. I was wondering if we could find out whether there was something at the bottom of it all, so to speak."

"Well, I guess we'll see."

They sat without talking as Tommy smoked his cigarette. The yard of the ranch house had a desolate feel to it, with no other vehicles in sight and no life evident in the house. The cheerless grey sky held a suggestion of snow, but the clouds were not moving.

Tommy got out of the cab, spoke to his dogs, and went to the edge of the yard behind the pickup. A couple of minutes later he came back. Settled behind the wheel, he turned to Wilf and spoke. "Do you think the boss gettin' shot had anything to do with that guy Palmer turnin' up dead?"

"You mean Parker?"

"Yeah, the one that shot the deer down on the hayfield."

Wilf pursed his lips. "No tellin'."

"You don't think someone did him in?"

"I don't have a real opinion on it myself, but I talked to Adrienne on the phone last night, and she read an article on the Internet from one of the newspapers down there. The coroner decided it was an accident. He ruled out homicide and says it didn't look like suicide."

"Yeah. I remember there was all three. What would have been the suicide motive, then?"

"Parker was divorced, and I guess his wife, or ex-wife, was causing him grief."

"Oh, maybe the boss had his nose in that."

Wilf shook his head. It didn't seem to fit, but he couldn't rule it out. "I don't know. My understanding was that someone else was in there ahead of him. Even at that, I don't know how that could cause him to get shot, if the ex-husband was already dead."

"Who knows? If someone shot him, they probably had a reason." Tommy looked at his rear-view mirror. "There ought to be a deputy out here pretty soon."

A few minutes later, a white Jeep Cherokee with a badge emblem on the door pulled into the yard and parked just ahead of Tommy's pickup. A heavy-set officer got out, a man with a flushed face and no hat or coat but otherwise in uniform, with name tag, badge, pistol, and a belt full of accessories.

"That's the guy that drove the pickup. Schultz." Tommy opened his door to get out, so Wilf did the same.

The deputy stood and listened, with the cold breeze riffling through his thinning hair, as Tommy told him what was up. The deputy went back to the Jeep for his hat, his coat, and a camera. He took a couple of pictures of the patch of dirt while

Tommy went to fetch two shovels.

Wilf dug first. The going was easy in the loose ground, but he took it slow, expecting to find something though he didn't know what. After he had dug about a foot, he jabbed the point of his shovel into the dirt and poked around. "Nothing so far."

"Why don't you let me try for a spell?"

Wilf stood back and let Tommy have a turn. Less than a foot deeper, his shovel clunked against something. Tommy looked at Wilf and then at the deputy.

He lifted the dirt out with more care now, until he exposed the upper half of a grey box wrapped in a clear plastic bag. Handing the shovel to Wilf, he said, "Looks like a safety-deposit box."

Tommy stepped down into the hole, with one boot on each of two perpendicular sides, and scooped away dirt with his hands. Then he rocked and wiggled the box until he pulled it free. He lifted it, dripping dirt from the folds of the bag, and set it on the grass at the edge of the hole.

Wilf knelt and pulled off the bag. He tried the latch, and it was locked. He looked at Tommy and then at the deputy. "That shouldn't surprise us," he said as he stood up.

Tommy stepped up out of the hole and lit a cigarette. "I'll go see if I can find a key."

"You don't have a search warrant," said Schultz.

"I'm not a cop. I work here. If I can look for a couple of shovels, I can do the same for a key."

Schultz took a labored breath and looked away. Wilf was afraid he would want to put the box in his car and drive off, but he also imagined the deputy was hoping to make himself look better back at the office and wouldn't want to take something that wasn't real evidence. As Tommy turned toward the house, Wilf said, "We need to see if there's something in there, and if there is, whether it's any of our business."

Tommy turned back. "You mean like a videotape of the boss in a blonde wig?"

Wilf raised his eyebrows and let out a short cough. "You've been watching too many movies, Tommy. And I hate to think what kind."

Tommy moved the cigarette from one side of his mouth to the other without touching it. "Like they say, you don't learn it all out of a book." He walked toward the house.

Wilf stood by the deputy without speaking. Then he knelt by the box again and rocked it back and forth. "Sounds like there's something in there." He stood and watched the door of the ranch house as Schultz took pictures of the box.

After about five minutes, Tommy came out on a fast walk. "I think this might be it," he said, flashing a short, thick key.

Wilf could feel his heartbeat go up as Tommy crouched by the box, fitted the key in the slot, turned it, and opened the door.

"Well, what have we got here?" Tommy took out two manila envelopes, each about five inches by eight, and handed them to Wilf. Then he stood on one side of Wilf as the deputy moved close to the other.

From the first manila envelope, Wilf took out a white business-size envelope. Inside of it he found a set of a half-dozen photos. In the first, Larry Wight was taking the panty hose off a blonde woman. She was reclined on a blanket on a green lawn, with flowers and a wooden fence in the background. It looked like a summer scene, well lit, and the photo quality was not bad. The other photos were of the same setting, further into the adventure.

"That's the other guy that came huntin'," said Tommy. "Who do you think the woman is?"

Wilf looked at Tommy and then Schultz. "I would guess it's Mrs. Parker."

Tommy let out a low whistle. "Oh, O.K. I follow you. Then the boss had these for a little leverage." He put on a thoughtful expression.

"I would think so." Wilf put the pictures back into the white envelope, tucked it into the manila envelope, and handed the pack to Tommy. Then he opened the other one, which also contained an envelope and photos, with no tell-tale notations of when or where they had been developed.

In the second set of pictures, the images were not as sharp, and they were not well centered. They seemed to have been taken in poorer light, and perhaps by a lower-quality camera, such as a hidden mini-cam. The prints were also a bit smaller than the first set, so they must have been developed in a different place.

The photos seemed to be taken in a motel room, as there were two beds with brown-and-blue-striped bedcovers and matching curtains in the background. In the first picture, Norman Lang lay naked on the bed closer to the camera, and a dark-haired woman, also naked, crouched between his legs as she slipped a condom onto him. Larry Wight, also naked, sat on the edge of the other bed, looking on with a frozen smile on his face. The next four pictures were a miscellany of the three people in various postures, without any clear sequence, so Wilf imagined that the photographer might have joined in at some point. The last picture showed Wight lying on his back with the woman on top, smiling, holding herself up with her hands on the mattress, while Wight, also smiling, had his hands raised and was holding a belt around the woman's neck.

Wilf's hands were shaking, and his heart was pounding. From the first picture he had known who the woman was, and he had tried not to look at her as he had flipped through the other prints.

"Same guy," said Tommy. "And who's the other? It looks like Norm Lang, a little pudgier with his clothes off."

"It is."

"And the girl?"

Wilf held out the last picture, which showed more of her face than the others did. "It's Heather Lea."

Tommy adjusted his glasses and said, "Jeez, it is."

Wilf's mouth had gone dry, and he was still shaking. He tucked the pictures away and went to hand the manila envelope to Tommy. Their glances met, and he handed it to the deputy, who accepted the one Tommy handed him as well.

Wilf looked around at the rolling hills, dark beneath the grey sky. "She's out here somewhere," he said. "Or Wentworth wouldn't have gone to all the trouble he did."

"What trouble is that?" asked Schultz. "Burying this box doesn't mean he buried the girl."

"I mean other things. Someone took the trouble to slip a .270 shell into my .30-06, and someone might have sent a goon on a snowmobile to harass me in my elk hunting camp. Wentworth's the only guy I know — or maybe him and Norman Lang both — who would have a reason to have it done. And like my girlfriend said, they wouldn't do it just because I squealed on a fixed hunting license."

Schultz gave a nonchalant look. "It sounds to me like

you're trying too hard to fit their motive to something that you can't really prove, and then on the basis of that, you say they've hidden this girl's body. Sounds to me like you just don't like these guys."

"Look, I've got the damn .270 shell, and you've got the pictures. But just forget about the first part. You've got the proof right there. Now we have to find her."

Schultz flopped the two envelopes against the heel of his left hand. "This is all good and fine that you boys dig up some pictures, and these ones of the missing woman tell us something, but I don't know how we can search this whole ranch when we don't even know there's a body."

Wilf could feel his anger rise. "Of course there's a body. Didn't you see that belt around her neck?"

"Sure. But she's alive in the picture. It's not a snuff film. They're havin' sex."

"Well, it's a little trick that some people like to practice. The guy in the picture might have heard about it from his friend, or taught it to his friend's wife, or who knows what. But it was something that some of the people in their group liked to try. The problem is, sometimes it goes wrong. I don't know where that motel room was, but my guess is it was in Cheyenne, and things went wrong there."

"I still don't see how things fit."

Wilf took a deep breath to calm himself. "Maybe I'm all wrong, but I think it might have gone something like this. I do remember that Wight came up here first. Then Parker and Newell. The visit was all arranged before. They were going to come up to hunt. I imagine Wentworth was going to let Newell hunt without a license because he owed him a favor for the pickup. But Wight came earlier, and he came by himself, probably for fun and games with this girl that Norman Lang knew." He looked at Tommy Tice. "Am I right on that?"

"On Norman knowing her? I think so. He's got an eye for all the women in the bars, and he was runnin' around when she was. He might not take her out for supper, but it would fit if he slipped off somewhere else."

"O.K. It could be Cheyenne, nice out-of-the-way place for those three guys, and she doesn't have to travel far. But it could be somewhere else—it doesn't matter a lot. Then we put this rendezvous a day or two before Parker and Newell show up. Things must have gone wrong with the girl, and they decided to take her up here to stash her. After that, Wentworth came to get me, to put a good face on everything, show that everything was out in the open. Then when they wanted to take the deer to the cooler and found out they needed a license, they went and got one. Wentworth didn't want any snooping. But he got some anyway, and he knew it came from me. Meanwhile, Lang acts funny around me, changing his tune, and then someone comes to harass me up in the high country. It just seems that Wentworth has had something big to hide, something he can blackmail these other guys about. Something to get shot over."

Tommy lit a cigarette. "You know, it does make some kind of sense. He does one thing, and then he does another. He talks about getting a housekeeper, and she never shows up. He says the pickup works, then he says it doesn't, when it does. He's gonna hunt without a license, and then he buys one."

Schultz looked at the envelopes and then at his watch. "What about the pictures of Wight and this other woman?"

Wilf shrugged. "The way I see it, Wentworth liked to have things to hold over other people. He liked control. For all

I know, he paid me with money he got from someone else, but my hunch is that he didn't put the squeeze on Wight earlier or he wouldn't have gotten him to play in the motel room. I'd guess he baited him into it, and then he got a bigger fish than he planned."

Schultz looked at the envelopes and the empty hole. Wilf could tell he was less confident than someone like Hopkins and would like to go back with what he had so far.

"I think she's out here somewhere," said Wilf. "And I think we should try to find her."

Tommy looked at the country around them. "This is a big place. Do we try to cover every square foot, lookin' for some more fresh dirt?"

"Think back, Tommy. Did he do anything else that stuck out? Something out of the ordinary, at about that time? Like give you a day off, or send you somewhere?"

Tommy took a thoughtful drag. "You know, there was one thing. He was practicin' with the tractor."

"To dig holes?" asked Schultz.

"No, to move bales."

Wilf turned to the deputy. "What do you think of taking another half hour while Tommy moves some bales for us?" He turned to the hired hand. "Do you know which stack he practiced on?"

"Yeah, that one where you guys killed the deer that first morning." He turned to Schultz. "Right at the bottom of the hill."

The deputy looked at his watch again and shrugged.

On the way down the hill in Tommy's pickup, with the deputy following, Wilf said, "You know, this goes back to something we talked about earlier. I don't think anyone killed

Parker. Wight wouldn't take that big a risk, especially if he was sitting on something else. He wouldn't plug Wentworth for blackmailing him about Mrs. Parker, but he might if Wentworth had two things to hold over him. Pushed him too far."

Tommy flicked the long ash on his cigarette. "So you don't think what's-his-name, Newell, was in on any of it?"

"Just the pickup and the license, but not the rest of it. He likes to be the smart guy, but if he had known about anything else when it happened, he would have been more careful with the license. If he'd gotten wind of it later, I doubt that he would have told me about Wight and Mrs. Parker, and he might not have called you this morning."

Tommy made a twist with his mouth as he rested his cigarette hand on the gear shift. "Could be."

As Wilf gazed at the long, tall row of bales, he had the sense that he was looking at them through new eyes. Two and a half weeks earlier, he had noticed the bales were crooked, and he had not given it a thought. Now, in this place where he had led Parker up to get a shot at the deer, and where he had cleaned the animal and thrown the scraps away in the tall grass, he could picture Wentworth practicing with the tractor.

Wilf stood by himself, a few paces away from Schultz, as Tommy picked up one bale after another and set it out in the middle of the field. When he had a few more than half the bales moved, he stopped the tractor, called out, and waved. Wilf and Schultz walked over to look at the ground where Tommy was pointing. He had uncovered a piece of bare earth that looked like the right size.

Wilf glanced at Tommy, who didn't seem to have much left in the way of jokes, and he turned to the deputy, who looked as if he had had a little bit proved and would like to see the rest. Wilf pivoted and headed toward Tommy's pickup to get the shovels.

The deputy took pictures of the rest of the haystack and of the disturbed earth. Then he stood back and let the boys work.

They took turns, as before. Wilf went first, skimming with the shovel and taking shallow scoops, trying not to point the blade downward. Tommy dug in similar fashion until the hole was dug out about two feet. Then Wilf took another turn, scraping sideways with the shovel, feeling no greater resistance than a dirt clod that rolled under or over the edge of the blade. Then he felt something.

He turned the shovel and skimmed lengthwise with the point of it. Something gave and moved. It was a piece of cloth. He scraped dirt aside, not bothering to lift out the loose soil, and the cloth moved. He got what looked like the waistline of it onto the tip of his shovel blade and gave it a shake. As the dirt fell loose, the cloth revealed itself as a black skirt.

Wilf glanced at the deputy, who had a dispassionate look on his face.

"I'd say that's far enough. I'm declaring this a crime scene. I want to thank you boys for your help." Schultz turned and walked to the edge of the field where the Jeep was parked.

Wilf looked at Tommy. "I'm glad we didn't dig any deeper. I didn't want to see her like this."

Tommy shook his head. "Neither did I. She was an all-right girl."

Wilf lifted the third strand of the fence wire and helped Adrienne crawl through. The two of them stood beneath the grey sky, watching the horses in the pasture below.

"It's too bad about Heather," she said.

Wilf took a broad view of the landscape, finding the hills in the distance. "Yes, it is. She couldn't have had any idea of what she was getting into, that's for sure." He shook his head. "They're really a chickenshit bunch. If it was an accident, they could have reported it. They'd have gotten in trouble, but it would have been the decent thing to do. Instead, they think they can get away with it."

Adrienne had a faraway look as she gazed out over the country and shook her head. "You want to blame it on the guys from Colorado, but Norman Lang is right in there with them."

"He is. Right here in your backyard, and just like them. And they know it better than we do." Wilf took a breath. "I keep thinking, how could I have done anything different? For her sake, I couldn't. It was already done when Wentworth came to see me. But all the rest of it has left me with a bad taste as well. The more I think of it, the more it seems my big mistake was having any truck with these guys to begin with. Of course, I wouldn't have stumbled onto Heather, but even before I did, I had decided I'd had it with all of this."

"You mean with guiding?"

"Right. With the business aspect. I'll still hunt, but I'm not into selling it any more and making things easier for these other guys. I really didn't like guiding anyway. It wasn't hunting, and it kept me from doing things the way I wanted. Someone else can do it. There'll always be customers who want to pay for it, and there'll be others who'll see it as just business, and that's all up to them. But I'm done with selling the gifts of nature. Those are the words I've put on it."

The horses were coming up the hill now, their hooves lifted above the ground as they floated in a lope.

"So what do you think you'll do?"

He looked at her and smiled. "Go back to working for a living. Like they say, I was looking for a job when I found this one." He patted the dark horse as it came up next to him. "I can still hunt for myself, and go camping. Take these guys along, go to the wilderness area, see what kind of a wrangler I can make out of you."

"What kind do you think?" She patted the cheek of the sorrel.

"Probably a pretty good one."

Adrienne smiled. "As long as no one else is looking on to know the difference."

Poacher's Moon

Printed in the United States
202628BV00001B/1-105/P